by Robert Bloch strained through a more literary—but quite welcome sensibility." —*The New York Times Book Review*

"Bahr writes like a demon, with a range from deadpan humor to living horror . . . Its haunting sequences may prove impossible to forget." —*The Wall Street Journal*

"A new noir classic. I loved it."
—Tod Goldberg, author of *Gangsters Don't Die*

"A worthy addition to the canon of country noir. Bahr's novel is eerie, dark, and disturbing in the best possible way."
—Ivy Pochoda, author of *Sing Her Down*

The DEAD RINGER

ALSO BY DANE BAHR

Stag

The Houseboat

The DEAD RINGER

A Novel

DANE BAHR

COUNTERPOINT

CALIFORNIA

THE DEAD RINGER

First Counterpoint edition: 2026

ISBN: 978-1-64009-754-4

The Library of Congress Cataloging-in-Publication data is available.

Jacket design by Victoria Maxfield
Jacket images of bell © iStock / ksena32, grave © Shutterstock / AdamBoor, forest © iStock / Vadim Misin, tree © iStock / Rixipix
Book design by Laura Berry

COUNTERPOINT
Los Angeles and San Francisco, CA
www.counterpointpress.com

Printed in the United States of America

1 3 5 7 9 10 8 6 4 2

This book is dedicated to
Tøren and Anders

Pensive and faltering,
The words *the dead* I write,
For living are the Dead,
(Haply the only living, only real,
And I the apparition, I the spectre.)

—WALT WHITMAN

Ring ring ring all night long. Maybe somebody wanted something bad.

—DALTON TRUMBO

PART 1

I was thirteen years old when I met my first bank robber. Of course, there were thieves I had been acquainted with but their larceny was petty in perspective. A chicken from a farmyard, for example, a piece of candy from a drugstore. Harmless acts committed by children. The actions of men, however, proved permanent, violent, and often without regret. These kinds of men reminded me of huge ships steaming full ahead only to ground themselves into the sand. Which is to say, they would not stop till they were forced to, and the bank robber was no exception.

The man of whom I speak was named Benjamin Kilt. He entered my life bloody and left it just the same. The ambitions of another are not mine to contend with so I will not pretend to know if his path was righteous or otherwise. Nor will I delude my humility and tell you the choices he made were incorrect. Every man and woman have their hopes for how their lives will play out. We are all working toward something after all. But everything endeavored has an end.

As a young girl I saw no good in anyone. The evils of this life seemed to purge the good. Flashes of grace were glimpsed for only the briefest of moments. Like how lightning brings out the details of things otherwise hidden in the darkness; what follows is the chuck of the thunderclap and the shuttering noise that ushers within us some unfounded fear. My years as a young girl were spent bracing for that thunder.

I am an old woman now, and though very little of my life was spent with Benjamin Kilt, his story is my story just as my story is yours. Nothing stays as it is, nor would we want it to. One must embrace the changes and in turn change with them. But this, I know, was a sentiment Benjamin Kilt was not willing to entertain.

Not a day goes by that I do not think about him. He cared for me, he was my salvation. The gratitude I carry for him is boundless, and if I knew then what I know now, I would have told him so. I know one day I will see him again, and I have that to comfort me.

1

(1935)

The orange light of a lantern appeared and then vanished among the caged trunks of ponderosa. The wind sawed through the black needles above. No stars to be seen through that wickered canopy. Skies so dark a chunk of coal might even glow. The lantern came into full view finally after its dubious rambling and all the prospector's tools and odd wares shown dim beneath the flame's anemic flicker. Importunate clanging of pots and pans, a rusted .30 Springfield tied all askew. A pickax, a dented shovel, and a sad-eyed pack mule being led under all this forsaken weight.

Cast in the frail light like some character out of Leroux, the prospector was masked in shadows. Mossed with grizzled hair and a sun-bleached beard full of tobacco stains that climbed to just below his pale eyes. He wore the pelt of a black bear cloaked over his shoulders and a shapeless greasy hat that seemed sewn from the same animal. He was stumbling a little and he would pause from time to time and tilt back a clay jug of corn whiskey. The warped image of the flame shuttered behind the glass of the lamp chimney and the lantern pendulumed above the mule from a wrought iron stand like it was weathering a great storm.

The wind strained through the branches and sounded like crashing surf. There was woodsmoke carried along from a burning forest over the ridgeline. The wind was loud but if one listened close enough they could hear this aimless prospector trying his best to carry out some warbly tune on a rusted harmonica. Clanking as he was through this abandoned wood and fumbling about on his improvised rendition he suddenly stopped. His ears were piqued by some odd foreign sound. Cocked an eye up at the trees and the clouds and the wind, chewing the air with his toothless mouth, and the dim-witted mule running into his back and not stopping, and the prospector calling out: Quit, donkey!

The mule finally understood and came to rest with the pots and pans ringing out in harried discourse till they hung still and went silent. For a moment the only sound in all that harbored darkness was that of the unabridged wind.

The prospector dumbly turned back to peer from where he had come but there was nothing there but the black stands of ponderosa. The clay jug was hooked on a finger and dangling at the end of his limp arm. The mule kept trying to urge him on.

Damn ye, donkey! he said, fending off the animal.

Then he heard the sound again.

And to prove he wasn't completely crazy he took his ear horn from his chattel on the mule's back and held it to his good ear in the direction he thought the sound was coming from. The mule jabbered and the prospector turned and said, I told ye to shut up!

The prospector poised the horn again and listened. Over the wind in the pines, faintly, he heard it once more. The tinkling of a tiny bell.

Dixon, he said to the mule. We ain't alone.

He lowered the ear horn and stood there idly but with a

certain amount of tenable suspicion. Then he hid away the ear horn and set his jug in the dirt and untied the Springfield from the pack and held the gun at his hip. He looked skyward and then again at the woods behind him. There was no reason for anyone to be tracking him but there was more than one not to risk it. He waited. He finally resolved he was alone and clicked his dry tongue and cradled the gun and tugged the mule along. Come on, Dixon, he said.

He tracked the sound like a drunk child. Getting lost and then stopping and listening again and pulling the mule in a new direction. He wasn't far off now as the sound was growing louder. But how the trees did gnash. The tops of the ponderosas and lodgepoles bent up there like the tips of bluestem in a prairie gale. The pine needles rained down upon him.

He took the lantern from its iron perch and held it before him. He stepped lightly, believing the smallest twig's snap would roar over the howling storm. Each time he stopped to check his bearings the mule would bludgeon its long face square into the prospector's back.

Damn ye! he shouted.

The bell rang out. It was constant now like an alarm sounding out there for anyone, anything to hear. Not far, the lantern caught sight of the sound and a little brass bell winked in the light. The prospector cautioned forward. He said: Who the hell's out there?

He didn't move.

He said it again. He called out: If anyone's hid out there I'll kill ye!

The prospector waited a long moment. He dallied the rawhide lead to a pine limb and told Dixon to stay. Then he set forth. He extended an arm with the lantern, and the orange pulse caught sight of the bell tacked in a tree five feet above the ground. From the bell was a thin string that worked furiously up and down. The prospector followed that string toward the earth where it threaded through the dirt and was lost from sight. The ground looked to have been recently excavated.

The prospector watched the string and the bell and said: Hellfire, Dixon.

The bell's tolling began to slow, began to soften. Then it rang once. Then once more. Then after that it went silent and then there was only the wind.

The prospector stood there not moving, looking down at the dirt. He finally said: Huh.

He set the Springfield aside and turned back to the mule and unlashed the shovel and stepped unevenly toward the string disappearing into the dirt and then drove in the tip of the spade. One shovelful and then another. Not long to follow he struck something and balked and fell backward in terror when the point of the shovel sank and cleaved away the trigger finger of a man's right hand. He skittered backward crablike till he ran into the mule. Then he stood and went to the body and looked down and wiped at his brow and the dirt from his hand smeared across his skin like paint.

The prospector finally reclaimed his courage and on his hands and knees went to work at the rest of the body, wiping away the dirt as gently as he could. The fabric of a jacket. Of a shirt. The oyster gleam of a pearl snap. Then the face of a corpse appeared. Mouth black with dirt. Eyes all sunk and skin waxen in the lantern's light.

Huh, the prospector said again.

He stood and went to the lantern and turned again to the body and held it over to better see all the dead man's features. On the wrist of his left hand a wooden case was manacled. The prospector toed it as if expecting the man to move. Then he stepped out of the shallow grave and went back to the mule and uncorked the jug of corn whiskey and sank a long drink. He wiped his mouth on the shoulder of his pelt. He spoke to the mule, said: Nary a dull moment, Dixon, is they?

He looked over his shoulder again and saw the mutilated hand reaching up from the earth as if in futile desperation. He turned back to the mule brandishing the subtle smile of an opportunist.

'Tis no mistake, Dixon, he said, we were meant to come upon this poor soul tonight. God is good, Dixon. God is very good.

The prospector took down a leather satchel in hopes of lifting anything of value and then unsheathed a bone saw with which to liberate the wooden case from the dead man's wrist.

But when he turned back with his arms full of implements the dead man was standing there in the grave. The prospector dropped the tools and the lantern and his eyes fell open wide in the same manner as his mouth at the man standing not dead at all but poised with a Luger pistol in his hand, his hand bleeding all over the gun, and then in some abrupt onset of rigor mortis the prospector stiffened and fell like a board in the wind.

The man stepped from the grave and stepped to the prospector and stood over him and looked down and in a dry voice said: Interesting.

He looked around at the blackness then he looked up at the sky and recognized none of it. And all the while the wind blew and the stars were raked through the darkness.

2

Kilt looked down upon the ruined prospector with neither contempt nor compassion. The lifeless eyes cast cloudward and void of cognition. His comic bearded jaw loose on its hinge and fallen open in a silent howl. Kilt nudged his ribs with the toe of his boot. The prospector's body was heavy with death and when Kilt pressed his boot it rocked like the carcass of a dead seal. Then with the point of his boot he snapped shut the prospector's jaw as if in objection to any protest the dead man might harbor.

Kilt looked down at the wooden case cuffed to his wrist. Looked at it like he'd never seen it before. With his damaged hand he lifted it. The words ST. REGIS SAVINGS & LOAN stamped across the front. His head was throbbing and he touched the lump behind his ear. Then it all started to come back to him.

Kilt went searching for a rock with which to break the chain and, finding one, laid the case on the ground and arranged the chain over the rock and with another struck down upon the chain. Yellow sparks lit up like fireflies. He tried it again but the chain did not budge. Once more and the rock he used as his hammer split in two. Kilt cursed under his breath and stood, holding the case like some ill-fated banker. He held his arm at length and let the case fall. With his other hand he aimed the Luger point-blank at the chain and fired. The shot rang out through the empty mountains. The mule stepped like it had heard thunder. The case dropped to the earth.

Kilt knelt with his knife and lodged the point between the lid of the case and twisted it. Snapping the blade, he rose with impatience and fired again at the lock of the case. The lid erupted and a fountain of Sears, Roebuck and Company flyers came forth and spread over the dark ground and raced off with the wind. He stood there a moment. And then it all came to him. He shook his head in anger.

He turned to the sad-eyed mule looking on with the placid gaze of an imbecile and Kilt raised the Luger and pressed the barrel just under and back of the animal's ear and angled the gun so the fired bullet would exit between the eyes to kill it quickly. He shied slightly so the spray wouldn't get in his eyes. All the while the dumb animal just watched him with eyes big as globes and therein Kilt saw the innocence of something not needing to die and if there was any empathy left in Kilt it revealed itself here. He let the Luger fall and he holstered it and took his bandana from his pocket and wrapped the remaining half of his finger in it. He knelt to scavenge through the prospector's pockets and coming up with 230 dollars and a rusted harmonica Kilt took up the braided rawhide and led the mule on, saying once or twice: Come on, mule.

Through the empty night, not a light on them. Clouds rushed through the sky like giant shoals of fish. The forest opened up and Kilt looked at the stars and traced a line from the tip of the Big Dipper to the North Star. Using it, he went south hoping to find the town of Missoula and his old partner and half brother, Sidney Bosco. The man who had stolen all of his money and buried him alive.

Kilt and the mule went on. The ominous roar in Kilt's ear of windward travel seemed to urge a flagrant warning to go no farther. The wind so loud the unlikely pair made not a sound as they traversed along. The clanging pots were beat out by the clapping trees. Kilt had abandoned the prospector where he had died. Not a burial or mark of remembrance. Just a heap of withering skin under all that bear fur. His soul maybe fleeing into the night toward the heavens. Maybe not.

At some desolate hour Kilt's legs gave in and he sat in the dirt. He needed water but he was too tired to search for any in the dead prospector's collection. He rose and tied the mule to a dogwood and walked to a felled pine and lay down and used the tree as a pillow and just as he was placing his hat over his eyes a cloud moved away and a big moon appeared and for a moment everything was awash in ceramic light. The shadows of the trees heeling in the wind looked like black flames.

Lying there and nearly asleep his finger began to nag him. He sat up against the log with annoyance and looked down at his hand. The bandana was slick with blood and in the moonlight looked like it had been soaked in tar. He unwrapped his finger and examined it. The bone was cleaved away at the first knuckle and the cartilage was pink.

Well, he said.

He rewrapped his finger and stood and got some twigs together. Pulled some dry grass from the ground. He balled up the grass and lay the twigs in a tepee shape over it. He moved around to the windward side to block the wind and took a pack of matches from his shirt pocket and popped one of them and cupped the flame in his hands but the wind snuffed it out. He lit another and this time the wind was gracious and the flame caught the grass and burned quickly.

Not too long he had a fire going. The embers pulsed a deep red. He wedged a stick into the fire's belly and watched it flame up. He waited till the tip was an ember and in the wan orange light he undressed his finger again. The light winked in the blood and against the fire's flames his finger looked like it had been dipped in gold. With his good hand he felt around for a stob of wood and finding one brought it to his mouth and bit down. He withdrew the ember from within the fire and in the cold air the thinnest thread of smoke twisted off the tip. The hot coal burned as a single point of light deep within Kilt's pupils like a lone satellite in some storybook sky. He tilted the ember to his finger and pressed the hot tip to the bone and the cinder hissed as it cauterized the flesh and Kilt winced and his teeth sank into the wood and when he finally took the stick away his finger looked like the end of an old cigar. He staggered up and went to the mule and found some remnants of whiskey in a tin flask and he drank till it was gone.

He went back to the fire and sat down heavily and watched the thin tips of the flames break off with the wind. He tore away a strip of his shirt and dressed his finger and lay back against the log with his brow sweating and his teeth hurting and his missing finger drumming out the phantom beat of his heart. He looked up to find the moon but the moon was gone and everything was dark again. He cradled his bad hand on his stomach and set a rock under his elbow so his hand wouldn't slide off and with his good hand he set his hat over his eyes and slowly the crashing of the wind in the treetops fell away as he drifted into tormented sleep, repeating the name Sidney Bosco over and over again.

3

A week before Benjamin Kilt was buried alive, he and Sidney Bosco were draining whiskey at the Pilgrim Saloon in Missoula, Montana. Between sips Bosco was spelling out his plan on how they were going to hold up the St. Regis Savings & Loan.

Easy peasy, Bosco said. In and out.

Not easy, Kilt said. And you know it. Calling it easy is dooming it from the get-go.

Nah, baby brother, Bosco said. Nothing doomin here. No doom for this outlaw.

He winked at Kilt and smoothed out his black mustache with his thumb. He shot down the rest of his whiskey then snapped his teeth at the air like a dog.

A pretty lady sashayed by and Bosco slapped her ass. She gave a little startle.

Don't be givin up that cootch before I get to you, he said. I don't want some dude's sloppys.

She was in a corset and tall stockings and she covered her face with a big Japanese geisha fan and when she failed to answer him he pulled her onto his lap and grabbed her face sternly at the cheeks and said: You hear me? No dicks unless it's the one you're currently sittin on.

She nodded shyly.

Good girl, he said. Now git.

She stood up and Bosco slapped her ass again.

When she was gone, Kilt said: Ain't got to talk to her like that.

Whore's a whore, Bosco said. Long as she's taking my money, I'll talk to her any way I want.

He looked around the place. He shook his head.

Could really go for one a them big ones, he said. They had a girl like that up in here about a month ago. Probably take the two of us to even lift her into the bed. Here.

Bosco handed Kilt a couple bills.

Be a good boy and fetch us another couple rounds.

I ain't your gofer, Kilt said.

You is when I'm paying.

Kilt didn't move and when he didn't Bosco gave him a look and then swept his fingers at the air as if excusing him. Kilt stood in a labored way like his bones hurt and with more than a little reluctance he got to his feet and took the money from Bosco's hand. The old chair whined as it slid over the wood. Kilt crossed the saloon toward the long walnut bar, his tall-heeled boots tapping against the cupped boards like some scorned flamenco dancer. He leaned against the bar and raised his eyebrows at Lonny the barman and Lonny came down and said, Another? Kilt raised his hand with his fingers in a V and Lonny nodded and poured the beer and then poured the whiskey and put it all on a tray and told Kilt he'd bring it over.

At the far end of the bar there was a woman with long dark hair and a long neck and big dark eyes who was cradling her chin in her hand. From time to time she would bound her forefinger in that long hair and look up at Kilt and when she did the whites of her eyes winked like coins in a fountain. Kilt watched her back. He didn't smile and he didn't frown. And he didn't look away from her till Lonny said again: I'll bring it to your table.

Still looking at the woman, Kilt nodded at him.

Back at the table Bosco said: What the hell?

What the hell what?

Where's the hooch?

Said he'd bring it over.

Kilt's head was turned. He was still watching the woman.

Who the hell you looking at? Bosco asked.

No one, Kilt said.

He looked back at Bosco.

You looking at Marie, ain't you? Bosco said. He shook his head. Who said they're bringing it over?

What?

You said he's bringing it over. Who's *he*?

Lonny. Ain't no one else working in here.

Lonny got some pussy he's hiding under that apron?

Didn't ask him that.

You know I got a thing about that.

Thing about what?

Being served whiskey by another man.

What kind of thing is that?

Gives the wrong impression.

What impression would that be?

Fuck, Bosco said. Gotta spell every damn little thing out for you, don't I. The cocksucking kind of impression, baby brother.

He held out his hand and let his wrist go limp.

Kilt said, You saying that if a lady brings you your whiskey she's probably wanting to suck your cock too?

No, Bosco said, I'm saying that men who do lady jobs probably like the same things as ladies.

Like sucking your cock?

They do it, don't they?

Don't mean they like it.

Then why do they do it?

Money, Kilt said. Because you pay them to.

Shit, Bosco said. You're giving me a headache.

Well, Kilt said, if you're so certain about this hypothesis—

This what?

Hypothesis.

What the hell's a hypothesis?

It's an unsubstantiated theory.

Quit using ten-dollar words.

My point, Kilt said, is that if you're so sure about all of this, let's ask Lonny if he enjoys sucking cock. What do you say?

Hell, Bosco said. I don't know. Shut the fuck up. I just like things the way I like them, okay? I like a woman to cook me my supper. I like a woman to launder my shirts. And I like a woman to serve me my whiskey. That all right with you?

Kilt shrugged his shoulders.

I'm starting to regret ever asking you to come along, Bosco said. Shoulda shot you back on the Triple Nine when I had the chance.

Ain't too late, Kilt said. He tapped his chest, pointing out his heart.

Hell, Bosco said, just make a bad mess for Lonny to clean up.

Kilt leaned back in his chair and looked over at the bar, at the woman still sitting alone. The way the late sun was slanting in and the light all amber from the wildfires, she looked like a bronze statue of a woman. One commissioned for a private collection. Hidden away and on display for only the luckiest of eyes. Kilt looked back at Bosco and said:

If it wasn't for me, you'd be pushing up dandelions somewhere outside of Bozeman.

Bosco turned in his chair and looked over his shoulder as if there were people eavesdropping. Then he turned back to Kilt and held a finger to his lips.

Goddamnit, Bosco said. Keep your voice down.

Kilt pressed a laugh through his nose.

You think the law's in here looking for us? Kilt said. Shoot, ain't no one out there looking for us. Far as the law is concerned we burnt up in that cabin they set fire to. We're ghosts, brother. Phantoms. Specters. Spooks. Anyone still looking for us is looking for ghosts.

You don't know that.

We got out of there pretty sweet, Kilt said. Not a dollar lost and everything else up in flames. Not even a shot fired.

You're all crazy, Bosco said. You know that? Fucking crazy person. Only thing you got from Mama is her crazy.

Don't talk about her like that.

Shit, Bosco said, I'll talk about her any way I want. What'd she do with me? Left me on some doorstep. That's what she fucking did.

No, Kilt said. I ain't crazy. Neither was she. Just trying to make a living. The both of us.

That's right, Bosco said, the whore and the bank robber. Salt of the fucking earth.

Kilt put his Luger on the table, standing it on the butt of the grip. Pointed it at Bosco.

Bang, Kilt said.

Then he set it down and spun it as if it were some child's toy. He looked one last time at the gilded woman sitting at the end of the bar. Then he stood up.

Where you going? Bosco asked.

Nowhere.

Uh-huh, Bosco said, tracing Kilt's glance to the woman. Bullshit, nowhere.

Kilt winked at him.

You forgetting something? Bosco said.

He pointed at the Luger on the table.

How many times I got a tell you, don't leave that unattended. Can't trust anyone these days.

Kilt took up the gun and holstered it. Swept his jacket over the gun.

Don't wait up, he said.

4

Kilt lay there in her bed with his back against the headboard looking at all her naked skin as she pinned up her hair. She was talking to him as she looked out the window. The morning sky was hazy and the sun was like a blood drop through the fire smoke. Up on the ridgeline of the Bitterroots the wind was blowing all that smoke toward Idaho. But in the Missoula Valley it was still and quiet and early enough in the morning yet that no one was in the streets. The saloon and the rooms above it were quiet and most of its patrons still drunk or asleep or both. Kilt watched her with reverence like the way one might watch the sun come up for the first time in their life.

Her silhouette was hourglassed against the window. A pretty shadow stamped in the early light. She turned slightly and the curves of her were backlit and he tilted his head as if to better take it in.

She caught him looking and she smiled and turned and covered herself with one arm, which did more to emphasize than hide.

You're staring at me again, she said.

I'm always staring at you, Kilt said.

Except when you're not.

And when is that?

When you're gone.

I'm only gone cause I need to be.

Because you need to be?

Yes mam.

Don't call me mam.

Come over here.

No.

Come here.

If I do, you going to stay this time?

Kilt was silent. He didn't look away but he didn't say anything either.

Uh-huh, she said. She turned back to the window, accepting his silence as her answer.

Uh-huh, what? Kilt said.

Her fingers were working through her hair. The two dimples above her hips were shadowed and many times Kilt had watched her sleep and imagined water pooled in that cupped skin and longed to lower his lips and drink from them.

She stepped into a cotton shift and pulled the straps up and slipped each arm through and then turned to face Kilt with her expression hidden by the paling light behind her.

You don't want me here, Kilt said. Not the way you think you do. I ain't that kind of man.

Don't give me a line, she said. It's insulting.

It's the truth, Kilt said. Ain't the staying kind.

You could be, she said. You could be that kind. To me you could.

You'd get tired of me, Kilt said.

Then let me try, she said.

Let you try what?

To get tired of you. You never even given me the chance.

I give you that chance and I might never see you again.

No different than it is now.

Be completely different, Kilt said.

She twisted her hair into a rope and wrapped it around and around on the top of her head and with a last pin she lanced the bun and smoothed up the fine hair of her neck.

How many you got pining for you? Kilt said.

Got no one pining for me.

You expect me to believe that?

I don't expect anything from you anymore.

There's no one else?

Her fingers kept brushing up her neck.

I don't believe that, Kilt said.

They don't count, she said. They don't mean a thing to me.

Same as me, ain't they? Money on the dresser. Pay to play.

You never paid.

You want me to?

No.

Then what do you want?

You know what I want.

And what's that, darling?

Don't call me that either. Not while you're still lying in my bed.

What do you want me to call you, then?

You could try my name.

Okay, Lindsay Marie.

The other girls like you calling them darling? she asked. Darling or sweetie or honey or whatever it is you want to call them that night.

Ain't no others.

You're a liar.

Ain't a liar, Kilt said. Just cause I go, it don't mean it's for someone else.

Then you're a fool, Lindsay Marie said.

Yes, Kilt said. Cause only a fool would leave this bed. Something which I seem to do with more and more reluctance.

Don't say that, she said. Don't say things like that unless you really mean it.

I do mean it.

Then don't, she said. Make a change. Don't leave it.

Stay in your bed forever?

Want me to tie you to it? she said. I will. I will if that's what keeps you here.

She walked toward the bed. Her breasts were loose under the cotton.

Make you my prisoner, she said.

Why don't you take that shift off and we'll talk about it.

I just put it back on, Lindsay Marie said.

Just as easy to take it off.

You're a coward, she said.

A coward?

You hide behind a bandana and that little gun of yours but I know who you are. I know the kind of man you want to be.

Of course you do, Kilt said. You're looking right at him. And I ain't never hid a thing from you.

I could just go to the law, she said. Tell them who I got in my bed right now. Bet they'd find that interesting.

Nothing interesting about me, Lindsay Marie. I rob banks. I'm a bank robber. Anyone could do it.

Then let someone else do it, she said. Let someone else run around for a change. Let someone else shoot at people.

I don't shoot at people.

How about shot *at*, then?

Occupational hazard, my dear.

Then change your goddamn occupation, Ben.

He watched her for a long silent moment. Then he said: What if this is the last one?

The last one what?

The last job I do.

You just got done telling me that's all you do, Lindsay Marie said. You're a bank robber, remember?

What if I do this last job, he said, and maybe I won't anymore. Maybe I'll stay here. Or better yet, I'll take you with me. Buy us a big house outside of Bozeman. I do this one last job and you won't have to lay down with anyone but me.

What if I want to lay down with someone else?

You don't.

How do you know?

Cause you just got done telling me you don't. The others don't count, remember? Don't mean a thing to you.

He looked at her for a moment with nothing crossing his face. And then the moment passed and she saw him grin.

So that's it, then, is it? she said. This is you being vulnerable?

He shrugged his shoulders.

Well, she said. She swiped her hands over the bedsheets as if to smooth out the wrinkles from all the hours and nights before.

If that's true, she continued, then you can leave the money on the dresser before you go.

She slid to the top of the bed and kissed him on the forehead and then stood up and looked down at him for a moment and then left the room without another word, leaving him alone with the red morning light seeping into the empty room, into that place more tender than the heart.

5

Morning rose cold and exhausted with the stilted lodgepoles half-burned around him like decrepit columns of some fever dream cathedral. He peeled his eyes awake and took stock at his surroundings. He wondered how far he had traveled the night before. He had the dead prospector's blanket donned about his shoulders and he rose to his feet in a languid manner, staggering once or twice as though he were drunk. He kept the edge of the blanket closed tight at his throat with his good hand. Looked down at the night's fire and toed the black wood in hopes of finding some pulse of heat therein but there was none. Not even the finest pinpoint of ember. Not even the smallest twist of smoke. All that stirred was a glaucous puff of ash, which itself was so lifeless that it settled back among the charred remains like sand.

The mule was tied to the tree where Kilt had left him the night before and seemed to neither relish nor protest its fate. At Kilt's awakening it simply turned its head and blinked at him. Kilt said: You got a name, mule?

The mule switched around its ears as if listening to something of interest. Kilt looked into the woods but saw nothing.

You hear something out there?

Kilt waited longer but nothing came. He walked a few feet away and switched hands on the blanket and with his good one opened his fly and took a leak on a bush. The ground was cold and the piss steamed. He finished and buttoned up the fly and turned again in a full circle with his shoulders hunched under the blanket. The sky was overcast and there was no help regarding a heading. A day so dark it seemed entirely vacant of a sun. A world of daylight in its most ambiguous form. A repudiation of light.

There was a light mist sifting down and within that mist were occasional spits of sleet. The dead prospector's wool blanket was damp and reeked of a wet animal. He had the sensation of needing to shit but the thought of dropping his pants in such cold and dismal air changed his mind.

He walked back to the mule and patted it with his bad hand. His nubbed finger throbbed. He looked down at it and tried to flex it but there was nothing there to flex.

He said to the mule: A gunslinger with no trigger finger. That's funny.

His head hurt, his mouth was dry, and he went around and rummaged through the prospector's collection in hopes of a canteen. What he found was a stained bladder made of some kind of animal organ and he uncorked the stopper and smelled the contents and then tilted what was left into his mouth. The water had a foul smell and tasted like iron but he drank it anyway. When it was empty he pitched the bladder to the ground and wiped away the wet with the back of his wrist.

He started searching again. He reached deep into a canvas sack and his thumb caught something sharp and he pulled his hand back like he'd touched a hot stove and his thumb came away with a line so clean that it took a moment for the blood to show up. He staunched it by stoving the thumb into his mouth and sucking on it like a child. He untied the sack from the mule's back and tipped it bottom up and spilled its contents over the sodden ground. All manner of trinkets lay strewn: a windup ballerina figurine in perfect pirouette, a copy of *Huckleberry Finn*, an ivory comb, several pictures of posing nude women, little tincture bottles of amber glass, and a Bowie knife half in its beaded sheath.

Kilt knelt to the knife and turned it in his hands and with his good hand he held on to the sheath and with his other pulled the blade free. The handle was made of elk antler. The metal of the blade was almost black. He sheathed it again and looked down at the red and blue beadwork. Thought it looked like it should be in a museum and not lost away in some dead man's satchel. Careful as he could he tucked the sheath and knife into the waist at the small of his back. He picked up the book and put that back in the satchel. Then he just stood there looking around at the quiet forest.

He had started searching for any little scrap of food when the mule's ears started moving again. Then it started to stamp its feet. Then it tossed its head. Its big dark eyes craned around toward the woods and Kilt looked there and took the Luger from his belt and thumbed off the safety and said: To anyone kicking around in them trees, I got some heat on you.

The mule brayed at something and tried to kick free but the knot held fast.

Go on, Kilt said to the woods. Best get it over with and show yourself.

The mule reared up and just then out of that dead quiet a raven came ghosting forth with its black wings chucking the air like someone swinging rope.

That's what's got you all hot and bothered? Kilt said to the mule. A damn raven? He shook his head at the animal and undallied the lead from the tree limb and clicked his tongue and led the animal away with the rawhide loosely gripped in his good hand.

The light was growing stronger and all the sleet had turned over to rain. He left the clearing and entered a thick wood of ponderosa. The undergrowth was scorched but the trees were intact with only a little black rising up the trunks. The canopy overhead was such that any rain trying to reach the earth had to work hard at it. The burnt grass was brittle and wet and fell apart under Kilt's boots. The black grass left charcoal smears on the leather and before long his boots were black as coal. The rain falling in the forest sounded like tiny pebbles being rolled up the shoreline of a beach.

He walked on over a ground upon which neither hoofprint nor animal track nor any sign of life was laid. Life itself seemed scoured from this place. A place of the past tense where the swaying trees merely took the shapes of trees.

What he was looking for was a creek or a stream. He was quite thirsty. He would also follow that water downstream till it converged with a river because he knew every river eventually flowed to a town. But flowing water here in this waste felt a thing of fantasy.

He stopped the mule and looked around again. He didn't know what exactly for since it all looked the same but still he looked. His eyes circumferenced this world and a chill drained down him and he shivered violently and pulled the wool blanket closer to his chin and tried to preserve any heat trying to escape. The mule blinked dully.

You ain't a complainer, are you? Kilt said.

He led the mule on. Gradually the land began to slope away. He'd slip occasionally over the wet ground, regaining his balance with the steadfast mule. He let his mind wander, trying to retrace the reasons for being here. What trickled through were dim auguries of Bosco and firelight and whiskey. Bosco's head raked back in crazed laughter like the hinged mouth of a ventriloquist's puppet. The bottle in a perpetual tilt. Bosco's left thigh wrapped in cloth, full of blood from the guard's bullet. The fire popping like fireworks. Bosco saying: Can't kill us, can they, baby brother? Bosco saying: We keep the company of angels. Then the black veil of drunkenness falling slowly over Kilt. Then all went black. Then awaking to another darkness, he recalled the thin string gripped between finger and thumb. The faintest ringing of a bell.

Yet here he was. Like some kind of refuted holy ghost. Some ill-granted second life. A cursed life in which the charge was to seek out the unnamable. He was just about to tell the mule of his perplexed fate when a noise came snarling through the trees.

6

The crash came from the woods behind him. Like rocks being trundled from a hillside. It made no noise other than that. Just like rocks tumbling. But Kilt turned at the very last moment to see the lion midair with its paws outflung and its yellow wild eyes. In what seemed the final second Kilt pulled the wool blanket from his shoulders and stretched it between his hands and threw it at the animal like a matador does a bull. The cat was netted in the damp fabric like some strange game fish writhing in contorted panic and came falling down upon Kilt blindly with its front paws snared and its teeth gnashing the wool.

The lion was trying to reach around but its feet were hung up in the blanket. The points of its claws punctured the wool and slashed at Kilt's arms. The cat made awful sounds that Kilt had never heard before. Sounds reserved for the gothic. For the darkest parts of the horror mind. Best he could, he held the blanket, cupping the lion's ears and trying to trap its head. The cat snapped at him. The mouth was clapping down on the wool. The teeth had come through and were lodged there like strange ivory stalactites.

The lion bucked oddly and its left front paw came around and tore at Kilt's shoulder. The pain was awful and he lost his hold on the blanket and with nothing to restrain it the cat laid its teeth with ferocious urgency into the soft muscle of Kilt's collarbone, its lower teeth sinking through the skin till they hit bone. The pain was like glowing rods of hot iron plunged smoking into flesh. Kilt felt his body going limp like he was drifting off to sleep. He looked up at the treetops. Ponderosa needles against all that gray. Branches upon branches of lodgepoles chevroned in the sky.

Kilt dropped his left hand and lay there. The lion thought he had won and had begun to move off with Kilt straddled beneath him, dragging him by the collarbone. Kilt felt the jaws of the lion flexing and unflexing against his flesh. There was a strange odor coming from the animal and Kilt didn't know if it was the cat or if he was taking in the scent of his own blood. *This isn't the way I die*, Kilt thought. *This isn't the way I die.*

Then with his bad hand Kilt reached behind to the small of his back and felt for the antler handle and pulled the Bowie knife from its sheath and in one quick motion arced the blade around and sunk it into the lion's side. The lion recoiled. It released Kilt and leaped into the air. When it came back down Kilt stuck him again. He got him in the belly and Kilt hauled against it in a garish design as if to open up as much of the animal as possible. He sunk the blade into the ribs. Then he sunk it again.

The lion leaned and then fell over. Kilt staggered to the side and the two fighters lay there panting and looking at each other in disbelief. There was blood escaping from the lion's mouth. Its teeth were stained pink. The gut was opened up and the stomach lining cut. Pale tubing like thick anemic worms spilling forth. Organs shaped like burgundy silk pillows lay steaming. The lion was trying hard to breathe but its lungs had been punctured and the air and blood came in bubbles through the openings like boiling water. Kilt lay there and watched its eyes go from yellow to black. Watched the life retreating in them like a light dimming out on a dark plain. The once caramel hide was now the color of chokecherry wine. The lion took a last labored breath and then it died.

Kilt rolled to his back. He looked up again at the sky. An exhaustion so great it almost felt profound fell over him. He touched his collarbone and his hand came away all full of blood. He let his hand drop to the dirt. He allowed the back of his head to settle into the wet earth as though the softest of pillows had been placed there. Felt the wet earth seep into his hair. It was the sensation of giving himself over. To submit entirely. To be engulfed. The treetops dimmed high above. He was suddenly very cold. He wanted a drink of water. He felt an icy wind blow along the forest floor as if in announcement of departure.

The mule came and stood over him and blew.

Go on, mule, Kilt said. Can't you see I'm dying?

The mule did not go. It stood there as though cemented in place.

Kilt closed his eyes but the mule reached down and Kilt felt the wet nose and he opened his eyes.

You ain't going to listen, are you?

Then he said: Okay, mule. Have it your way.

He labored into a sitting position. Held his shoulder and using the mule's bridle rope lifted himself to his feet. He pulled a long piece of fabric from the dead prospector's stores and best he could he wrapped it round his collarbone and chest with several painful passes and then tucked the bitter end into the sling. He was in no state to walk so he took the knife and cut the latigo that held all that weight to the mule and in a pitiful execution pushed all of it to the ground.

Hold on, mule, Kilt said. Don't go moving on me.

Kilt lay his chest into the mule and with his neck and his left leg he swung himself up and with his free hand he took a fistful of the animal's mane and said: Okay. Slow now.

As if the mule understood it started down the mountain for lower country. Kilt tottered atop the mule's back, falling forward constantly and then catching himself in the last moment before he fell off. The mule had a proclivity toward good nature and it seemed to step delicately down the grade. Kilt could feel the blood running out of his shoulder and down his chest toward the waist of his pants. He looked once and saw the blood gathering there. The dark stain widening. He resolved to not look down again. His head bobbled and then he closed his eyes and slumped forward against the mule's neck and to anyone who might have been watching it looked like the mule was carrying a dead man.

7

Only a few nights before, Sidney Bosco was sitting against a log with one leg wrapped and outstretched and the other bent up with his hand on his knee, the other holding on to a small entrenching shovel, saying, We done did it, baby brother. I told you we had it. What did I say? I said easy peasy. I said nothin to it.

Kilt squatted at the fire, tending the flames, looked up at Bosco, and said, That your version of nothing to it? You nearly bleeding out up here in the mountains, a couple guards lying in pinewood boxes. I wouldn't be surprised they got a posse together, getting their hounds out. Hunting us down right now.

No one saw our faces, Bosco said. Don't even know who they're lookin for. Besides, got the money, didn't we?

Can't spend money when you're dead.

We ain't dead, Bosco said. Not yet, we ain't.

What did I say? Kilt said. I said calling it easy is dooming it from the start.

You said the get-go.

Start, get-go, that's the same damn thing. I thought we had a plan.

We did have a plan. And we followed that plan.

Nothing about any of that was in the plan, Kilt said. The plan was to get the money. That was the plan. You just went in there shooting.

Bosco eyed him for a long moment. Like he was full of suspicion.

Thought you ran out on me in there, Bosco said.

I didn't run out on you.

Where'd you go, then?

I was there the whole time.

Shooting starts and you're AWOL.

Bosco lifted the bottle from his side and drank and held it out to Kilt but Kilt didn't move so Bosco drank again and then set the bottle back in the dirt.

You been getting squirrelly lately, Kilt said. Like you got some bone to pick with everyone.

I'm a outlaw, baby brother. You don't get to being a outlaw by saying please and thank you.

No, Kilt said, you get dead. That's what it gets you.

Relax, baby brother. Calm yourself. We ain't dead. I don't know about you but I ain't dying today. Nah, Benji, what we've got are angels. We keep the company of angels out here.

Bosco raised the bottle again and held it out to Kilt.

Go on, baby brother, he said. Get you a drink. We need to celebrate.

Bosco shook the bottle at him. Kilt spit into the fire. Then he reached for the bottle and sank a long drink.

There you go, Bosco said. Go on and git you some.

Kilt swallowed and winced at the heat of it. He tried to pass the bottle back to Bosco, but Bosco said, Nah nah nah. I've been plenty greedy enough with it. Kill er off. Got anothern in the bag there.

Kilt stood and drained the bottle and pitched it off into the woods.

Since you're just standing there, Bosco said, throw another log on.

Kilt tossed on a couple more. The sparks burst into the dark air.

Probably shouldn't get this thing too big, Kilt said. Don't want to burn up the valley. Or worse, let someone know someone's up here.

Hell, Bosco said, it's already burned. Going a rain here soon anyway.

Kilt went just outside the light of the fire and took a leak. While he was standing with his back to him, Bosco said, You think that'll be enough?

Be enough for what?

To retire.

Who said anything about retiring?

You did. Just the other day. What you told Lindsay Marie, wasn't it?

What are you talking about?

Thought that's what you said. This is the last one, ain't it? Do this job and retire. Move away together. Buy some big cowshit spread. Make a honest woman out a her. Ain't that what you said?

She tell you that?

Shit, baby brother. Known you all my life. I know what you're angling for. Hell, I know you better than you know yourself.

You do, do you?

Yessir.

What am I thinking right now, then?

Well, Bosco said. You're holdin your pecker so you're probably thinking about sweet Lindsay Marie's golden pussy, and how all that money your sweet big brother stole for you is going a buy the two a you a whole new life together.

You got all that from watching me take a piss?

Shit, brother. I'm as clairvoyant as they come.

Kilt shook himself and did up his pants and turned back to the fire and came into the light and spit into the flames and sat down and said, Look at you learning new words.

He could feel Bosco staring at him and when Kilt turned and asked him what the hell he was staring at, Bosco said: You think it's going a be enough?

Enough?

Money. To get out a here? Take Lindsay Marie with you? She's got it in her to be one a them fancy kind a women. Not easily satisfied, if you catch my net.

Kilt spit.

Yeah, he said. It'll be enough.

What if you had all of it?

All of what?

All the money. What if you had all of it?

Don't need all of it. Right down the middle. Like we always do.

Sure, Bosco said. But what if you had all of it? That kind of money could buy a empire.

I don't want an empire, Kilt said. Just want some land. Enough of it to where I don't have to see anyone unless I want to.

Don't you think Marie's going a get lonely living that kind of life?

What are you saying?

A gal in her line a work?

That better be the last you say on that.

She's social, Bosco said. That's all I'm sayin.

That's enough.

Bosco tossed up his hands. He labored to his feet. Went to the satchel and retrieved the fresh bottle. He uncorked it with his teeth and spit the cork into the fire. He sank a good drink and then handed it down to Kilt. He sat again with some effort. Then took a heavy breath.

How's your leg? Kilt said.

Never better.

Bosco watched Kilt drink. Then he said: You know. When Mama left me on the steps all them years ago, all I could think about was getting back at her for it.

She was just a girl, Kilt said. We've talked about this. Only a kid. She was scared.

Scared. Pssh. Shit, so was I.

Kilt looked at him. Bosco had his hat low and his eyes were hidden in shadows. Only his black mustache could be seen. His teeth flashing amber in the firelight. Kilt said, I get the feeling you're aiming to tell me something.

All I wanted, Bosco continued, was to get some kind of revenge on her. Then when Wainwright told me who you were when you first showed up at the Triple Nine all I wanted to do was kill you. Here comes the boy Mama decided to keep. The one she decided to love. Shit, the way I was feelin, the devil himself would've gone easier on you. And then Wainwright up and does the same thing.

You stole from him and lied about it.

I was a kid.

Stealing is stealing.

Wainwright's got his coming too.

He took a pull from the bottle.

So why didn't you? Kilt said. Why didn't you kill me right then and there?

I do not know, Bosco said. Had a whole plan too. Several plans. But then one day I reconciled it wasn't your fault. Hell,

I figured I could always do it later. Might make the event even better.

You telling me you still haven't ruled it out?

Nothin's set in stone, baby brother.

Bosco smiled oddly.

And now here we are, Kilt said.

Here we are, Bosco said. Couple a outlaw brothers on the lam.

You ain't going to get all mushy and tell me you love me, are you?

Bosco tipped his hat back and winked at him. Then he said, I'm going a get us some grub. This outlaw is starving.

He started to stand but Kilt said: Stay put. I'll get it. Don't want you losing any more blood over me.

Kilt stood and went to his bag and knelt at it and opened the flap and looked through it. He called out a few things, asking Bosco's preferences. Kilt said, I know we were being chased out of there but we should've stolen a couple steaks on the way. What do you want?

Kilt heard Bosco's boots scraping over the dirt. Kilt said, I told you I got it. Go sit down.

And Kilt was just turning back to his brother when the side of the entrenching shovel came down behind his ear and it all went dark.

8

In the soft wind of the dream he was walking in a field of tall grass just as the sun in the west was going down behind a distant hill covered in wildflowers. The sun going down made the tall grass look like lavender and he walked slowly with his hands held out on either side and the soft points of the grass brushed against his palms like the tips of kitten ears. The smell rising from the cool earth through the grass was so sweet he would lick his lips sometimes in hopes of tasting it. He heard his name called and he turned and saw Lindsay Marie standing in the grass with the hill and the sun behind her. The light daubed any detail of an expression she might have worn but her hair was loose and it rose and fell in the wind and her arms were bare and the falling sun shone upon them. He turned and tried to walk to her but his feet did not move and when he looked down the grass was no longer sweet smelling but black with dead fire and when he looked toward Lindsay Marie again the sun was aflame with a corona of vicious spines and seemed to be approaching. The heat gathered and a line of fire heralded the sun's coming. He was hit with a wall of hot wind and called Lindsay Marie's name but she did not hear him and the line of fire reached her and she burst into flames and he fell to his knees in despair and then he woke up.

His eyes snapped open and he came awake gasping. He tried to sit up but a hand held him down. He blinked about furiously trying to reckon any logic in this new shadowed place he found himself in. He was lying in a bed with a straw mattress. He was naked to the waist and a moth-bitten blanket covered his legs. The room was a one-room cabin with bare logs and mud chinking. Along one wall there was an enormous hearth blackened with soot and the air smelled like cooking meat and woodsmoke and a little like wet dirt. There was a giant moose shed hung on the wall and a bearskin rug with its taxidermized face in a perpetual roar on the floor near the fireplace. The flames danced in the little glass eyes. The floor was old pinewood planking and cupped in places and reflective in others where decades of bootheels had worn the wood to a dull gloss. There was a gun over the mantel. A gun propped near the door. Another just lying on the table in the center of the room. There was a stack of wood near the hearth and a stout ax leaned against that. His Luger and holster were piled near the rifle on the table.

Kilt tried to sit up again but the same hand held him. Kilt squinted up. There was a girl of about fourteen sitting there on the bed next to him. She had a basin of water and a hand towel in her lap. The water in the basin was pink with his blood. The girl dipped the towel and dabbed lightly at his shoulder. Kilt tried to speak but she just said: Shh.

What the hell am I doing here? he said.

I found you, the girl said.

Rain was tapping against the thin-paned windows and the twisted image of the room was reflected all wonky in the glass.

What do you mean you found me?

I was out fetching water and I found you.

Where did you find me?

You were sitting on a mule.

Where's the mule?

In the stable.

Where am I?

You're at his house.

Whose house?

What were you doing out there? the girl asked.

Doing out where? I don't even know where I am.

Sitting on that mule, she said. You looked dead.

I feel dead.

Well, you ain't.

Kilt stretched his eyes and his view adjusted to the almost dark and he looked at her sitting there. There was an old-fashioned hurricane lantern on the table. There was another near the bedside. And along with the fire in the hearth that was the cabin's only light.

The girl had black hair and black eyes and dark skin. Her hair was shining in the hurricane lamplight. Her eyes flashed with the light just like the water in the basin flashed with light.

Where am I? he asked again.

You mean the town?

Is there a town?

No.

What's the closest town?

Which way you going?

I don't know.

She pointed. She said, That way is St. Regis. That way's Missoula.

St. Regis, Kilt said.

Uh-huh.

Kilt said, You Flathead?

Maybe.

What do you mean maybe?

Maybe.

Am I in some Indian camp?

The girl shook her head.

Then where am I?

You're at his house, she said again.

You got others here?

No, she said. Just one of you.

Just you and your daddy here? Kilt asked.

He ain't my daddy.

Granddaddy, then?

No.

Where's he at?

The girl didn't answer. She squeezed the hand towel into the basin. The water made a light sound as it fell in. Then she dipped the towel and pressed it softly against Kilt's collarbone.

You got bit, she said.

Yeah, Kilt said. I got bit.

Lion get you?

How'd you know it was a lion?

Cause it looks like a lion bite.

You come across lion bites often?

No, she said. You were lucky it was just a bite.

Lucky, you say.

It could have been a lot worse.

Kilt looked around at the room. Then he looked down at his wrist where the manacle had been.

What happened to the cuff? he said.

She nodded to the table. The manacle was lying open next to his gun.

You get that off me? he said.

She nodded. Then she said: What happened to your finger?

Got cut off.

How?

I don't know.

He watched her a moment. Then said: You want to tell me where I am?

He said to keep you comfortable, she said. You comfortable?

No, Kilt said. He around here somewhere?

No.

Where'd he go?

Just run off somewhere.

You don't have any idea?

He just runs off sometimes. He'll be back. He always comes back.

I was here when he left?

Of course.

When's he coming back?

Might be tonight. Maybe tomorrow.

You don't seem all that saddened by it.

She shrugged.

Does this happen often? Just leaves you here alone?

Sometimes, she said. It's better when he does. You want some whiskey?

You got some hiding around in here?

The girl nodded.

Okay, Kilt said. Thank you.

The girl rose and went to the cupboard on the far side of the room. Kilt watched her go. She was wearing a cotton dress with thin straps and the back was open. The way her hips shifted under the dress Kilt knew she was naked under it. He thought it an inappropriate thing to be wearing for a girl so young. When she got to the cupboard she scooped the hair over her shoulder so the entirety of her back was showing and she craned her neck around to see if he was watching, and if it seemed like something she had done before it was because she had.

She opened the door to the cupboard without making

a sound. She reminded Kilt of a mouse in the middle of the night. She took down a bottle and a glass. The rain had picked up and the wind blew it in sheets against the windows. The wind whistled in the flue. Whistled through all the gaps. She said: Do you take water in it?

No mam, Kilt said.

She came back with the bottle and the glass and sat down on the bed and poured the whiskey into the glass and then handed the glass carefully across the bed. Kilt tried to reach for it but as he did he winced with pain.

Here, she said.

Like a nurse she held one hand behind his head and with the other tilted the glass to Kilt's lips and helped him drink. After he swallowed she said: More?

Kilt nodded.

She leaned toward him and when she did the front of her loose dress drifted away and Kilt caught sight of her breast. It was small and firm. Like it wasn't completely formed. It did not go unnoticed to the girl. She said, Have as much as you want. Told me to make you comfortable. Whatever you want.

He had another sip and as she helped him she leaned with her chest nearly touching him and when Kilt moved his hand she thought he was going to touch her but when he didn't she leaned back and opened her eyes.

That's enough, Kilt said. Thank you.

She sat on the bed holding the glass in one hand and the bottle in the other and a confused look drew across her face. As if maybe he was playing some kind of game with her. As if it were some kind of trick.

You want anything else? she asked.

One of the straps had fallen off her shoulder. The lantern light was coruscating off her skin and he looked at her shoulder for a second and then back at her eyes.

What're you asking me? he said.

Asking if there's anything else you want?

Kilt reached out and hooked his finger in the fallen strap and slid it back up over her shoulder, and then shook his head and leaned back into the pillow and closed his eyes and feigned sleep.

She sat there in silence for a moment. She was wondering if this was all a part of the game. She thought at any second he would open his eyes and she would acquiesce with his desires, which seemed to be every man's desire, but he did not. Finally she said: Are you hungry? Got some elk stewing.

Kilt peeled open one eye.

Stewing?

Yessir.

Smells mighty good.

Been stewing all day.

The day I say no to elk stew is the day you can take that Luger of mine and shoot me with it.

The girl almost grinned. She stood from the bed. She crossed her arms before her and rubbed the skin of her arms. Kilt said, Here.

He pulled the shawl that was laid over his knees and handed it to her.

Too cold in here to be going around bare armed.

She took it reluctantly.

Go on, Kilt said.

She wrapped the shawl around her shoulders.

Thank you, she said.

Don't have to thank me, he said. It's your shawl.

The corner of her mouth curled up.

There we go, Kilt said. Haven't seen one of them awhile.

Yessir, she said. I'll get you some stew.

Ben, he said.

What?

Ben. That's my name. Benjamin Kilt.

Ben Kilt, she said. She smiled and he saw her white teeth flash in the firelight. She said, Been brought back to life is more like it.

He squinted at her. Then he laughed through his nose.

That's funny, he said. You're a funny girl.

You sure you don't want anything else?

Just the stew would be fine.

She went to the hearth where the stew was simmering in a large blackened pot. There was a metal ladle hanging from a hook over the fire. She licked her fingertips then touched the ladle lightly to test its heat and then took it down and dipped it into the stew and stirred it. The steam billowed up. The girl turned as she stirred and regarded him oddly. It wasn't a frown but it was something like it. Kilt waved at her. She turned back to the stew.

No idea when your daddy's getting home, huh?

He's not my daddy, she said.

He got a name? Got to thank someone for the hospitality.

You can thank me.

Done that already.

He rearranged himself with his back against the wall.

Would you do me another favor? he asked.

Okay.

There's a book out in one of those packs on the mule. Would you bring that in for me?

She hung the ladle up and crossed the room and went out and then came back in after a moment and handed him the book.

Thank you, he said.

He folded back the cover and started to read.

Need more light? she asked.

I'm fine, thank you.

She stood there watching him read. She cocked her head at him.

What's it about? she asked.

All kinds of things.

Like what?

Like how the world is, Kilt said. Or was. Answers, I guess. It's got a lot of answers.

She went back to the fire and took down the ladle and began to stir again. She was squinting at the steam. Then she looked back at him like she had too much on her mind. Like she didn't know what to get out first. He looked at her and put the book in his lap.

Cat got your tongue? Kilt asked.

I can't figure you out.

How do you mean?

Can't figure you out is all.

Of course you can't.

Why not?

Cause you just met me. If you had me all figured out already, I'd be a pretty boring person, wouldn't I?

Are you?

Boring?

The girl nodded.

I may be a lot of things, kiddo, but one thing I ain't is boring.

What makes you not boring?

A lot of things.

Name one.

Kilt pursed his lips like he had to think about it.

I rob banks, he finally said. How about that? That ain't boring.

You rob banks?

Uh-huh.

Like you're a bank robber?

Bona fide.

What's that mean?

Means the real deal, kiddo. Tried and true.

I don't believe you.

Kilt shrugged.

Prove it, she said.

Prove that I'm a bank robber?

Yes.

How am I going to do that lying here? No banks in here that I can see.

Where's all your money, then?

It's gone.

You spent it?

No.

Then where's it at?

Stolen.

Your stolen money got stolen?

Ironic, ain't it?

Who stole it?

A bank robber.

When'd it get stolen?

I suspect a few days ago.

Before you were attacked?

You mean by the lion?

Yes.

Money ain't much use to a lion.

So who stole it?

My brother.

The guy you rob banks with is your brother?

Half brother. Robbed, anyway. Don't think there's much of a future for us now.

I don't believe you.

Okay.

What's his name, then?

The bank robber?

Yes.

Sidney Bosco.

That ain't your last name, though.

That's the half of it.

That really his name? Sidney Bosco?

You know him?

No.

Probably better for it, Kilt said. Not a very nice guy. He robs banks, you know.

So do you, the girl said.

That's true.

You seem nice enough.

That's because you're being nice to me, Kilt said. Just reciprocating the favor.

What does that mean?

It means you ain't giving me any reason to be mean.

Why you telling me all of this?

Because you asked.

No, I didn't.

You asked if I was boring.

Aren't you worried I might tell someone?

No.

Why not?

Trust, I guess. I guess I trust you.

So where's he at?

My brother?

The girl nodded.

Kilt pointed. He said, I suspect Missoula.

The girl said, That's St. Regis.

Kilt pointed the other way.

The girl just stood there with the ladle hanging limp at her side. Kilt pointed at it.

You're dripping stew on the floor, kiddo.

She gazed down at it as if she had no idea why she was holding it. No idea what a ladle even was. She said: What if I was mean to you? What then?

You wouldn't be.

How do you know that?

Cause I ain't dead somewhere in the woods, that's how I know.

That's a pretty simple reason, she said.

Just because I'm not boring doesn't mean I can't be simple.

Later that night Kilt awoke to the sound of a man's voice that was low and rumbling like thunder in the distance. It was coming through the closed door of the only room. The voice wandered and strayed but its intent had a kind purpose that could only be described as sinister. Kilt blinked to adjust his eyes to the darkness. Both of the hurricane lanterns were out and the only light was the dull glow of dying embers within the stone hearth. Not even enough there to make a shadow. Hardly enough to even be called light. The rifle on the table was gone. So was his Luger and holster.

He tried to sit up but the pain did not allow it. It forced him to lie there and only guess at what might be being said behind the door. The boom of the voice rose suddenly and then he heard the delicate sound of the girl's voice gasp followed by the unmistakable noise of violence. The man behind the door shouted again and again. The girl must have been hit. Kilt heard the girl begin to cry.

Then the door to the room burst open and captured within that brick of soft light was the man doing up his belt with his back to Kilt and the girl naked and trying her best to cover herself with her small hands. A single lantern was lit in there and it filled the room with orange light and it spread over the girl's skin and the bruise under her eye and the bruise on her chest looked almost like shadows but Kilt knew better. She had tears in her eyes and her cheeks reflected the lamplight.

She caught Kilt watching them and she shied and pulled a thin blanket from the bed with which to hide behind, and seeing this the man turned and looked Kilt in the eye. He staggered from the room and swayed there for a moment before muttering something and then crossed the room to the front door where his mackinaw coat and hat were hung and he put them on and opened the door where the rain was turning over to snow, and right as he stepped out he regarded Kilt a final time and then slammed the door. A moment later Kilt heard the motor of a Ford Coupe start up and then the car clattered off until it faded altogether and then all was silent again. Kilt looked back into the room and if he didn't know any better he would have said it was empty. Then the girl appeared in the doorway for a moment before she closed the door. The bar of light under it lingered for a second. Then the light went out.

9

Morning broke early and white. It had snowed in the night and the white light off the snow flooded through the thin glass panes. He blinked like his eyelids had frozen. He tried to lift his head from the pillow. Then he tried again. Each time his head falling back into the meager pillow with defeat. Again he tried and this time labored with a great amount of pain and sat up and swung his feet from under the blanket and swung them off the bed and placed them on the cold wood floor. His toes curled in discomfort like the skin of dried fruit.

He attempted to sit up straight but that was wishful and he folded into himself. His eyes welled involuntarily. His nose became clogged. His arm was across his belly and his face between his legs as though suffering from stomach flu. He breathed a rancid breath through his knees toward his palsied feet on the floor. A small miasma of smoke in the cold air. He coughed and expected to pull away with his lap all full of blood but he raised up and found none and standing there before him was the man from the night before.

Sleep good? the man asked.

Kilt closed one eye as though looking into the sun. Or some glaring sunlike reflection. But despite the snow-bright room Kilt could only make out a dark outline of the man. A figure towering toward the ceiling in shadowed exaltation.

No, Kilt finally said. No, I did not.

Pity, the man said.

You the one I have to thank for the hospitality?

Not me, he said. We don't thank anyone out here. No one to thank.

You want to tell me where *out here* is?

She didn't tell you that last night?

No, Kilt said. She did not.

Huh.

The man took a chair from the raw pinewood table and spun it like a dance partner and sat down heavily with the chairback facing Kilt and finally sucked his teeth.

She tell you anything else? he asked.

No, Kilt said. She said she wanted to make sure I was comfortable.

Were you?

No. Kilt pointed to his collarbone. Got attacked, he said. Hard to be comfortable after being attacked.

The man rose from the chair and crossed toward the bed like a litigator approaching someone on the stand. He stood over Kilt and with a finger pulled aside the stained cloth and saw the purple bruised skin and home-knit sutures the girl had administered, and he studied them a moment then took his hand away and crossed back to the chair and sat down. The man tilted his head back and scratched his whiskered neck without taking his eyes from Kilt. The light caught his rotten teeth. His eyebrows stood long and crooked like the legs of dead spiders. A raven's nose like Poe would fantasize over. The man leveled his gaze on Kilt in the bed. His eyes were dark and hooded.

What're you doin all the way out here? he asked.

Not sure.

You oughta have a little knowin.

Wish I did.

The man nodded. You mean to tell me you just stumbled upon us out here?

That's not the way I'd describe it.

How would you describe it?

I do not know, Kilt said. This being the first time I've found myself in some abandoned cabin, I don't think I can give you a satisfactory answer.

This ain't abandoned. This look abandoned to you?

The man waved his hand about.

Again, Kilt said. I do not know.

I'm here, ain't I? the man said. My things are here, are they not?

Okay.

Seems to me you don't have a good idea of what abandoned means.

Semantics, I suppose, Kilt said.

What?

Not important.

What're you playin at?

Not playing at anything.

The man squinted his narrow eyes. Stirring within that wet alchemy he had the confused look of a drunk viper. Finally said: Ain't abandoned.

Okay, Kilt said.

Again the man scratched his neck. Then he leaned back in the chair and reached into his waistcoat pocket and produced a pouch of tobacco and some rolling papers and pulled one of the papers from the sheath and creased it lengthwise and set the V of paper on the table. He removed a pinch of tobacco from the pouch then picked up the paper and dolled the shreds down the middle like he was sprinkling salt and then licked the leading edge and rolled it between his fingers and thumbs. He put the cigarette between his scaled lips and went to the fire and knelt and lodged a stick into the flames and removed the burning end and held it to the cigarette. Then he came back to his chair and sat again. Not saying anything for a long moment, only watching Kilt in the bed and smoking slowly. Then he said: I want to know what it is you think you saw last night.

Last night.

That's right.

What I saw last night is none of my business, Kilt said.

She try anything with you when I wasn't here?

Try anything?

That's right.

I'm not sure I understand the question.

She use her body in any way?

Oh sure, Kilt said. She walked from there to here and back again couple times. Got me some stew. A little whiskey. Very helpful, that body of hers.

You think you're bein cute.

No sir.

She's mine, you know.

Yours?

Mine. Fair and square.

How do you mean fair and square? You win her off someone?

That's exactly what I did.

Some kind of prize?

Took her off some riverboat captain over in Idaho.

Took her? I thought you won her?

Took her, won her. Same thing. Fair and square.

I've never known anyone to win a little girl off anyone before.

She ain't that little.

Pretty little.

That captain told me he bought her off some reservation up in Canada. That's a transaction. Personal property.

And he just gave her over?

Pssh. The man grunted. You think squaws like that grow on trees? Shit. Captain got to beggin and pleadin with me. Got all kinds a tore up about it. Said I cheated him. Well. Can't have that kind a talk, can we.

So you reasoned him out?

Shit. Reason had nothin to do with it.

You must be awfully persuasive.

Not me, the man said. Guess you could say he lost his head over it all.

Lost his head. That some kind of innuendo?

A what?

A joke.

Shit. No joke about it. Blew his head clean off. Property's property and winning is winning.

Fair's fair.

Fuckin right.

How about that fancy Coupe you got out there?

What about it?

You win that too?

He sucked his teeth again. He nodded.

You ain't so bad, the man said.

Oh, thanks, Kilt said. Means a lot coming from a guy like you.

I tell you what. You want a little go with her, I won't object. A little poke. Hate to hog a fine piece of ass like that. What do you say?

That's very generous, Kilt said. But I like mine a little longer in the tooth.

Have it your way.

The man stood from the chair. A cloud of smoke hanging in the dank air and he rising into the toxic pall to be daubed of any detail again.

Fine piece of ass, he said again. You just think about it.

Then he strode off to the door and opened and closed it behind him and a moment later Kilt heard the Coupe start up and rattle off, farting its blue smoke into the distance till it finally all went quiet.

10

He slept through most of the day and in the last hours he rose in the drawn light and found his boots near the hearth where the girl had stood them to dry and lifted each and brought them to the table and sat in a chair and struggled into them one at a time. The dry leather was tight on his swollen feet. He had no socks but the fire had warmed the boots and he moved his toes in them like someone might in a pair of slippers.

He stood there in silence and took stock of the empty cabin. There was a washbasin but no running water. A bucket and ladle only. Near the basin was a woodstove which served as the oven. Blackened cast-iron skillets, a dirty kettle, and bellied-out Dutch oven. He looked at one of the windows and even from his place in the middle of the room he could see daylight through gaps so wide you could slide mail through them.

He crossed his arms and went to the door. The bolt-action handle was levered closed and the door in its jamb was all askew and the bolt took some effort to slide free. The cold air hit him and he looked out on the quiet forest all white with snow. He stood there on the crooked porch. He looked cockeyed at the sun where it lay huddled behind the meshwork of pines. The sky overhead was the blue of veins.

He walked to the far end of the porch and leaned his good shoulder against the post. All over the bone-colored snow were the tracks of small animals like sutures in a skull. There was a small shack maybe fifty feet from the cabin and the flimsy plank door had only one hinge keeping it from falling off. The door was open and Kilt squinted his eyes and saw a buck strung up by its antlers and skinned from its neck down. Just the deep maroon of frozen flesh. The pale arrested lines of sinew. There were chunks cleaved off and he suspected the stew the girl had served him the night before was not elk but deer. He wondered how long the animal had been dead for.

Kilt stepped from the porch into the snow. The cold came through the boots instantly. The slick sole of the boots made it hard to walk and he slipped like a court jester. More than once his arms flailed and the pain was so incredible that he swore aloud, cursing both his curiosity and the fates that divined him here.

He stepped into the shack and stood before the ruined animal. He gazed upon it as if it was a martyr displayed on its altar. Strung up in this hermetic grotto like it might predict some ominous portent. The dirt below the carcass was dark with dried blood. The ground was sprinkled profusely wiıth mouse shit. He pressed his fingers into the ribs of the animal and it was like touching a cold piece of granite.

The carcass swung in a morbid pendulum. He finally gripped the deer like a boxer hugging his bag, calming it to a standstill, and examined the inner workings. The ribs carved away. The belly hollowed. The mouth fallen open and the tongue cut out. An empty mouth tenanted only by rutted teeth the color of tea.

Dead is dead, Kilt thought. *Everything dies.*

He turned back into the light and was startled by the girl

standing there with her arms at her side. A stubby saw dangling limp in her right hand.

Sawing wood? Kilt asked.

No, she said. She nodded to the deer behind him.

Ah, Kilt said.

The girl's eye was swollen and the color of a beet. Her bottom lip was split. Kilt narrowed his eyes. Said: He do that to you last night?

No, she said, not taking her eyes from his, as if to break contact would give her away.

You going to tell me you fell? Kilt said.

That's right, the girl said. I fell.

Hell of a fall.

The girl shrugged.

What's your name? Kilt asked.

My name?

Yes.

Why do you want to know my name?

So I can call you something. Address you properly.

She squinted at him.

You do have a name, Kilt said. Don't you?

I got a name.

Okay.

Bonnie, she said.

Bonnie, Kilt said. Bonnie what?

Bonnie Grace.

Bonnie Grace.

It's the one they gave me.

Who's they?

The ones at them Indian schools they send people like me to.

You run away from it?

Yeah, she said. I ran away.

You want me to call you Bonnie?

You couldn't say my real name.

Why not?

Your mouth doesn't work like that.

Okay, Kilt said. Bonnie it is. He do that to you often, Bonnie?

Do what?

What he did last night.

Didn't do anything last night.

You telling me I made it all up? Telling me I was just seeing things?

Maybe you were.

How long you been telling yourself that?

I don't tell myself anything.

Not the truth anyway.

What's that supposed to mean?

You in the habit of lying?

You calling me a liar?

Yeah, Kilt said. I'm calling you a liar.

She stood there unmoving. Her fingers flexed around the handle of the saw. Then finally her eyes fell.

I'm sorry, Kilt said, I'm in your way.

He stepped out from within the shack. The stark light made him wince as if expecting pain. Bonnie moved past him into the shack. She stood there a moment letting her eyes adjust. She reached for the deer like a blind person. When she touched it she raised the hand with the saw and held the frozen carcass almost in an embrace. Then she began to cut.

I'll leave you to it, then, Kilt said.

He was turning to go but she spoke and her words stopped him.

Last night, she said.

Yes, he said.

He turned back to her. She was talking while she was cutting.

When I was helping you to drink the whiskey, she said.

Yes?

You took a peek.

I apologize for that. Sort of a knee-jerk reaction, I suppose.

How come you didn't do it?

Do what?

Bonnie stopped her sawing. She spoke with her back facing him.

Touch me, she said. The way men like to touch sometimes.

What way is that?

She got mad and she turned to face him but she saw a little flicker of something in his eye.

He smiled and shook his head and said: I didn't touch you because for one I was just mauled by a lion and left for dead till you came along. And for two, you're just a child. And that's all anybody needs to know.

I ain't little.

Kilt looked her up and down and nodded.

Yes, you are, he said. And I didn't say little. I said a child. And that's as far as it should ever go.

They just watched each other and they didn't say anything and then Kilt finally nodded and for a second time he turned to go and for a second time she stopped him.

Why you being so nice to me?

Am I?

Yes, she said. Why?

Well, Kilt said, I suppose I haven't been able to be nice to anyone in a while. You're just giving me the opportunity.

He nodded at her. He gave her a small grin that formed in the corner of his mouth.

I'm going to go lie down now, he said. Arm's going numb.

11

Night fallen and the man and Kilt at the pinewood table speaking little if at all. The man wavered with drink where he sat. Blinking as though his papery eyelids were seized in glue. Staring at the fire like some carnival geek. Bonnie went about her evening work sticking to the shadows and coming forth into the light diminutively only when she had to. Arms burdened with pans. Fingers black with soot from tending the scullery fire. In her drab finery she looked like a forgotten anchorite vowed to a dismal penance.

Kilt watched her with his head turned down pretending to clean the dirt from his fingernails with the point of the Bowie knife. He had his bad arm in a paltry sling, which was ripped from the hem of one of the girl's pale cotton shifts. Bonnie stole glances at him as she moved. Her eyes jumping like a songbird on the ground.

Through the window to the east the silver moon rose like a white sun's replica to blue the snow beneath it. Some omniscient fabrician's dye bleeding out on all that dead white.

The quietude was broken with the shattering of a clay bowl

slipping from the girl's hands. The man was lurched from his torpor and lashed out howling at the girl. He flung the first thing his hand clamped down upon which was his wooden cup of whiskey and cast it end over end at the girl. The whiskey being flung like blood spray against the fire's light.

You best pick that cup up, the man said to the girl.

The man looked at Kilt. The fire was sawing in the man's soapy eyes. His beard had a tobacco stain running toward his chin.

You got sumpin to say?

Kilt merely shook his head.

The man looked back at Bonnie.

Go on, he said. Pick it up.

Bonnie went to the cup on the floor and knelt without taking her eyes from the man like some belittled fighter retrieving their weapon. She lifted it carefully as if she feared it might break and then stood there watching him as though she was unsure of how to continue.

Well, the man said.

The girl didn't move.

You gonna bring it back?

Bonnie moved toward the table. She was stepping delicately as though on a thin skin of ice. She reached out with the cup in hand. Nothing about her trembled. She set the cup down and just as she was taking her hand away the man snatched her wrist and pulled her close and with his other clutched the back of her neck and forced her head down so she was looking over the empty cup.

What do you see? he said.

She didn't answer. Kilt could see that her eyes were closed. Pinched tight. Little crow's feet spreading out at the corners.

I said what do you see? the man said. Open them damn eyes, girl.

He gave her a little shake.

Go on, he said. Open em.

She looked into the cup.

You see anything in there?

The girl shook her head.

That's a problem, he said.

Again she remained silent and again he gave her a shake.

What're you gonna do about this?

She whispered out something that was barely audible.

Hmm? the man said.

He leaned his ear to her lips.

Get more, Bonnie said.

She was speaking as if there were an infant asleep in the room.

That's right, he said. Get more.

You have to let go of her first, Kilt said. His first words.

The man turned his attention to Kilt. A look of bewilderment overtook him. As if Kilt had suddenly appeared across the table. As if the voice had been conjured out of the black air.

What're you sayin to me?

Still picking at his fingernails with the knife, Kilt said, Said you have to let go of her first. If I were you, I'd let go of her.

And as calmly as placing a fork beside a plate Kilt laid the Bowie knife on the table. The firelight leapt on the metal. Kilt looked at the huge knife then he looked up at the man.

You tryin to tell me sumpin? the man asked.

Kilt looked back at the knife and shook his head.

No, Kilt said. Just can't do much if you don't let her go.

The man let go of her wrist with reluctance. Like a spoiled child giving up a toy. The skin on her wrist was white from his grip. Bonnie went to lift the cup but he placed his palm over the top. He snapped his tongue at her.

Where you takin my cup? he said.

Getting you more, she said.

It's my cup, he said.

I know.

You know? Then why you tryin a take it?

I—

You bring the bottle, he said. Cup stays here.

The man looked at Kilt.

How about you?

How about me what?

You want any more?

I haven't had any yet.

You want some?

You got another cup?

The man looked at the girl.

Get another cup, he said. And bring the bottle.

They watched her go. When she came back she went to pour the whiskey into the man's cup. But again he held his hand over the top.

Pour his first, the man said. Then the man looked at Kilt. He's our guest. Don't want to be rude.

Bonnie came around the table and set another cup before Kilt and uncorked the bottle and poured in three fingers.

Thank you, Kilt said.

Bonnie nodded with tight lips. She went around and poured for the man. He lifted up on the bottle, tilting it as she poured.

Good girl, the man said. Now run along.

The man slapped her ass as she went. Kilt watched her go. She walked into the bedroom and closed the door. The only noise was the popping fire. Kilt sipped his whiskey and then set his cup next to the knife. The man took a long pull off his and then set his own cup down and wiped his mouth with the back of his hand. He nodded wordlessly at the knife.

Hell of a knife, the man said.

Thank you.

Who you steal it off of?

Who said I stole it?

Seems to reason.

Based on what?

Based on what you do for a livin.

How do you know what I do for a living?

Girl spilled the beans.

Did she.

Heard St. Regis Savings & Loan just got robbed.

Oh?

Wouldn't happen to have anything to do with that?

No idea, Kilt said.

The man nodded.

So how you get into it?

How'd I get into what?

That line a work.

I didn't.

You either do or you don't.

It chose me.

Chose you.

Like anything divine, I suppose.

Divine?

Yes.

You kill many people?

No.

Guess God might frown on that, eh?

God? Kilt said.

Yeah.

You a believer?

A believer?

A Christian. Devout. Fire and brimstone and all that?

Well, sure, the man said. What else is there?

Kilt made a face like it was the first he'd ever considered such a thing.

Adaptation, I suppose, Kilt said. That's something to consider. Adaptation.

Materialism, Kilt said.

As in what I see is what I get?

Sure. All boiled down. Sure.

A guy can . . . what's the word you used?

Adapt.

Yeah. That word. What's that mean?

It means evolve.

You like your big words, don't you.

It means get used to. Change with your surroundings.

So it's one or the other?

God or evolution, you mean? Kilt said. God or adaptation?

Yeah.

Sure.

Okay, the man said. I can agree with that.

Kilt shifted his eyes between the man and the Bowie knife.

But remember, Kilt said. If you believe in adaptation then you also have to believe in maladaptation.

I don't know what that means.

I know you don't.

So what's it mean?

It means things evolve solely for the outcome of their own destruction.

I don't believe that.

So you believe in God?

Yeah.

But what if I don't?

Then I guess you'll burn in Hell.

Kilt smiled at the man. He sipped the whiskey. He said: Do you carry a gun?

A piece?

Yes, Kilt said. A gun. A piece. Whatever it is you want to call it.

This is Montana, Mister. You know that. Everyone carries a piece.

And what is that gun's purpose? The one you carry.

Its purpose? the man said. I guess its purpose is to smoke any fucker dumb enough to try and smoke me first.

So protection, then, Kilt said. Its purpose is protection. That what you're telling me?

Yeah, the man said. Protection.

Kilt said: Let's say the man down the bar has a gun.

There ain't no man down the bar. Hell, there ain't even a bar. Just you and me.

Well, let's say there is. For the sake of this example. Say the man down the bar has a gun and he gives me the same answer as you just did and you decide to pull your gun on him first and he uses his gun to protect himself, and when there were once two men with guns now there is only one. And let's say this pattern repeats itself indefinitely till there is only you left. One. One man with a gun. And that gun, remember, was invented by man. A species, according to some, believed to have evolved or adapted. Now, would you say this is a maladaptation?

You sayin we evolved or whatever only to destroy ourselves?

I don't know, Kilt said. That would be a discussion on directed evolution.

On what?

Anyway, Kilt said. I hope not.

You hope not what?

That we are maladapting.

Why not?

Because I don't feel like dying today. Do you feel like dying today, Mister . . . Say, what is your name anyway?

Santz.

Mr Santz. Do you want to die today?

No. No, I don't.

Kilt nodded. He sank the rest of his whiskey and grabbed

the Bowie knife and stood from the table and sheathed the knife and stuck the sheath in his waist at his back.

Where you goin? Santz said.

Think I'll hit the road.

Right now?

Yessir.

Middle of the night.

There's a moon.

Santz nodded.

You have my gun? Kilt asked.

Santz nodded at the hearth. The holstered Luger hung from a peg. Kilt went and retrieved it and slung it around his good shoulder and looked at the man sitting at the table.

Good thing you got attacked, Santz said.

Why is that?

Might try and shoot me.

Kilt smiled at him.

Wouldn't even have to try, Kilt said.

At the door he hefted on Santz's coat.

That's my coat, Santz said.

You ain't going to need it, Kilt said.

Then Kilt threw the prospector's old bear pelt around his shoulders and walked out the door without turning back.

12

The girl in her room heard the cabin's door open and then saw the flame of the guttered candle on the nightstand bend with the vacuum and then right again with the door's closing. Then it was all quiet. She sat on the bed with her head all askew like a curious dog, listening as she was. Her eyes darted back and forth across the dull wood floor. She half waited for the man to storm into the room as he often did after a night of whiskey and half waited for something else. Some kind of pardon maybe. Some kind of deliverance from all the squalor in which she found herself. But nothing came, not in any form. Not a voice, not a whisper. Nothing. Only the unwavering silence to which she had been inured seemed to hold true.

She finally stood from the bed. She faced the door. When she opened it she found the man passed out, face down on the table. She stepped into the room cautiously as if the floor might creak and snap him awake and send him into some dolorous rage. She watched him, she waited. When certainty of his state codified itself she walked past him. The man's swollen tongue choked his breath and he gagged histrionically and his head rose up like some botched exorcism to which Bonnie froze in fear. The man's head craned about like a broken toy and his pearled eyes blinked wildly as if underwater and a spill of slurred fragments warbled from his lips with spittle leaping forth to hang like dust. But it was short lived and all at once he collapsed back onto the table like he had been stripped of his bones. The girl walked on and opened the cabin door and looked back at the man at the table and then stepped into the night and closed the door behind her.

Through shadows and moonlight cutting the canopy, Bonnie saw Kilt loading something onto the mule's back. She stood on the porch and watched him. She was almost afraid to call his name. Her arms slack at her side. Her shoulders sloping like melting wax. Kilt looked up and saw her there and came around the mule and stood waiting as if she might say something. Nothing came and so he said: You're just standing there.

Yeah, she said.

Why?

Where are you going?

Nowhere, he said.

Going somewhere.

East. I suppose.

It's the middle of the night, she said.

There's a moon.

Well, what's east?

Kilt shrugged.

Must be something special, she said. Taking you out in the middle of the night as it is.

I suppose.

What's so important you got to leave like this?

Something that belongs to me.

You weren't even going to say goodbye.

Didn't know you wanted me to.

Can't it wait till the morning?

No, Kilt said. I don't think it can.

It could if you say it could.

Just cause I say it, doesn't make it so.

Maybe you wait till the morning anyway.

I'm already out here.

You could come back in.

Kilt looked up at the moon. He looked off down the dark road.

Good moon tonight, he said.

Stop saying that, Bonnie said.

You got something you want to say to me?

Don't go, she said.

Don't go.

Yeah. Don't go.

I have to go.

Then I'll come with you.

That's not a good idea.

Why not?

Cause you'll get into trouble.

I'm in trouble here.

Bonnie stepped off the porch into the blue snow. She stepped quickly toward Kilt.

What're you doing? he asked.

I'm coming with you.

No, you ain't.

Please.

I'm not arguing about this.

We don't have to argue.

I know it, Kilt said. Cause you ain't coming. And that's that.

He turned back to the mule and walked around it and with his good hand continued to cinch up the guy rope with strained jerking motions to which the mule blinked mutely and its ear twisted around.

So that's it? she said. You just going to let him keep doing that to me?

Her voice seemed composed of the palest colors. Kilt's hand fell still. He didn't look up at her immediately. He stared at the dirty chattel on the mule's back as if contemplating some question proposed in scripture. One of which has no answer. Or worse, he'd known all along but was too afraid to face. He turned his eyes up at her and the words formed on his lips and his breath drew inward and his lungs filled in preparation but nothing was said.

You ought to get back inside, Kilt said. You'll catch your death standing out here.

Kilt lifted the rawhide bridle rope and tugged at the mule and man and beast set off one before the other over the snow with their shadows leaning long over the isabelline ground. The pots starting up their clanging and Kilt's boots and the mule's hooves punching through the snow like odd teeth into old bread. He didn't look back but he knew she had not moved. And wouldn't till her bare feet went numb and tears began to rim her eyes.

13

The moon rode high in all that vaulted dark with the stars in their enormity swinging in slow carousel. Kilt came into the moonlight from time to time where the trees thinned and he gazed up and noted the North Star and then went on again. He looked back occasionally to see if his trail was being followed. He would halt the mule and wait for the pots and pans to cease their racket and stare back into the darkness with his head cocked slightly. Sometimes waiting a very long time as if his hidden tracker might grow weary of it all and announce themselves. But each time he was met with nothing but shadows and silence. And it was those shadows and that silence that dealt the guilt upon him. Even the sad-eyed mule seemed to have an opinion.

What? Kilt said to it.

The mule did not look away but instead blinked its huge wet eyes.

It wasn't my business, Kilt said. Girl's got two legs. She can run out of there anytime she wants. Now come on.

He jerked the mule on but it refused. Its long neck stretching like taffy.

Fine, Kilt said. Suit yourself.

Kilt dropped the lead and let it fall to the snow. He went around to the chattel on the mule's back and untied a leather bag and labored it down. He took the Bowie knife and stowed it in the small of his back and then swung the leather bag onto his shoulder and walked back around to face the mule.

Adios, Mule, he said.

He set off and only once did he turn to see the mule still in its place. Standing like the granite statue of a mule. Some queer monument hewn and left there for the benefit of the forest.

He kept on. The road fell down the mountain. There was ice in all the mudholes and the air was cold and his breath smoked all around him. He shivered violently at one point and tightened the bear pelt best he could at his throat.

The cold was unnerving. With no clouds to blanket the earth the temperature dropped out. Whatever moisture in the air had crystallized to anything it could and the moonlight winked in it all like some palace of ice in a child's dream. The limbs of ponderosa bejeweled and frosted like enormous sticks of rock candy. It would have been beautiful if not for his state. If not for his predicament.

He stopped where he stood and looked down at the ground. Then he turned and looked back from where he'd come. He could no longer see the mule. Swallowed up by some void of ill fortune. Lower on the mountain now the snow was thinner and the tire ruts from the man's Ford Coupe had cut a pair of lines in the frozen earth. Kilt kept to the tire ruts. His footprints all but vanished. He thought about Bonnie. About her standing barefoot in the snow. Her small voice asking for salvation, pleading in her own way. Pity or guilt or both rushed at his conscience and he made some kind of sound akin to an annoyed bear. He turned back to the road ahead but he didn't go on.

It ain't my business, he said aloud. His breath hung before him. So thick it was he could no longer see the road. So thick he took his good hand and swiped at it like someone swiping at smoke. When he did, the pelt slipped from his shoulders and fell to the snow. Kilt cursed himself and the pelt and the cold. He bent to retrieve the pelt but his slinged shoulder throbbed to do so. He tried again. This time dropping to one knee. He lowered his bad shoulder to the snow and with his good hand he attempted to pull on the pelt. It did not work well. Finally he fell to both knees and lowered his forehead to the ground like a penitent. With his good arm all askew he tugged the pelt over his back like some carnival ape trying to hide. His breath spilled over the snow like rolling fog. Bowed there as he was he closed the pelt at his throat and raised up and still on both knees gazed moonward. The pines towered. He looked down the road and then he looked behind him.

You got me on my knees, he said.

He saw her again, standing alone in the snow. Just a child. It was a feeling he was familiar with. He had no intention of going back but maybe that's what did it. The image of a child being left behind. Maybe that's what finally got to him.

Okay, he said. Have it your way.

He stood in a clumsy manner taking care not to lose the pelt again. His feet were cold in his boots. Seemingly lost of their joints, he stepped like a marionette.

He started back up the road. Back toward the cabin. The moon was behind him and his shadow stretched out and rippled over the uneven snow. He kept his head down as if to return was a shameful act.

The mule came into view up the road. It was standing just as Kilt had left him. Its long face staring at him as though waiting. As if knowing he'd be back. The mule watched him approach and as Kilt came up upon him it turned to look. Kilt stepped into the snow to walk around it. When Kilt was past he stopped and turned to see the mule's eyes looking sidelong at him. It's stout neck in the shape of a U. Kilt clicked his tongue and said: Well. Come on, then. And like a dog the mule turned and began to follow with the pots and pans starting up like some ridiculous wind chime.

Half an hour later Kilt could smell woodsmoke from the cabin. A little farther on he could see the thin twist of smoke rising up through the trees, suspended in the still air. Then finally the cabin appeared. Huddled in the blue snow, its dark wood the black of ink. Save for the orange square of an oil lamp stamped dimly behind a warped pane, it looked abandoned.

Kilt stopped and studied the house. The mule stopped behind him without being told. Kilt squinted an eye as if reasoning out his improvised plan. Like coming to a wide river with no way to cross it.

You wait here, he said to the mule.

Kilt stepped lightly as he could, keeping his head tilted and a little turned not knowing if the man was passed out inside the cabin or set about the darkness in some drunken vagary.

Kilt crept up behind the Coupe. He leaned his good shoulder against the metal frame and peered into the glass. He didn't know what he was looking for, but he looked anyway. Just an empty carriage. A blanket balled in the back. Several empty bottles. He came around the car and kept on toward the cabin. He looked up once more at the pearl-colored moon. Bright and full, it was like some luminous jewel set against the smoothest of dark skin. Then he heard it, stealing his attention away from the sky.

He looked back at the mule thinking it had nickered or sighed but the mule stood stock-still. Then he heard it again. It came from inside the cabin. Muted through the wood but unmistakable. Kilt reached for the Luger and unholstered it and thumbed off the safety and started for the cabin, never taking his eyes from the front door.

His pace quickened. He knew what was happening but he didn't know where inside the cabin. If it was in the main room or the bedroom. At the door he stopped and with his slinged hand he struggled with the bolt latch, keeping the Luger poised in his right hand with his middle finger hooked through the trigger guard. Kilt had to raise up on his toes to help lift the latch and then twist his whole torso to slide it free. The door eased in and the rusted hinges moaned like oars in their chalks.

The fire in the hearth was dying and the room was empty. He looked at the bed in the corner of the room where he had slept. That was empty too. Just as he had left it with the single pillow folded against the headboard and the wool blanket all sideways on the mattress. The bedroom door was closed and a thin bar of orange light ran along the floor. He could hear the man in there and he could hear Bonnie's voice and Kilt knew exactly what the man was doing to her.

Kilt crossed the room taking care not to make a sound. The tortured voice of the girl would ring out suddenly and then fall back into silence with only the man gibbering some unintelligible orders like some kind of vile commentary. Kilt was just on the other side of the door, not an inch of plank wood separating them. He leaned against the door and with his slinged hand turned the knob with his fingertips. He winced as if the door would make a sound and give him away. But no sound Kilt made could overcome what was going on in the room.

The man had his pants wadded at his ankles. He still had his boots on. The girl was beneath him and her legs flung all akimbo. Her hands were pressing against the man as if she were caught beneath a drunk steer. Impossible to know what the girl was looking at if anything at all. Perhaps her head was turned and she was watching the wall, the shadow play of them acting out some fiendish scene. That enormous dark hulk writhing out amid the candlelight in its single violent purpose. Or maybe her eyes were closed in an attempt to believe it wasn't actually true. That it might be yet another horrible dream from which she would awaken if only she pinched her eyes together tight enough.

But in that last moment Kilt suspected she was looking straight at him because she screamed as half of the man's face erupted in a plume of gore and fled sidelong to collide against the wall. The dead weight fell down upon her and she screamed some more. Kilt stood with the Luger poised a moment to make sure the man was not going to move again, and when the man didn't Kilt went and rolled the dead man to the floor, him landing on his back and staring up at the ceiling, a visage even in its lifelessness tantamount to evil.

The man's only eye was wide and he stared up like some freak cyclops, unblinking and aghast. There was a hole in his left temple where the bullet had entered. The right side was missing and the blood was bubbling like a garish stew. The wall shined with blood. There were bits of brain tissue and fragments of skull stuck in it and it looked like a kind of gruesome stucco.

Bonnie was spackled in the man's blood. She peered down at the man on the floor and then up at Kilt. Then she slid up the bed against the headboard and pulled her dress down over her legs. The blood seeped from the ragged opening like a burst yoke and congealed with the shards of bone, still warm with the heat of the now halted heart.

You shot him, Bonnie said.

Yeah, Kilt said. I shot him.

You said you don't shoot people.

Did I?

Is he dead?

He ain't alive.

Kilt looked him over. He stepped to where the man's right

hand lay motionless on the wood. Kilt knelt and set the Luger on the floor and lifted the man's hand and turned it and the candlelight caught the jewels of the ring and threw little shards of light against Kilt's face. He laid the man's arm on his thigh and then trapped the arm between his elbow and leg and in an odd manner he tried to free the ring from the finger. The dead man's fingers were bloated and pink. Kilt made some kind of frustrated sound and let the hand drop back to the floor. He stood and reached behind and pulled the Bowie knife from its sheath and knelt again and raised the knife and swung it and cleaved off the finger. Bonnie flinched. The hand bounced oddly, like cutting the head off a dead fish. The girl looked on, not knowing what to say. Then finally: What'd you do that for?

Need a little walking-around money, kiddo.

He slid the ring free and dropped the finger to the floor and put the ring into his pocket. Then he swiped the blade flatwise on one side then the other against the man's shirt and then he sheathed it. Then he lifted the Luger from the floor and holstered that too. He looked at the girl.

You all right?

Bonnie shrugged. I don't know, she said.

Kilt nodded. Well, he said. Then he turned toward the door and when he didn't hear anything behind him he stopped and turned and said, You coming?

14

Outside Kilt untied the chattel from the mule's back and pushed it all off and slapped the mule on the rump. Told it to git. Then he walked to the Coupe and turned to the girl and said, Come on.

The Coupe bucked down the guttered road sliding and skittering over the trenched snow. Bonnie sat beside him with her hands in her lap saying nothing and thinking only of the cabin and the dead man inside of it.

After a long moment she said: I don't understand men.

What?

I don't understand you.

Me?

Any of you.

Nothing to understand, Kilt said. We're an open book. Hell, you don't even need to open it. It's all right there on the cover.

You want me to buy that?

I don't care if you buy it or not, Kilt said. It's the truth. And the truth don't care if it's bought.

All you men do is destroy each other, she said. If you were to leave it to women, the world, that is, women looking after it all, you wouldn't have any of this destruction.

That's probably true, Kilt said. He looked at her. I hope this hasn't sullied your image of me.

My image of you? I don't even know you.

Listen, he said, sometimes good people have to do bad things.

Is that what you are?

Is that what I am what?

A good person. If I'm coming with you I want to know if I'm riding with a good person or a bad person.

Well, Kilt said. What do you think?

She didn't answer him. She just looked straight ahead. The headlights lighting up the snow.

If it was up to me, Kilt finally said, I wouldn't have done it.

Done what? she said. Shoot him?

Her voice was tired sounding.

No, he said, I was always going to shoot him. Just not on top of you like I did.

But you ain't sorry that you killed him?

No.

Kilt looked over at her. She still had some blood at her temple, a little over her left eye. Kilt said, Here, and handed Bonnie a handkerchief.

She took it and wiped at her skin.

Gone? she asked. She turned her face in the moonlight.

Yeah, he said.

They drove off the mountain and into the valley and the snow was all melted out. They came to a road that went east and west. Kilt stepped on the brakes and leaned over the wheel. Looked right and then looked left.

How do I get to Missoula? Kilt said.

Bonnie pointed to the left. Kilt sat there with a hand on the wheel. He said, You okay?

Yeah.

You sure?

Yeah.

Okay.

Why we going to Missoula? she asked.

Going to surprise someone, he said.

Who you going to surprise?

My brother.

He don't know you're coming?

That would ruin the surprise.

What's the surprise?

I'm going to kill him.

15

Well past ten when they got to Missoula. Kilt parked the Coupe in front of the Pilgrim Saloon and turned off the engine. He sat back in the seat. The girl had fallen asleep and when the engine cut she lifted up from her place against the door and rubbed her eyes and said, Where are we?

You stay in here.

I'm coming in.

You're staying here.

But before he could protest she had already left the car. Kilt sighed and got out. He followed her in through the front door. The place was raucous. There was a man playing the piano. Several tables with men playing stud. The whores in their garish makeup and finery floated about the room like they weren't even touching the floor. Everyone shouting over each other. Kilt pointed with his chin to a table as far from it all as they could get and said, Sit you down over there, kiddo. I'm going to go get some answers.

Kilt went to the rear of the saloon and climbed the steps and in the dim stairwell he passed a couple of whores who called him baby and kissed the air at him. Top of the stairwell the hall unraveled before him. A red carpet ran down the middle. The walls were affixed with a few electric sconces. He passed several closed doors before he came to the one he sought and stood a moment with his hand poised at the doorknob as if working out his next move, and then abandoning it completely, he knocked on the door and waited and knocked again.

The room was empty. A lamp had been left on and threw long shadows over the wood floor. He stepped in and pushed the door shut behind him. He took off his hat and crossed the room and ran his fingertips along the bed frame. He gripped one of the posters and looked up at the lacy canopy and he ran his fingertips through that too. He went to the bureau where she normally kept her jewelry and perfumes and the little music box with the miniature ballerina but all that was gone and all that was left was the lace doily it all sat upon. He went around the bed and opened the drawers at the table there but there was nothing in them. He took a quick stock of the room then pulled the chain on the lamp and then went to stand by the window in the dark.

He stood there with the lace curtains folded back in his hand and he looked down at the street. The red light of the Pilgrim Saloon's sign bled into the dark room. The white sheets on the bed and the white lace above it looked to have been stained with watered-down blood. There were people holding hands down the sidewalks. There was a boy hawking cigarettes. Kilt slid open the window and listened. Then he slid shut the window and went and sat on the bed. A car horn squawked and a dog started to bark. After a while he stood and put his hat back on and crossed the room and opened the door and then pulled it shut behind him.

Kilt went back down to the bar and leaned against it on his good elbow. The barman looked at him and his eyes flared.

The barman rubbed his chin and nodded at some man and set the glass of beer down before him. Then he came down the bar, rubbing his hands together like he was working out arthritis.

Ben, the barman said.

Lonny. Where's he at?

Where's who at?

Don't be cute.

Lonny answered him without a hint of sympathy.

This wouldn't have anything to do with St. Regis Savings & Loan, would it?

Don't know anything about that.

Sid said you were dead, Lonny said.

That's not an answer, Kilt said.

Told me he was the one who put you in the ground.

I'm sure he was. Where's he at?

I don't know.

What do you mean you don't know?

I ain't in charge of him, Ben. Lonny looked down at Kilt's mangled hand then up at his arm in the sling. Then he looked over at the table where Bonnie was sitting with her hands in her lap, half looking out at the room, half looking at Kilt.

Lonny said, That little squaw must be quite the tomcat in the sheets. Tearing you up.

Kilt ignored him and said, When was the last time you saw him?

Been a few days.

He say anything to you?

Said a lot of things to me.

Cut the shit, Lonny.

You want something to drink?

Not really.

Have something to drink.

Lonny reached under the bar but Kilt stopped him by setting the butt of the Luger on the bar top. Clicked his tongue at him. Said, You want to surprise me with something you can surprise me somewhere where I can see your hands.

Lonny held up his hands then turned to the backbar mirror. Stared at Kilt as he reached down a bottle of whiskey. Reached down a glass. He turned again toward the bar and uncorked the bottle and poured three fingers. Slid the glass toward Kilt with the tips of his fingers. Lonny looked down at the Luger pointed at him, said, Moren a few cowboys in here that would probably take offense to that Kraut sidearm you're pointing at me. Might see you as some kind of Gerry sympathizer.

You going to tell me where he went or not? Kilt said.

Lonny hadn't taken his eyes from the gun. Not the first time a gun had been trained on him, but it still made him uneasy. Lonny might have been dumb but he wasn't stupid.

What do you say you put your iron away and drink that whiskey instead. Help with the pain of it all.

I never said I was in pain.

I just figured you might be, Lonny said. A man's brother running off with his woman? Hell, it makes me mad just to think about it, and I ain't even got a woman.

A defeated expression fell on Kilt, like all the wind had been taken from his lungs. Like he some kind of cruel manifestation set aside only for the ill-fated.

Where's Lindsay Marie? Kilt said.

I just told you, Lonny said. Gone. G-O-N.

Kilt clicked off the safety of the Luger with his thumb. Lonny took a step back with his hands held in something like surrender.

Come on, Ben, Lonny said. We've known each other a long time. I ain't the one that did it.

Where are they?

Told you already.

You better formulate an answer pretty darn quick or I'm going to put a hole in your stomach.

Goddamnit, Ben! For Chrissake!

Five.

Ben, goddamnit!

Four.

Said something about the Triple Nine.

Three.

Goddamnit! That's all I know!

Two.

His countdown was interrupted by the crashing of a chair at Bonnie's table. Kilt turned and saw three men standing around her. Mean-looking guys with beards and black cow-puncher hats. One of them wore a slicker and that one had his hands on his waist with an evil and long-standing hatred in his eyes. The chair next to Bonnie's had been thrown from the table. She sat there huddled like she was waiting to be slapped around.

When Kilt looked back at Lonny he was gone. All the faces at the bar were focused on the table and what might be coming next. The man in the slicker bent to speak to Bonnie in a tone only she could hear. And when Kilt shouted at him the man lifted his head and faced around with ominous intent. Kilt moved away from the bar and squared up with the man and then moved toward the table in a studied saunter.

When he got to the table Kilt said, Bonnie, you all right?

But before she could answer, before she could even offer the smallest gesture, the man said, No Injuns allowed.

His voice sounded like boulders tumbling underwater.

Kilt leaned and looked at the toppled chair. He pointed the pistol at it. He said, I was sitting there.

You hear what I said?

No, Kilt said. Can you repeat it?

The man stepped toward Kilt. The other two closed in around to either side to flank him. Kilt glanced sidelong at each in turn. First to his left then to his right. Then Kilt looked straight ahead at the man in the slicker.

I don't recognize you fellas, Kilt said.

That's cause we ain't from around here.

Then how do you know the rules of this place?

No Injuns, he said again.

Then Kilt started to shake his head. He holstered the Luger at his chest under his jacket. It looked as if Kilt might even start to smile.

What's so funny? the man said.

Nothing, Kilt said.

Then why the hell you smilin?

Am I smiling? I'm sorry, I didn't realize I was.

This squaw belong to you?

Squaw?

The girl. The Injun.

Belong to me? No. Just traveling together.

Well, you best travel your ass right on outta here. Take the bitch with you. Fuckin animals belongs outside.

Fucking animals? Kilt said. Like having sex with animals? That belongs outside?

What the hell you takin about?

You said fucking animals belongs outside. You said belongs. With an S. Is that your thing? Fucking animals?

I said animals belong outside. He pointed at Bonnie.

Huh, Kilt said. He popped his lips. Squaw you say?

That's right.

You know, Kilt said, you're the second guy to call her that in as many days.

I tell it how it is, the man said.

Like calling the sky blue because it's blue.

What?

Looks like a duck and quacks like a duck . . .

It's probably a fuckin duck, the man said.

There you go, Kilt said. Ain't as dumb as you look. Now, that name you're appointing to that girl there, however. Squaw. That name is a derogatory one.

A what?

Not nice, Kilt said. That name represents a loose woman. A whore. And when I look over there at her, I don't see any kind of woman. I just see a girl. Hell, I just see a child. So if we're going to keep standing around talking about her let's at least assign her a more fitting title.

And what title would that be?

You could call her by her name.

Squaws don't have names.

Kilt winced like he'd just heard metal grinding.

You said it again, didn't you? Kilt said. Then he looked at Bonnie and said, What's your name?

The girl said nothing.

Go on, tell him your name, Kilt said. He ain't going to hurt you.

Bonnie, she said. She spoke softly, with her head tilted forward, speaking at the table.

Bonnie, Kilt said. Yeah. But what's your Cree name?

The girl was silent. The men around Kilt shifted on their feet. The man in the slicker hadn't blinked once.

It's all right, Kilt said. No one's going to hurt you.

So she said it. Her eyes shifted up at the men then at Kilt. Kilt winked at her.

Now, Kilt said, you know her name. You can call her that or you can continue to call her squaw just like the other guy did and roll the dice.

The dice?

Forgive me, Kilt said, you were playing stud when we come in, weren't you. I'm mixing my metaphors. See what you're dealt. How about that?

And what was the other guy dealt?

He folded.

The man looked at his friends to either side. He smiled, said, Never seen a white man stick his neck out for a Injun like this before. Must be some sweet squaw pussy she's got between her legs.

Bonnie looked at Kilt and saw his jaw flex. His once calm and warm eyes changed. Like clouds washing over a peaceful field of grass. Like all the lights going out in a house all at once.

Say her name, Kilt said. His tone was flat.

Fuck you, the man said.

Say her name.

The man spit on Kilt's shirt. The foam bubbled like acid on the fabric. Kilt tilted down his face and just looked at it. Then in a deft motion pulled the Bowie knife from the sheath at the small of his back and with the butt of the handle popped the man in the nose with the cartilage snapping and the skin erupting in a spray of blood. His friends balked backward, their eyes going wide for a brief moment before Kilt's bad arm sprung from its sling and he unholstered the Luger and shot them each through the forehead. They collapsed to the floor without ceremony. Kilt knocked the man with the busted nose to the floor and fell upon him with his knees trapping the man's arms at his side. The blood from his nose was streaming into his eyes turning them red. He attempted to blink the blood away but it was useless and his black pupils just swirled around in it, shifting wildly in fear.

Kilt lowered his face to the man's. He said, Open your mouth.

The man either didn't listen or he didn't hear. So with the point of the knife Kilt turned the man's face to the side and wiped the blood out of the man's ear. Kilt leaned down to speak into it.

I said open your mouth, Kilt said.

Bonnie had stood from the table and watched on with neither horror nor awe. Almost expressionless, like she was standing at the rim of a deep canyon and just staring off into it.

Ben, Bonnie said. Her voice was soft.

Hold on, kiddo.

The man finally parted his lips ever so slightly and when he did Kilt jammed in the knife and levered his jaw open and took hold of his tongue and was about to cut it out when Bonnie shouted.

Benjamin!

Kilt turned. She was silently pleading for him to stop. He could see it in her face. The way her eyes didn't move. Her lips poised to speak but unable to deliver a word.

Kilt let go of the man's tongue.

You better thank her while you can, Kilt said.

Then he popped the butt of the knife into the man's jaw. It ruptured in blood with a quick snap.

Kilt stood from the man's chest. The saloon was entirely silent, only the man writhing in agony on the floor. No one said a word. No one dared to. The man's wet face shined in the saloon's tawdry lights. Kilt eyed the patrons like they were wooden cutouts and then back at Bonnie who too had not moved. Then Kilt looked down on the doomed man and shot him twice in the chest. Then he trained the Luger at his face and shot him between the eyes.

PART 2

I do not like to talk about violence. More and more it seems an obsession of the human race. We ingest it as if it were good for us. We make time in our day to revel in it. Perhaps we cannot help ourselves. Or perhaps to dwell is merely a way of trying to understand it. Like solving a difficult math equation or building a tower in the sky. We look for answers to these things and in time we are rewarded. The problem with violence is that there is no answer and we know the outcome and yet we continue to puzzle over it, continue to engage knowing it only ends in sadness and pain. It is something that has plagued us for too long.

You have to remember my part in all of this was as a young girl. Of course I did not see myself as such, but when one lives a life that is longer than one might think or hope, the small years that seem endless when living them are condensed to a blink. Yet, I can still see every flame, every bullet, hear every word spoken, every vow abandoned.

I do not like to talk about violence but I can't not talk about it if I ever want to talk about Benjamin Kilt. He was wed to it in a certain way. It was the way he acted around it. Like it was a snake he had danced with many times. He moved with it because he had to. But he also laughed at the snake. And made the snake ashamed of itself for ever trying to strike him. I know I will dwell on violence in the future because I have not been able to rid it from my past. But for the moment I'd rather think of something else.

16

Turn of the century. 1909. A harbor town in Northern Minnesota. Someplace where the ice stacks on the frozen shores and the winds howl. A place where the blowing snow pales everything, leaving nothing for the eye to look at. Maybe smoke churning from one of the many pulp towers, only slightly darker than the snow. Maybe. Picture in this: a brick building six or seven stories and on the fourth Benjamin Kilt was only seven years old.

His mother loved him, his father didn't even know he had a son. Kilt had a half brother somewhere in the world. Four years his senior he had heard. Kilt's mother had left the newborn child on the steps of a church in Minneapolis and returned to Duluth and that was that.

His mother would come home late and her sleeping boy in the only bed in the only room would be curled there under the thin covers. The heat turned off for the night. She would take off her petticoat and drape it over the child. She would then turn away and undress at the washbasin and wet a rag and pull one strap of the slip off her shoulder and set to cleaning herself.

Kilt would lie there with one eye open only a slit, watching his mother. Her skin was translucent. Almost iridescent. He would count the bruises each night as she washed. The fresh ones all pink and raised up. The older ones going yellow, the color of jaundiced eyes. Once or twice she would turn back to see he was not watching. And then kneeling over him would kiss his forehead and say: The meek will never inherit anything. You'll be bolder than me. One day you will get to choose your life, baby boy. You, and no one else.

And then she would crawl in behind him and wrap her arm around his thin belly. The boy would open his eyes now and wait till his mother was asleep. And only when he knew she was would he close his eyes again and fall asleep too.

When his mother died he was only nine. She had taken a bath and opened her wrists and closed her eyes in all that red water. A girl named Sylvia found her. The other girls of the place took care of him, making sure he wouldn't see anything. They said sweet things about his mother. They were affectionate. They said she treated all of them like sisters. Said she would have done anything for them. He watched two men load her in a truck. She was under a blanket. One of the girls told him the blanket was so that she wouldn't get cold.

He quit school after the second grade. Went to work cleaning the saloon in the mornings. Sweeping the floors. Taking out the trash. Whatever Mr Thompson asked him to do. Sylvia took it upon herself to teach the boy to read. She gave him a copy of *Moby-Dick* and read from it every night. They read it front to back and then they read it again. Even if you never have money, she told him, at least you'll be smart.

Winter gave way to spring, and Kilt turned ten. With the warmer weather a young man appeared one day at the bar. Maybe twenty-five years old. Sat in the same stool every night for almost a month and a half. Never drank more than a glass of beer. Made that glass last for hours. None of the girls ever had a bad word to say about him. Always a gentleman, they said.

He looked like a cowboy but not full cowboy. Wore boots but not the hat. Had the kind a stevedore would wear. Always wore a tie and a clean white shirt and a leather jacket. He didn't talk much. Just sat there studying the room through the Brunswick backbar mirror.

It was a Saturday when he first spoke to Kilt. 1912. A horn bellowed as a big laker steamed into the canal off Lake Superior. The crowd at the bar stirred and everyone left their glasses there on the bar to watch the freighter come in. Everyone except Kilt and that man. The man squinted at Kilt.

Ain't you wanting to see that boat?

Seen them before, the boy said. He had his head down, sweeping the floor with a broom.

It's one a them big ones.

Seen big ones.

You're a hard worker, he said. Been watching you.

Kilt stopped and looked up.

You want a pop? the man said.

No, thank you.

Come on. Take a break. Come get you a pop.

Kilt didn't move.

What, you don't drink pop?

I do.

Then come get you a pop.

The man reached over the bar and opened the ice chest and fished out a bottle. He sat back in his stool and set the cap on the corner of the bar and thumped his hand and the cap sallied through the air and spun edgewise on the floor like a coin. He held the bottle out for the boy. Already the glass was sweating in the muggy heat.

Go on, he said. Don't let it get warm.

Kilt set the broom against the bar, not taking his eyes from the man. He came forward cautiously and the man held the bottle by the neck and Kilt took it with equal caution then finished it in two drinks and then the man nodded, saying: Good?

Kilt nodded.

You want another?

Kilt didn't answer.

Okay, the man said.

So again he reached over and opened the ice chest and performed the same thing, handing the bottle to the boy by the neck.

What's your name? the man asked.

Benjamin.

Benjamin. Benjamin what?

Benjamin Kilt.

You that boy without the mother? That one who used to work here?

Kilt nodded.

Uh-huh, the man said. That's a sad story. Boy losing his mother.

Kilt was silent. He drank from the bottle.

I lost my mother too, the man said. How old are you? I bet you're about eight.

Ten.

Eight's about ten. Shoot, you're a little feller.

Kilt squinted. The man waved a hand.

Ah, didn't mean nothing by it. Being big ain't all it's cracked up to be. Look at me.

The man stood from his stool.

I look big to you?

Kilt looked him from boot to hat. He nodded. The man sat down.

That's just cause you're a kid. All adults look big to kids. Well, I'll tell you. I ain't big either. My name's Nick. Nick Mercy. Called me Nicky when I was your age. Nicky Mercy. It's got a ring to it, I guess. But you grow up, you know.

I don't mind it, Kilt said.

Don't mind what?

The name. Nicky.

That's cause you're a kid.

Mercy looked at the boy as if he had just prophesized something. Mercy took a small drink off his beer. He made a gesture like conceding to a long-held debate.

How much are they paying you here, Benny? Can I call you Benny?

Okay.

How much, then?

Thompson gives me a dime a day.

A dime?

Yessir.

That ain't much for a day's work. Thompson the owner?

Kilt nodded.

Sounds to me like old man Thompson is ripping you off.

Ripping me off?

Ain't giving you your cut. Your fair share.

Mercy took off his hat and combed his hair with his fingers and then put his hat back on.

Can you drive a car, kid?

I don't know.

What do you mean you don't know?

Never been in one before.

It's easy. You just press a pedal. Turn a wheel.

Why you asking?

Mercy smiled. Lifted his beer. Drank half the glass in a single pull.

Tell you what, Benjamin, Mercy said. You meet me in the alley in one minute and I'll teach you how to drive a car. Make more money in a single afternoon than you ever would a lifetime working for old man Thompson at a dime a day. How's that sound to you?

The boy stood stock-still. The Coca-Cola bottle dripping in his small hand. Mercy stood from his stool and placed a bill on the bar top. Took a couple coins for the Coca-Cola and put them on top of the bill.

Nothing free in the world, he said. He looked at the boy standing before him. Mercy stood from the stool and straightened his tie. Then he straightened his hat. Looked down at the boy.

You've an endearing quality to you, did you know that?

Kilt only stared at him.

You know that word? Endearing.

Kilt shook his head.

It means you're easy to like.

Mercy reached out and tousled the boy's hair.

Come on, Mercy said. Let's teach you how to drive a car.

17

The car Mercy taught Kilt to drive was a Cadillac Model 30. A 1912. Dark red, almost black. A true getaway car, Mercy said. Want to take a seat in her? Fire it up?

I never cranked a car before, Kilt said.

Mercy smiled at the boy. Said: Kid, you don't crank this one.

How you start it, then?

Mercy took Kilt around and opened the engine. He pointed at a box with some wires coming off it.

See that? he said. That's an electric starter.

That starts the car?

First of its kind, Mercy said. That's the future right there, Benjamin Pretty, isn't it?

The boy nodded.

L-head straight four, Mercy said. Bored out to 286 cubic inches.

What does that mean?

Means it's fast. Mercy shut the hood. And I'm going to teach you to drive it.

They went around and Mercy opened the door for Kilt and told him to get in.

Slide on over, Mercy said. Go on. Grab that wheel.

The boy craned his neck to try and see over the wheel.

How's that feel? Mercy said.

Kilt only nodded.

Don't be nervous, Mercy said. It's only a machine. You tell it what to do.

How do I start it? Kilt asked.

All right, Mercy said. It's a bit of a process, so pay attention. I want you to memorize this. Burn it into your brain, okay?

The boy nodded.

Okay, Mercy said. First things first. He leaned over the boy. Wiggled a long silver lever. This, he said, is the shifter. Make sure it's in neutral. Now take a look down there at your feet. Three pedals. That one on the left is your clutch. The one next to it on the right, that's your brake. And that smaller one below those two is your throttle. The clutch engages the engine to the transmission. The brake stops the car from running into anything. And the throttle makes us go vroom vroom. You following me?

Kilt nodded again.

Now over here, Mercy said, pointing to a curved black box to the left of the wheel, that's the magneto and ignition switch. Flip this to mag, he said. Any guesses as to what that does?

Makes it so we don't have to crank the engine?

Mercy smiled at him.

That's very good, Benjamin. Quick learner. Okay, we got it flipped to mag, now we go down here.

Mercy pointed at a black button between his legs.

You press this to energize the system. Now you see that little mark on the wheel? That little C? That indicates top dead center. So we swing this little silver arm up to that mark. Now we're at top dead center. Now, keep your foot off that clutch for a second. I'm going to push that button in again. All right, go ahead. Step on that clutch. There you go, all the way.

When Kilt did, the engine turned over slowly. Once, twice. Three times.

On the fourth rotation the engine caught and the boy's eyes lit up.

Now bring that silver arm back down, Mercy said, trying to be heard over the engine.

The boy did but did so too quickly and the engine died. Kilt looked at Mercy as if Mercy was going to scold him. But he didn't. Instead he raised his hands in a kind of shrug.

Let's try it again, he said.

So the boy did. This time Kilt brought it down slower and the engine evened out. It sounded like boiling stew.

Not bad, Mercy said. See that short lever on the steering column? That's the choke. Make sure that's perpendicular. Okay. Want to take her for a spin?

Kilt gripped the wheel.

Push in the clutch, Mercy said. Swing that shifter down and toward you. That's first. Up and to the right and up again is second. And down from that is third. Three gears. You ready? Push in the clutch, put it into first. Now let out the clutch.

Kilt let out the clutch abruptly and the car bucked forward like an unbroken horse and they sped off down the alley.

Yeehaw, Mercy said, holding on to his hat.

Kilt looked at Mercy with his eyes huge and his mouth dropped open.

Don't look at me, Mercy said, look where you're going.

The alley ended and they shot onto the street with a few people having to leap out of the way. One man shouted a line of profanities. Mercy just waved at him.

Let's head on down the way a bit, Mercy said.

They practiced every day for three weeks. Mercy in the

passenger seat. Kilt at the wheel. The boy was getting pretty good. A muggy day and they drove up the lakeshore and pulled into a roadhouse. Kilt shifted it into neutral and Mercy flipped the ignition.

They sat in silence for a moment. Finally Mercy looked at him and said, Was that fun?

Kilt was smiling. Yeah, he said.

That's good, Mercy said. Life's meant to be fun. And ain't no one will suspect you either.

Suspect me of what?

Of being my getaway driver.

Get away from what?

The banks. The scene of the crime. The big show. You're about to earn some real money, kid.

Mercy could tell Kilt was confused. Could see it in his face. Mercy nodded.

Maybe I should've been clearer on that.

On what?

On what it is I do for a living.

Mercy sat back into the seat. He took out his tobacco and rolling papers and made up a cigarette. He lit it and then lay his arm across the back of the seat.

Do you know how much this car cost? he asked Kilt.

Kilt shook his head.

This car cost two thousand dollars.

That's a lot of money, Kilt said.

Dang right, it's a lot of money. And you know how a young guy like me got enough money to buy such a nice automobile?

Mercy took a drag on his cigarette. Kilt just stared at him.

I robbed a bank, Mercy said. Hell, I robbed several banks.

You rob banks?

Mercy nodded. Hand to God, he said.

How come you ain't got caught?

Cause I'm good at it.

Ain't you worried that you will?

No, Mercy said. He sat and smoked and looked at the boy.

You kill people? Kilt asked. In the banks? Do you kill the people?

No, Mercy said. Heck, I don't even have a gun.

Then how do you rob the bank?

I talk to them.

Talk to who?

The people at the bank. I tell them that I'm not there to steal their money, I'm there to steal the bank's money. The bank's money is insured, which means they're not losing a penny and anything I take will be returned to them free and clear. All debts paid in full. God bless America.

Mercy saluted the air.

Ain't they scared? Kilt asked.

Do I look like a scary man to you? No, Benjamin, no sir. I ain't no bogeyman. Not a dang thing scary about me.

Mercy smoked and blew rings into the air.

Look, Mercy said. I sprung it on you. Wasn't entirely forthright, and that ain't fair. You probably thought we were just out having a good time, burning off some gasoline. So I tell you what, you want to walk, okay. That's fine with me. No hard feelings. We'll just head on back to Thompson's, get some grub. You can go back to swinging that broom for a dime a day. We'll call it good. Even Stephen.

Kilt had not taken his eyes from Mercy. The boy had no reason not to trust what Mercy was saying.

It was getting on early evening and the sky to the north was darkening with clouds. The air was still and the birds were calling in the trees the way they do before rain. Mercy looked up at the sky, the towering clouds over the tree line. Then the first sound of thunder rippled out. As if a giant hammer struck some black-iron anvil deep within the cloud's center.

Going to rain soon, Mercy said.

How come you want me? Kilt said.

Huh?

How come you want me to do this? Why me?

Mercy smoked thoughtfully. He picked a piece of tobacco from his tongue. Flicked it away.

Well, Mercy said. I think it's because I see a little of myself in you. The way you are, I guess. You remind me of me.

What does that mean?

It means I want things to be different for you. I've watched you sweep those floors for Thompson going on a month and a half now. Ain't got so much an atta boy for it. From him or anyone. Doesn't have to be like that. I picked you because I think I can help change it. Can help change the way your life might turn out.

Stealing things don't seem the right way, though, Kilt said. Stealing don't change nothing.

No, Mercy said, but that money on the other end of it, that changes things. That money changes everything.

Another roll of thunder came and Mercy stared up. He spoke to the sky. Said: So what's it going to be, kid? You want to drive a Cadillac or do you want to push a broom?

A couple came out from the roadhouse. The young woman on the man's arm. The man had his hat at an angle. She was urging him on but the man stopped next to the Cadillac and said: That's one hell of a car, slick.

Thank you, Mercy said.

The man looked at the boy sitting behind the wheel.

He your chauffeur?

Mercy turned to Kilt and took a smoke.

That's up to him, Mercy said.

Shit, the man said, I'd pay *you* to drive that car around. Lucky kid right there.

Pssh, Mercy said, luck's got nothing to do with it.

18

Two weeks later ten-year-old Kilt was sitting in the driver seat of Mercy's Model 30 across the street from Hibbing First National. The instructions from Mercy were simple. Said: You just keep your eyes on that door. When you see me I'm going to be coming out of there very calmly like I've got every right in the world to be there. This gladstone here's going to be full and I'm going to set it in the back seat. Then I'm going to get in and you're going to drive just like we practiced. Can you do that?

Kilt nodded.

Good boy, Mercy said. And keep the engine running. Do it just like I taught you. Starts to stutter or hiccup at all, just push the throttle here closer to TDC till it evens out. Okay?

Okay.

Good, Mercy said. Here's the clock.

Mercy handed Kilt his silver pocket watch.

Watch that long hand, he said. I'm going to leave the car when that hand hits the three. If I'm not back by the time that hand hits the V, what're you going to do?

Drive, Kilt said.

What else?

And don't look back.

That's right, Mercy said. And you ain't going to stop till you get back to Duluth.

Yessir.

But you don't have to worry about that because that ain't going to happen.

Yessir.

Okay then, Mercy said. I'll see you in a bit.

Mercy reached across and tousled the boy's hair and then he got out of the car. Kilt watched him cross the street with the gladstone in his hand. Only once did Mercy turn back to look at him. When he did he winked.

At the door of the bank Mercy stopped to let an older woman enter before him. He held out his hand like an usher. He touched the brim of his hat and held the door for her. Then he walked inside behind the woman.

Kilt looked down at the pocket watch. The second hand was moving as it always did, without falter, but it seemed slower now. The minute hand moved like it was gummed up in molasses. The boy sat there behind the wheel, shifting his eyes between the door of the bank and the minute hand of the clock. The street was quiet. Hardly a soul out. He was looking down at the clock when a birdcall made him look up. The sky was blue and the air was heavy. Not a mention of wind. On the roof of the Colonial Hotel there were a few crows, all evenly spaced, stamped against all that blue. Kilt counted them. Six in all. They perched up there not moving, more like stone figurines of crows. Then he heard a muffled pop. Then another. Then several more in quick succession. Then the door of the bank swung open and he heard his name called. He saw Mercy limping across the street. The gladstone was full. He was carrying it in his right hand and in his left he was holding a Luger Po8 and was making somersault motions with the barrel.

At the car Mercy set the gladstone in the back seat and got into the passenger side and set the Luger on the seat between himself and the boy. Kilt saw Mercy's lower leg was covered in blood.

Let's boogie, he said.

Kilt pushed in the pedal but stalled the car. The engine sputtered then died. He looked at Mercy. Mercy's jaw flexed. He looked back once at the bank and then back at the boy.

Don't panic, Mercy said, his voice level. Here. Jiggle the shifter. Make sure it's in neutral. Good. Now swing the throttle to TDC. Keep your foot off the clutch. Push in the button to energize the system again.

He saw the boy's hands tremble.

Just keep calm, Mercy said. You're doing fine. Take your finger off that button. Now push in the clutch.

The engine turned and turned. Finally it caught.

Now bring that timing back down.

The boy swung the lever too fast and the engine died again. Kilt looked at Mercy. There were tears starting to form in his young eyes. If there was any anger or frustration within Mercy he did not show it. He almost seemed to grin at the boy.

Do it again, Mercy said. You're doing fine.

Kilt had started to repeat the process when there came a noise at the bank's door and both Mercy and Kilt turned at the commotion. There was a guard stumbling into the light, squinting at the sun, with a rifle in his hands. The shoulder of his tan uniform was full of blood. Without looking back at the boy, Mercy said: You just get her going. You focus on that.

Mercy limped out of the car and next to the gladstone in the back seat he lifted out a Madsen LMG. He came around the car with the gun at his waist, hobbling on his bad leg. He snapped in the magazine and pulled the bolt. Kilt looked at him with something between horror and awe etched in his face. Mercy looked at the boy and saw the boy's fear and in a very pacified voice said: You just get her going, Benjamin. You're doing fine.

And then Mercy turned back to the guard and the bank and opened it up. The guard barely had time to hit the sidewalk before the bullets were ripping holes into the brick. The shots were deafening but Mercy didn't so much as blink. The guard army-crawled along the bank's wall with the Madsen's rounds pitting the stone like a perforated line. Mercy didn't stop shooting till the guard had retreated around the corner and the magazine was dry. He levered out the empty and snapped in a fresh. Then he started shooting again. By the time it was all said and done the bank looked like some wartime ruin. Mercy stood there with the hot barrel smoking in the daylight. Nothing moved out on the street. It was like a ghost town. Absolutely quiet. Mercy with his back to the boy looked like a statue. The peace was broken by the engine firing and Mercy turned to look at the boy sitting behind the wheel. Mercy limped to the car and set the gun carefully next to the gladstone. He took a seat beside Kilt.

Smoother on the timing, Mercy said. Nice job. Now let's skedaddle.

19

They stuck to the back roads going back to Duluth. Mercy had his foot up on the dash. He had torn his shirt into strips and had his leg wrapped in one of them. Every so often he would remove the strip and it would come away glistening and full of blood. The boy, watching the road through the gap in the wheel and the dash, would steal glances. First at the gunshot wound then at Mercy's face. His forehead was sweating. He was a little pale. Mercy would wince as he pressed a finger against the tender skin.

Does it hurt? Kilt finally asked.

Nah, Mercy said. Could've been worse.

Looks bad to me.

That's cause you've never been shot before. This ain't nothing.

Mercy took a clean strip from the seat beside him and wrapped his leg in it. The bloody strip he threw out the side.

I figure we'll get back this evening, Mercy said. Have a steak dinner to celebrate. That sound good to you?

Kilt couldn't take his eyes from the bloody leg.

You keep your eyes on the road, Mercy said. And quit

worrying about it. I'm going to be fine. We'll get back, eat, lay low for a few days.

You want to go back to Thompson's?

Sure, Mercy said. Got all my stuff there. Anyway, I suspect the girls are probably worrying about us. Especially you. I reckon the one who looks after you—

Sylvia, Kilt said.

Yeah, Sylvia. When she sees all this she's going to tan my hide.

They drove on in silence for a while. There were stands of pine and the roadsides were thick with ferns. There were maples and elms and everything was in full green. Where the sunlight fell through the canopy the radiant bands held whorls of tiny flies. There hadn't been any rain for a few days and the dust from the dry road rose behind them like smoke. Mercy tied off a fresh bandage and leaned back into the corner of the door. He watched the boy.

What is it you're wanting to ask me? Mercy said.

Kilt looked at him.

Ain't wanting to ask you anything.

Yeah, you are, Mercy said. I can see it. Hell, I think I even know the question you're wanting to ask.

Ain't got a question.

You're wanting to know if anyone is dead back there. That's your question.

Kilt stayed silent.

Mercy nodded and took out his tobacco and papers and rolled a cigarette.

You want one? Mercy said.

Kilt shook his head. Mercy put the cigarette between his lips and pulled a small box of matches from his pocket with a little effort. He lit the cigarette and then sat back into the seat and closed his eyes.

How old do you think I am? he asked the boy.

How old?

Yeah. What would you guess?

Kilt shrugged. Maybe forty? Forty-five.

Shit! Forty-five, you say? I look that bad?

I don't know, Kilt said.

I'm twenty-six, Mercy said. That seem old to you?

Kind of.

Yeah, Mercy said. I suppose it does to me too. It's just a number, though. You're ten. I'm twenty-six. Only numbers. Mercy shrugged, smoked. Speaking of numbers. You want to see it all?

Mercy sat up and reached into the back seat and pulled the gladstone forward. He set the bag between them and unbuckled it.

Pull over here, Mercy said. Don't want you getting distracted and running us off the road.

Kilt pulled the car to the side. Mercy reached over and killed the engine. The silence of the woods swelled around them. Only birdsong, a cricket or two in the tall grass. Mercy tugged at the mouth of the bag and opened it wide. He reached in and took out a stack that was bound with a blue money band. Handed it to the boy.

That's a strap right there, Mercy said. A strap of ones. One hundred bills to a strap. What's that make?

He could see the boy trying to do the math. Mercy smiled and smoked. He said: One hundred.

One hundred?

And that's just one strap. Mercy leaned to look into the bag. He dug his hand in like he was lifting sand. Got a whole bag of straps. Don't we?

Mercy took out a few and handed them to Kilt.

Here, he said. Take a couple. Just in case something were to happen between now and Duluth. We'll divvy out the rest over some steak.

Mercy buckled the gladstone shut.

Okay, he said. Let's shake a leg.

Kilt didn't move. Just sat there behind the wheel with a strap in each hand. Mercy watched him and smoked.

You ever held that much money before? he asked.

Kilt did not answer.

Hell, Mercy said, you even seen that much before?

It's a lot of money, Kilt finally said.

Just for driving a car.

Mercy patted the boy's head.

Come on, he said. Let's go. I'm starting to get hungry.

They passed through the town of Cloquet a little before five. The town was preparing for the Fourth of July. Flags in the streets. Banners in all the hanging flowers. Every building on Main Street adorned with bunting.

Almost the Fourth, Mercy said. Say, you thirsty?

Kilt nodded.

Pull in there, would you? Run out and grab us a couple pops.

Kilt parked the car at a soda fountain and ran in and ordered two Cokes. He came back out and handed one to Mercy. Mercy held out his bottle to Kilt and said: To robbing banks.

They sat there in the parking lot saying almost nothing. A couple of young women passed their car and eyed the two of them sitting there. They frowned slightly at the sight of the boy at the wheel, Mercy with his bloody leg. Mercy winked at the prettier one. Both covered their mouths with a hand and then went into the fountain.

You like girls? Mercy asked.

I don't know, Kilt said. Not really.

Makes sense. A bit young yet.

Do you?

Kid, I can't get enough of them. If it wasn't for this damn leg, I'd be in there right now.

What would you say to them?

I got a whole list of things I'd say to them. Most of which I can't repeat in front of you.

How'd you learn it?

Hell, Mercy said, I'm an outlaw. I was born with it.

He winked at the boy but could see that the joke was lost on him.

You ever been to Montana? Mercy asked.

Kilt shook his head.

You even know where Montana is?

Again Kilt shook his head. His eyes were big. No one had ever talked to him like an adult before.

It's west, Mercy said. He pointed a finger in the direction of the sun. West, he said.

Is it far? Kilt asked.

Yeah, Mercy said. It's far.

What's in Montana?

Nothing, Mercy said. Indians and a lot of sky. And that's about it.

You've been there? Kilt asked.

Shit, kid. I was born there.

You didn't like it?

No, I liked it just fine.

If you liked it then why'd you leave?

Because sometimes you got to leave places.

Why do you have to do that?

I don't know, Mercy said. To be able to go back, I guess. Anyway, it was in Montana. Where I learned to talk to girls.

Were you married?

Hell, I'm only twenty-six. Got my whole damn life ahead of me.

He watched Kilt try to process all he was saying. Mercy

was struck by his innocence. A horrible feeling of guilt for ever bringing him into this overwhelmed him. For a moment he wished he hadn't even spoken to the boy.

No, Mercy finally said. I wasn't married. I wanted to be.

You had a girlfriend then?

Had, yes.

She's not your girlfriend anymore?

No, Benjamin, she is not.

Why not?

A lot of things.

Like what?

Well. Like I caught her.

Caught her?

Yes. I caught her.

Caught her doing what?

He looked at the boy and smiled. Said: Rolling in the haystack.

Mercy laughed through his nose.

Maybe we'll go to Montana one day, Kilt said.

Yeah, Mercy said. Maybe.

Mercy drank some of the Coke and then set the bottle between his legs.

Getting back to your question, Mercy said.

What question?

The one you've been wanting to ask since we left the bank.

I didn't have a question.

But Mercy ignored him and said: The answer is no.

No?

No, Mercy said. There's no one dead back there. Everyone's fine. Safe and sound.

What about that guard?

What about him?

He was bleeding.

I don't know, Mercy said. People bleed, I guess. Bleed all the time. Look at me.

Mercy lifted his leg.

Then Mercy nodded and finished his Coke and threw the bottle out and it shattered on the ground.

No matter how all this turns out, Mercy said, you get yourself into a jam, I want you to head to this little place in Montana. Little ranch outside of a town called Black Elk. Place called the Triple Nine. There's a fella there, Royal Wainwright. You tell him I sent you.

Why do you want me to go there?

I think there's someone who you might like to meet.

Okay.

They'll get you all straightened out. Get you some answers.

Yessir.

Mercy pointed with his chin at the soda fountain. Said: Here. Take some money. Run in there and grab us some grub before we hit the road. Get whatever you want.

Kilt took the money and went inside. He stood in line with his back to the storefront window. At the counter he ordered two roast beef sandwiches. The woman working the register asked if he wanted pickles. He handed the woman the money and then asked if he could use the restroom. She pointed down the hall. When he came back out the food was wrapped in brown paper. He took the sandwiches off the counter and thanked the woman. He walked out the door and looked up and where Mercy's Cadillac was supposed to be there was only a rucksack. Kilt went to it and knelt and opened the mouth of the bag and found the Luger Po8 laid atop several straps of bills.

20

The sun was falling and Kilt was walking with his back to it. The dirt road stretched on before him. The colors of the sky pinked everything they touched and the robins in the trees were warbling their evening songs. He was looking down at the dirt. He had one of the roast beef sandwiches in his pocket. In the other pocket were the straps of money. The Luger was jammed into the front of his waistband. Cloquet to Duluth was twenty-some miles, too far for anyone to walk. Let alone a child on their own.

He thought about Mercy and he thought about what Mercy had told him about not using a gun and he thought about the noise the Madsen had made and he remembered how calm Mercy had looked walking out of the bank and he remembered the fear on the guard's face and he remembered the heat from the sun and the crows on the Colonial Hotel and the blue peaceful sky. He felt a profound loneliness he had not known since his mother had died. He thought about her face and he thought about all the nights she would come home and sleep beside him and he remembered her smell and the way her voice sounded when she said his name and how she had portended this very moment.

How the meek inherit nothing. How he would be bolder than she. But what she got wrong was that no one chooses their own life. The road had already been cut. Free will and fate running in parallel equity, never to meet or diverge. The boy wanted nothing more than to see his mother at that moment. To be wrapped in her warmth. To be saved from the world's wrath.

He was on the verge of tears when something not of the natural setting caught his eye. Trapped in the grass, fluttering in the soft wind, was a twenty-dollar bill. Kilt stopped in the road and looked down at it. He knelt and picked it up and held it with two hands in front of his eyes. His hands fell to his sides and he looked down the road. There was another twenty-dollar bill maybe ten feet away. Another, a few feet from that. He walked on, kneeling at each. He came across more, scattered on both sides of the road. Some were in the ditch. Some snared in the ferns, the branches of the trees. Ahead, the road bent and he followed it, collecting the bills as he went.

At the bend in the road he stopped. He was looking at three cars parked along the side of the road. There were six men standing around. Some with their arms crossed. Some with their hands on their hips. All of them in uniform. All of them police officers. Kilt quickly pulled the Luger from his front and jammed it into the small of his back, flipping his shirt over it. One of them turned and shouted: You! Kid! Get over here!

Kilt didn't move.

I said get your ass over here!

Kilt made his way slowly toward the officers. All of them had turned to eye the boy. They had made a kind of wall, blocking out the ditch behind. In the gap between two of them Kilt saw the undercarriage of a rolled car.

What're you doing out here, boy?

Kilt was silent.

You deaf? one of them said.

No sir.

Then answer him, said an officer.

Just walking, Kilt said.

No shit, one said. Where the hell you walking to?

Just down the road.

Just down the road.

Yessir.

Awfully late to be just walking down the road. How old are you?

Fourteen.

Bullshit you're fourteen.

Where's your mother? asked another.

At home.

Ain't she worried her little boy is out so far from home?

Maybe.

Maybe? Goddamn. If my boy was out doing this shit I'd belt him one.

Yessir.

Yessir what?

I don't know. Nothing, sir.

Goddamn.

What happened? Kilt asked. His voice was soft and light.

What happened? The officers jostled a little. A few of them snickered. What happened, he said, was justice, young man.

Another said: Does the name Nicky Mercy mean anything to you?

No sir, Kilt said.

That's good. Because Nicky Mercy was a bad man. Been tracking him down for months now. Bank robber. Nasty son of a bitch.

He robbed banks?

Robbed one this morning. Back in Hibbing. Shot up the place. Killed everyone inside. Some sweet old lady, seventy-five years old. Took a bullet right between the eyes. The officer tapped his forehead. Pow, he said.

The man was a maniac, another officer said.

Was he alone? Kilt asked, worried.

A guard said he thought he saw someone in the driver seat. But who knows. Poor fucker was taking gunfire from a light machine gun.

How did you find him? Kilt asked.

Sheer dumb luck, an officer said. Someone heard he might be staying at some whorehouse in Duluth. Who knows. Got him now, though. Smoked the fucker.

Another officer said: Now get out of here, kid. Go home. Tell your mother you're sorry for making her worry.

Yessir, Kilt said.

He walked through the line of officers with all of them shaking their heads in disapproval. Kilt looked down into the ditch at the overturned car. Steam was rising from the engine. It smelled like gasoline. Fifteen feet or so from the car was Mercy's body lying in the grass. In his back there were about two dozen bullet holes. His face was turned toward the road. There was blood coming from his mouth and where his left eye should've been the skull had been blown away from behind. Kilt paused only a second before one of the officers said: Git on!

It took him all day and most of the night to reach the outskirts of Duluth and when he did the faintest paling in the eastern sky was leaching over the lake's horizon and the last of the city lights were burning out under the gray dawn. He sat in the dirt of a ditch and set the rucksack between his feet and opened it and looked in at the money. The straps of twenties and loose bills rested in the bottom motionless but somehow terrifying. He thought about what the police officers had told him. About how Mercy had shot them all. The money felt cursed. He was overcome and he vomited at his side. His stomach wretched and his eyes welled. When it was over he wiped his mouth and stood and stuffed the pistol in his trousers at his back and slung the rucksack over his shoulder and started off again.

Around noon he walked through the doors of the Laker Inn and found Thompson wiping down glasses and looking at him like the boy had never left.

He nodded at Thompson and crossed the bar floor clutching what little he had at his chest and then started up the stairs without a word and found his room down the hall. He closed the door behind him. All was as he had left it. The unmade twin bed, the open drawers, a few clothes on the floor. He went to the bed and slid the rucksack with the money and pistol under it. Then he tidied the sheet and smoothed it with a hand and then stood back and studied it all to make sure nothing looked wrong.

For four years he stayed there and never did anyone say the name Nick Mercy and never did anyone mention his likeness. It was as if the man were some kind of fabrication, a chimera within the child's mind. A thing antecedent to a greater darkness of which neither boy nor anyone could foretell.

Four years after returning, Benjamin Kilt left for the last time, thinking of what Mercy had told him. Of Montana. Of the town of Black Elk, and of the Triple Nine where there was nothing but answers. He said nothing to no one. Four years and he hadn't spent a dime of the stolen money. Maybe afraid someone would know where it came from. Maybe afraid someone would come asking. He pulled the rucksack from under the mattress and walked to Sylvia's door and knocked and when she didn't answer he went in and set the sack on her bed. He left it there with a note that read, simply: *Thank you, love Ben.* Then he stuffed the Luger in the pocket of his trousers, got his coat, the tattered copy of *Moby-Dick*, and left.

21

That fall the autumn colors were brilliant against the open northern sky. The gales of the first storms stripping away the leaves, leaving the bare limbs to quake like tremored fingers. The brilliance gone. Dour days the color of gutter water. Then the frozen winters full of wind and cold. Fields of dead corn with the tortured remains spiked from the deep snow, lodged there like some infinite bed of nails. Nothing stays like you want it to and for everything unwanted, that changes too.

He had never heard of Black Elk, Montana. Never seen a mountain. He hitched a ride in the bed of a truck that took him as far west as Detroit Lakes. From there he hopped a train. The open boxcars rattling over the iron. The rare companion not unlike him. A few possessions wrapped in cloth and clutched tight at the chest. A few of them with nothing at all. Sometimes only a face appearing above the boards to gauge the setting, to heed some baleful warning and flee without a sound. Others embracing their bony knees in the darkness of the car with teeth chattering despite the warmth of the night and staring painfully out the open door or at their feet, seeing things the rest of the world had not and never would.

Kilt had his corner and slept sitting up with his back against the wall. When he wasn't asleep he watched the black country scroll past under the clouds. When it rained the rain fell sideways past the open doors and the boy didn't know if it was from the squalls or the speed of the train. When it was clear the moon rode full and white over the prairie. So bright you could count the rows of wheat by it. Kilt saw farmers at work in the row crops and if the boxcar was empty and he was alone he would stand and go to the door and sit and dangle his feet and watch the tractors move about in all that open country using only the moonlight to guide them. The dust risen in the spectral light gave the boy an uneasy feeling like a strange kind of homesickness. It made him shiver to watch it and he would retreat to his corner and try to sleep only to be shook awake by the lurching of the slowing train as it came into another town at which point the boy would leap from the car because he knew better. He would hide where he could and watch the bulls with their search lamps and clubs, sometimes having to hide the night long, sometimes having to watch the train depart without him and hide till the next came through. So went these capricious days moving west.

One morning a red line stretching on from the rising sun cut through the open door and lay across the oiled boards of the boxcar and half within that red light Kilt saw a man who must've hopped while he was asleep in the night. The man wore a greasy Stetson with the crown belled out. There were blue and red and yellow Indian beads for the band. Half his face was hidden in shadows but the one eye in the light was staring right at the boy. The man was smoking and the smoke lingered about him. His one eye was black and shining. It looked like some kind of polished stone. So polished it was that even from across the empty boxcar Kilt could see the sun boiling within it. The man held his gaze and Kilt was arrested in some kind of terror cognate to Satanism. The man only stared and smoked. The boy clutched the Luger in his lap and the man said, That'll blow a hole in yeer gut. He said, Slide it to me, boy.

Kilt didn't move.

I said slide it here.

Kilt took the Luger from his lap and tried to remove the magazine. The man laughed. His voice was hoarse and quarrelsome. The man said, There's bullets in that magazine.

I know, Kilt said.

Ye ain't gettin that magazine out unlest the magazine is empty.

I ain't going to give you my gun.

The man smoked and tipped the ash with his pinky finger then smoked again and blew the smoke through his nose. The man smiled.

Slide it here, he said. I ain't given ye no reason not to trust me.

Kilt stared at the man. The iron wheels tapping in a kind of staccatoed rhythm. Humming occasionally like the ringing of batted ears.

I'll come over there and take it from ye, he said.

When he motioned to stand, Kilt said, Okay.

He slid the Luger over the floor with reluctance, with the gun spinning like a dancer till it collided with the man's boot and came to a stop. The man put the cigarette in his mouth and reached down for the gun. He lifted it and held the gun in his palm. He had huge hands. Did a motion like he was seeing how much it weighed. His black eye shot up at the boy. He said, Where'd ye get a gun like this?

Just found it, Kilt said.

Bullshit ye jest found it.

I did.

Ye killed it off a someone, didn't ye?

No sir.

How old are ye?

Seventeen.

Bullshit ye are.

I am.

Yer seventeen as much as I'm the king a England.

Kilt didn't say anything.

The man looked down at the gun. Said, This is a war kind a gun.

Okay.

Ye headin south to fight them Mexicans? Put a hole in ol Pancho Villa's belly?

No sir.

What if I told ye I was goin keep this gun?

Ain't yours.

That wudn't my question.

My gun, Kilt said.

The man stood without effort, like he was just squatting on his hams. He was wearing a tattered poncho and his trousers were mended in all manner of patches and his boots were held together with wire. He stood in the corner, half in that malignant red light. He swayed with the motion of the train. Then he took a step toward Kilt. As he did his full face came into view, enameled in the hard light, and Kilt could see that he had no left eye and a deep scar fell from his brow to his chin and his jaw under his left ear looked to have been clouted in and the skin there hung like the folds of a hound. He started toward Kilt with measured steps. He came upon the boy and stood looking down on him. He had a biting, sour kind of smell to him. Like sweat and wet animal fur. The man reached down with the gun, holding it by the barrel. He said, Ye be careful with this. This gun was only made fer one thing.

The man walked back to his corner and sat down as effortlessly as he had stood, coming to rest with one leg bent up and the other laid out across the boards.

How far ye goin?

Montana.

Montana is a big place.

Ye got anythin to eat?

No.

I ain't askin ye to share. Jest askin if ye do.

Well, I don't.

Ye ain't too smart, are ye?

Sir?

Ye deaf?

No sir.

When was the last time ye ate?

Two days ago.

Where was that at?

Detroit Lakes.

Ye been ridin since Detroit Lakes?

Yessir.

The train swung and the line of red fanned across the wall and floor like some kind of useless spotlight. And with the train steady in its new heading the line of early sunlight stayed locked in the middle of the boxcar, fencing the man from the boy with each of them huddled in their respected corner. The plain beyond the boxcar was without end. To the north in what might have been Manitoba there were clouds with flat bottoms and the bottoms were dark from the rising angle of the sun and the green of the prairie was still against the windless morning and the grasses were mottled with the shadows of the clouds printed upon them.

The man was watching Kilt and then he turned his attention to the country without and said, It's goin a rain today. Ye see them clouds shaping up the way they are?

Kilt leaned and looked out.

Yessir, he said.

It'll rain, the man said. By day's end we'll see rain. Ye best be off this train too. They don't like folk like us gettin no free rides. Meaner than dogs, they is. Want nothin more out of life than to stove yer face in. Laughin when they do it.

You've seen it?

Seen it? Shit.

The man turned his face to Kilt and ran a gnarled finger from his brow to his chin. He said, Jest don't let em catch ye.

The man took a pouch of tobacco from his person and rolled a cigarette. Then popped out a match and lit the cigarette and closed his eye as if to savor the first pull. As if all the finery from his life had been taken from him and he reduced to the most primitive of rewards. Or perhaps what the boy saw was a life in ascension, cleaved of concern. A life divining the simplest of pleasures. The man sat smoking. Then he opened his eye and faced the boy.

What are ye runnin away from? he asked.

Ain't running from nothing.

Bullshit ye ain't. Why is it ye goin to Montana, then?

Kilt watched the man for a moment. Then he said: Someone told me I should.

Who tell ye?

Someone.

Yer daddy?

I don't have a daddy.

Everyone's got a daddy.

Not me.

Yer like Jesus Christ, then?

That's blasphemy, Kilt said.

Only if ye believe in it.

You don't believe in God?

No.

You don't think you're going to go somewhere when you die?

I'll go into the ground.

Then where?

I don't care.

Why don't you care?

Cause I'll be dead.

It don't worry you?

Worry me? Shit.

You got to have some thought about it.

Boy, he said, the dead don't worry and the dead don't have no opinions. Dead is dead.

He finished his cigarette and flicked it out the boxcar door. He looked at the boy and squinted his eye.

Ye don't belong here, he said.

No sir.

No, the man said. I don't mean this train. I mean here.

At this he made an encompassing motion with a long, gnarled finger.

Ye don't belong *here*.

Then he pulled his hat over his face and lay flat against the floor, crossing one boot over the other and setting his knapsack under his head, punching it like you would a pillow, and very soon he was asleep. Kilt listened to him snore. He thought it was odd how quick a man could fall asleep in the presence of a stranger. Kilt resigned himself to the pact of not falling asleep, as the man, he figured, was liable to do anything. The thrumming of the train wheels over the rails, however, lulled the boy and he tried his best to keep his eyes from falling shut but he did not succeed and soon he was asleep and when he was finally roused by the shuddering of the slowing train the nameless drifter was gone and Kilt was alone in the boxcar. Beside him was a wrapped piece of linen and Kilt reached for it and unfolded the corners one at a time and resting within the piece of cloth was a piece of bread. Kilt ate it. Then he stood and gathered his things and leapt from the train.

22

Two days later he arrived in the small cattle town of Havre, Montana. He found a place to sleep in the broom closet of a saloon. The owner reluctant to offer it up. Saying: You don't have any money?

No sir.

You expect me to just give you a place to stay?

I was only asking.

The owner eyed him.

You can work for it, I suppose.

Yessir.

Can you push a broom?

The boy spent four weeks there. Kept awake upstairs by the moans heard through the closed doors. The broke gamblers and lonely cowboys exiting the rooms when they had finished, stamping their feet like they'd just come in from bad weather, buckling their belts, squaring their hats. And all of them squinting hard at a boy standing in the hall with the broom in his hands. Some of the men nodding or saying howdy but most saying nothing at all as if to conceal their embarrassment or shame or mistrust of seeing a child in such a place.

At night Kilt would come downstairs to watch the men gamble and drink and fight. Their tongues beginning to slur with the hours and the inevitable venomous curses spilled from the lips bringing forth the iron at their hips.

Despite all this the boy felt safe. He wandered the halls like he had done in Duluth. The girls smiling or offering him their leftovers of supper. The oldest among the whores had taken a quiet liking to him. Never addressing him, but watching him like someone watches birds. She wasn't exactly shy but she took a kind of care around the boy. As if she might scare him away.

Kilt sensed she was lonely in some way but he was too young to know why. She often sat alone. Either at the far end of the bar or in a smoky corner on a damask sofa. She was dressed nicely, though. Always in a black dress with black lace gloves reaching halfway to her elbow. A plunging décolletage and alabaster skin. She drank brandy and Kilt knew she drank it but the glass always appeared full. Night after night she sat alone while the younger girls came and went and caroused and giggled behind their supple hands.

Then one night she stopped him as he passed the open door of her room. She sat in a wooden chair wearing a white silk Japanese robe with her auburn hair laid over her shoulder and she was combing it as if to soothe it, the comb brushing down and her other hand following in a gentle way like rubbing the back of an infant. Kilt had only glanced into the room briefly while working the broom but in that quick moment their eyes had locked and the woman said, Can I ask you something?

Kilt stopped in the doorway and looked in and they watched one another through her bureau mirror.

Mam?

May I ask you a question?

Yes, he said. I mean, yes mam.

It's going to be direct.

Okay.

What are you doing here?

I'm not sure I understand what you mean, mam.

Here. In this place.

You mean Havre?

I mean Havre. I mean this brothel. I mean here. You're only a boy. Havre isn't where you're trying to get.

No mam.

So where you trying to get to?

I guess that'd be Black Elk.

Why are you going to Black Elk?

Kilt only stood there. He shifted on his feet.

You're the one from Minnesota.

Yes mam.

Black Elk, Montana, is a long way from Minnesota.

Yes mam.

So why are you going? You must have a good reason to go all that way. A boy your age.

I should get back to work, Kilt said.

That's what they tell us, she said. Isn't it?

Mam?

That we must work. The virtues of work. Have you ever wondered who it's for?

I guess I haven't.

She was still seated at the vanity table. Still speaking to him through the mirror with her back turned and combing out her hair.

Do you find me attractive?

Mam?

I suppose that's an inappropriate question to be asking you. You just a child and all. You know how old I am?

No mam.

You want to take a guess?

I don't know.

I just turned forty.

Okay.

Do you think that's old?

I don't know.

I suppose everyone is old to you.

The woman nodded and set down the ivory-handled comb and pulled her robe tight and stood and went to the window. She took a pack of cigarettes from her pocket and gently pulled one free like she was selecting a single flower from a bouquet. It was a thin cigarette like the kind they enjoyed in France and she lit it and crossed one arm over her chest and smoked. She stood smoking, looking down at the street below.

It had just started to rain and the rain began to pattern the dry street. The rain in the far distance looked like fog. In the failing light of the day she could see where the wind was gusting and the rain that was gathered up in those gusts looked like shoals of fish. What small crowds there had been were now gone because of the rain and the street was empty and the rain was falling on all the parked cars and against the glass of the window. The woman smoked and blew the smoke into the air above her.

Kilt watched her back. The silk robe hugged her body and he could tell she was naked beneath it. Kilt watched her and only her as there was little of anything of interest in the room. Only the bed, the vanity. There was a plain wooden chair in the corner. A Victorian lamp with a fringed shade. An oil painting of a dog. He stood and waited, not knowing if she wanted him to stay or leave. And then she said: I was married once.

Yes mam.

I was only sixteen. Just a girl. Not much older than you. When I look at you I see now that that was crazy. Irresponsible even. Children aren't supposed to get married.

Yes mam.

He was twenty, she said. Pretty much a boy himself. A cowboy, believe it or not.

She half turned and raised her eyebrows and widened her eyes as if to reinforce the sarcasm in her voice. Then she turned back to the window.

Got into the rodeo, she said. Used to travel all over with him. You know who William Cody was?

No mam.

Buffalo Bill. The whole Wild West show? He was a part of that. Did that for years. And then I turned thirty and it was like a switch going off. He told me it was because I couldn't give him a child, but he didn't want a baby. Men like him never do. That was just something he said. An excuse. One day he was just up and gone. I heard about it three months later. That he'd bunked up with some nineteen-year-old down in Laramie, Wyoming. Fifteen years his junior. Why are men always doing that?

Doing what, mam?

Bunking up with younger women.

I don't know, Kilt said.

You think it's because they need someone to fawn over them? Dote on their needs? Tell them they're big and strong? Take care of them in some way?

Kilt did not speak. The woman smoked. She blew out the smoke and did not bat it away. Just let it hang about her. Let it conceal her. Let it daub out the details of her face and her hands and her hair. She said, Or is it just the opposite?

Mam?

Is it about control. Do they feel they can control a young woman more than they can an older one? Young girls are stupid. I can say that because I was young once, and stupid things can be controlled. Made to do things they might not want to.

I don't think I understand, mam.

Have you ever had sex, young man?

No mam.

It's an incredible thing. The sensation, the feel, the power that goes along with it. When I was younger I felt it was an act done only *to* me. That I was there for *his* whims. *His* desires. What I didn't know was that at that age all the power was mine. See, now I'm forty years old, I know what I had. But now I'm afraid it's too late, and all these men, all they want is something younger, something to coddle them. Men are terrified of smart women. Threatened somehow.

She smoked again. She said, You know I haven't been kissed in five years. Not really kissed, that is. The men who come up here and lay in my bed, all they want is a poke. They don't want to kiss. A good kiss takes time. You got to be patient with a kiss. They just want me to lay there or get on my hands and knees. A poke is all they want then they're out the door or snoring drunk.

She turned back to the boy and half smiled. Turned back to the window, said, Five years without a kiss. I'm afraid I might have forgotten how to do it.

She put the thin cigarette in her mouth and untied the robe and slipped it from her shoulders and let it fall to the floor to pool at her feet. She stood naked at the window. Only moving her hand to take the cigarette from her lips.

I'm here, she said, to be seen. I won't spend the rest of my life hiding.

She turned toward the boy and began to walk toward him. He took a step back. She reached out and took the door in her left hand. She said, Thank you for listening to me.

Then she closed the door and he was left alone in the hall.

23

In the morning he awoke to noises like clumsy movers and voices full of accusation. When he finally came into the hall the entrance to the woman's doorway was clogged with the girls of the house still in their nightgowns and the ones not in the room were flooding out along the wall. The boy only had to look at any one of them to know the story.

Kilt pressed through the crowd as if invisible. At the doorway he peered through the caged window of legs to see the dead woman hanging from a beam in the center of the room. The other girls were crying. The saloon's owner was hugging the naked body around the waist as the sheriff's deputy stood on a chair and sawed at the rope. The dead woman's hair trembled as he sawed and then the rope gave and all her dead weight went limp into the saloon owner's arms and he struggled and nearly collapsed with her atop him. They laid her on the floor and took a sheet from the bed with which to cover her and then both men stood looking at each other with the saloon owner's fists balled on his hips. The boy heard the deputy say: I'll go get Mack. You keep these girls outta here.

Kilt left that afternoon. The sun was in his eyes. The green hills rose and fell out in front of him and the sky to the north and the west was so dark with weather that it looked like it was painted there. He walked down the road. He stumbled into a ditch and sat in the dirt and cried. He thought about life and he thought about death, and as he was only fourteen years old death seemed far away but also he didn't know why it stayed so close. He wanted to know why his mother did what she did and he wanted to know why that woman hanged herself from the rafter. He rolled to his side and used his arm as a pillow and he cried till he was too tired to cry anymore and then he slept.

When he woke the sun had slipped. Maybe an hour had passed. He rose from the dirt and walked back to the road. Not long a man and a woman passed him just outside of town and pulled the truck to the shoulder and waited for him to catch up, and when Kilt was alongside the woman leaned over and asked where a boy his age was going. They offered him a spot in the cab but Kilt said the bed was fine. More than once the woman looked back at him and smiled with her lips all wonky and her face distorted through the glass of the dusty window. The miles ribboned on. Havre faded in the distance.

That night he camped along the shores of Bearpaw Lake. The mountains to the north of Warrick lay silver under the moon. The dark clouds Kilt had seen earlier that day had moved off and the sky was awash in starlight. In the lavender dusk he had broken twigs from wind-bent willows and stunted pines and gathered up a nest of dry sage and tepeed the sticks over it. He'd gotten his flint to spark it and the spark set the brush on fire. The wood took quickly and soon he could feel the heat on the skin of his cheeks.

With the fire certain he went hunting more wood and after a while came back into the firelight dragging with him an old juniper stump full of burls. Kilt heaved it on and an eruption of sparks showered the air followed immediately by a glaucous cloud of smoke. Kilt stood fanning the coals, afraid he had just put out the fire. Then he got down on hands and knees and blew at the smoke and the coals. The smallest little flicker appeared and the grass took and soon too did the branches. He stood and coughed and looked up at the stars. Then he sat down and cradled his knees against his chest.

All the heat had gone from the day and the night had turned cool and the stars were swinging slowly toward the west, the great constellations being dragged over the black edge of the horizon. Kilt built up a great bonfire with the cedarwood popping and the sparks leaping and swirling like swarms of iridescent flies. For the first time that night he inched away from the fire as the heat was starting to bite at his shins. His pants were hot. He looked off across the dark lake and printed upon the black water was the sky in reverse. All the thousands of stars trembling and quaking back at themselves. Then the lightest of wind arose and all those stars were washed away.

Kilt watched the fire with his knee held tightly and his chin resting on his folded arms. The fire sawed in the wind and the flames heeled like the glowing sails of little burning boats. Past the fire the boy could see the lights of town winking in the distant dark like jewels displayed on a sheet of black velvet. Kilt was hungry and his stomach moaned. The woman from the truck had given him a dried beef sandwich but the boy had long since eaten it. He'd a can of beans and a tin of Vienna sausages in his knapsack and pulled them free and opened them and laid both in the dirt to simmer just beyond the flames of the fire. The flames blackened the metal and Kilt pulled his sleeve over his hand and turned each till both were boiling. Then he lifted each out and stood the cans at his feet.

In the hills beyond the lake another fire caught Kilt's eye, burning in that broad expanse like the reflection of his own fire and he watched it with an unsettled feeling. Then like some diminished thunderclap came the report of a single rifle shot somewhere in those hills. With nothing to deaden it, the sounds raced off into the night. And then it was all quiet again.

Looking into the fire Kilt thought about the days that had been and he thought about the dead woman and he wondered why people do the things they will. He watched the fire like it might offer an answer. Like it could foretell events to come. Like it harbored some great, unknowable secret. Thought about all that for the better part of an hour. But the fire was only a fire and it had no answers, and this much he knew.

He was laying another chunk of pine on when from out of the black a hulking figure formed. The sight caught Kilt's breath. First the shining black nose and then the yellow eyes wherein the flames danced wildly. With half its body now in the fire's glow, the wolf stopped in its limp and gazed at the boy. The animal seemed to study him as if it had not seen a human before. As if the boy were the first human in existence. As if the wolf, up until this moment, believed itself to be the sole inhabitant of the world. Kilt did not move for what felt to be a long time. The shoulder of the wolf's foreleg was slick with blood. The blood was black and shined like the fur had been lacquered with oil. Kilt reached for a stick lodged in the fire and the wolf peeled back its lips and snarled. The hackles rose up. Kilt laid down the stick and moved his feet beneath him. The wolf took a cautious but labored step forward. Kilt got his footing and crouched and said: I ain't going to hurt you. And in some strange unspoken accord, the wolf retired its posturing and the eyes of the animal softened and looked almost domestic. Kilt stood and for a moment he and the wolf just watched one another.

You're hurt, Kilt said.

He said: You're bleeding all over.

The wolf craned its head and licked the patch of blood at its leg. Then it licked at its lips to clean them.

Kilt said, You don't have to stand. You can lay down if you want.

The wolf blinked tiredly and when it did a second shot careened out of the darkness and the wolf collapsed just beyond the fire and died.

24

The sound of the shot scared Kilt and he had closed his eyes and when he opened them again he saw the wolf on the ground and a man with a big-bore rifle at his shoulder with the barrel still trained on the animal walking into the firelight. When the man was satisfied the wolf was dead he unshouldered his weapon and cradled it in his arms and turned to the boy and said, Fucker really took off on me.

Kilt shifted his eyes between the wolfer cradling his weapon and the dead wolf lying unmoving just across the flames. The man had shot the wolf in the heart and from the hole the blood drained out and matted the fur and seeped into the earth. The eyes were still open but flat now and black and the colors of the fire rippled in them.

What're you doing out here? the wolfer asked.

Kilt couldn't speak.

You ever seen one up close? the wolfer asked.

Kilt blinked and looked at him over the flames.

What?

I asked if you ever seen one up close?

No sir, Kilt said.

You can pet it if you want, the wolfer said. That'd be tolerable.

Pet it?

Well, sure, he said. Ain't goin a bite.

Kilt looked back at the wolf.

Well, go on, the wolfer said. Come on around here. Go feel its ear tips. Softest thing you'll ever touch. Go on now.

Kilt rose slowly. The man was smiling down at the slain animal like it was some kind of beleaguered surprise on display for Christmas morning. Like the man had been waiting a very long time to show him this. Kilt moved around the fire. When he passed the wolfer, the man reached down and tapped the boy almost paternally on the shoulder. He sensed the boy's reluctance and said, Go on. Nothin to be afraid of. Then he gave Kilt a shove.

Kilt stumbled before the wolf and knelt and got down on his knees and put his small hand on the wolf's stomach. Its body was still warm and Kilt half expected it to lurch at him but it did nothing.

Go on, said the wolfer. Pet its ear.

Kilt obeyed and ran the ear tip through his fingers.

What'd I tell you? the man said. Soft, ain't it? All right now, kid. Shake a leg. Get outta my way.

The man stepped to the wolf. He laid his rifle in the dirt beside the animal and unsheathed a long thin knife from a buckskin scabbard.

What's the knife for? Kilt asked.

You don't think I'm takin the whole damn thing?

Kilt only stared at him.

They don't pay by the pound, kid.

Pay?

Shit, yes. This ol boy's got a bounty on him and I'm aimin to collect. This fucker'll get me close to four dollars. Can you believe that? Four bucks just for pullin a trigger.

The wolfer let out a guttered laugh and then fell to coughing. He punctuated its finale with a wad of phlegm spat into the darkness without.

Here, said the wolfer, hold its head still.

Kilt didn't move.

Don't look so sad, kid. Only a wolf. Thousands of them out here. Now hold its head.

The wolfer pulled its tail and when he did the whole animal slid over the dirt.

Damn it, kid, he said. I told you to hold its head. Now hold its damn head.

Kilt did as he was told and again the wolfer raised the tail and cut a circle around the animal's anus and then drew the knife up its belly, spilling the organs to roil and steam over the ground. From the belly he cut a line down each limb, exposing the sinew, and when that was done he began to peel away the hide from the flesh. He continued this work till he got to the base of the skull at which point he stopped and looked at the boy with a strange gleam in his eyes and said, Here we must be delicate. And using the tip of the long knife he began to separate the skin from the skull. The hide was clumped like a bloody rug. The body of the skinned wolf was red and white and smoking in the firelight, the shadows lapping against the dead muscles, the quieted punctured heart. At the tip of the nose the wolfer gave a final tug and the entire pelt came free.

He stood with it gathered up in his hands like he was holding soiled laundry. He jostled it, guessed at its weight, said: Four bucks, kid. What remained of the wolf looked like some kind of grotesque embryo, disemboweled and still weeping blood from its new death. The wolfer turned and vanished into the darkness leaving the boy to stand over the animal.

The man was not gone long before he returned into the ring of firelight. He put his hands on his hips and picked his teeth with his tongue and regarded what was left of the wolf and then nodded and said: Mm hmm. He bent and took a hind foot in his hand and started off toward the lake. Kilt watched as the skull dragged over the ground with its tongue aloll and going black with dirt. Almost immediately the man was only a silhouette against the blacker lake and at the shoreline he knelt and took the dead animal in his arms and pitched it into the water. The surface exploded and the rings of it rippled out wider and wider, expanding evermore till the far shoreline swallowed them up, and then the surface of the lake was still again.

The wolfer knelt and washed his hands and turned from the lake and came back into the firelight with his shirtsleeves rolled to his elbows. He wiped one side of the blade and then the other against his pant leg. He picked up his rifle and expelled the spent shell and then levered in a new one. With the gun over his shoulder, his hand on the barrel and the butt skyward, he looked down at the boy and said, Hope you weren't plannin on stayin here tonight.

What do you mean?

I mean I fucked it up for you. Ain't safe anymore. Kiyotes'll be all over this blood. You're here when them bastards show up, they'll tear you to pieces.

He nodded down at the boy's small knapsack.

That all you travelin with?

Yessir.

Well, go on and pick it up. Where you headin anyway? Little kid like you.

Black Elk.

Black Elk, Montana?

Yessir.

Shit, kid, you're lost.

The wolfer sucked his teeth and stared at the boy as if making up his mind. As if resolving some conflict.

I suppose I could go to Black Elk, he said. Ain't been in a while.

You ain't got to do that, Kilt said.

I know I don't. But I think I will. Got to make a stop in Bozeman first. Got to collect this bounty.

Yessir.

Okay, then, he said. Let's get on.

25

The light was just coming on when they reached Wilsall. The Bridgers were dark and silhouetted by the paling sky. The last of the stars were dying out in twos and threes till finally there were no stars and an aurora bloomed on the horizon and the new light spilled across the plains and coppered the valley. The clouds at that early hour were lavender and orange and the sky was a faded blue and the Bridgers to the west turned orange like the clouds.

Kilt had fallen asleep and came awake suddenly as the truck lurched to a stop. The wolfer sat with his hands on the wheel and his chin resting on his hands and his eyes were red and brittle and his eyelids looked paper thin. Kilt sat up and wiped the spittle from the corner of his mouth. He immediately reached for the knapsack and the Luger and the wolfer said, Don't worry, kid. Ain't goin a rob you.

Kilt blinked and rubbed his eyes.

Where are we?

Little place called Wilsall.

The wolfer sucked his teeth. The truck was parked in front

of a café. There was a long hitching post and half a dozen saddled horses dallied there with their long tails whipping at the early flies.

You hungry, kid?

Kilt didn't answer.

Of course you are. Come on. Get some grub in us before we go get our money.

They took a table along the wall and the wolfer took the seat facing the door and he eyed it like he was expecting bad news. He took off his hat and set it on the table and ran both hands through his black hair and then looked at his hands as if his hair might have left some kind of stain. Then he laid them on the table and turned and watched the waitress. The waitress was a lanky thing who called everyone *hun*. There was a line of cowboys seated at the long counter with their hats pushed back on their heads. All of them wore spurs and pistols. Some of them poured whiskey in their coffee. The wolfer watched the crowd as if he had already insulted them and was awaiting some kind of assault. But mostly he just watched the waitress.

There was a folded paper on the table near the wall and the wolfer turned it with his fingertips to read the headline. He took his papers and tobacco from his waistcoat pocket and rolled a cigarette and lit it and then sat back and smoked. Then he flipped the paper over and pushed it against the wall.

A moment later he leaned forward and waved the boy closer. He said, She says anything about wolves, you just keep quiet.

Why?

Cause I told you to.

The man winked at him and leaned on his elbows and smoked some more. He looked around the café and when he looked back at Kilt, the boy was still watching him.

Wolfers don't draw much water in these parts, the man

said. Most of these here cowboys don't take so kindly to trapping. You think they would but they don't. See it as cheatin or something. Got no problem shootin one a the sumbitches, but you put out a trap . . .

He shrugged his shoulders.

But you didn't trap it, Kilt said.

Not that one, I didn't, he said. Anyway, she'll ask you. She'll ask what you're doin out here with me. You just keep your mouth shut.

The waitress came over with a pot of coffee and turned the enameled mug set before him right side up, and all the while she looked at him sidelong like she was formulating how to start it all. Still pouring the coffee, she said: Where you been, Virgil?

He smoked and plucked a piece of tobacco from his tongue.

No hun?

She looked at the boy.

Who you got here? she asked.

Don't know, as a matter of fact. What's your name, kid?

Benjamin.

Benjamin, the waitress said.

Yes mam.

How do you know Virgil?

I don't.

Then why you sittin at this table with him?

He's giving me a ride.

A ride.

Yes mam.

Where's he givin you a ride to?

Black Elk.

Why you goin to Black Elk?

Kilt didn't answer. The waitress looked at the wolfer.

Why you takin him to Black Elk, Virgil?

Cause he needs a ride.

She pursed her lips and nodded. She looked out the window at the parked truck. Said, What do you got in the back a that truck?

The wolfer didn't answer. She said, You trappin again?

He only looked at her and grinned. She looked at the boy.

He got a dead wolf in the back a that truck?

Kilt looked down at the table. She said, How'd he do it? He trap it or did he shoot it?

Still the boy was silent. The waitress nodded. Mm hmm, she said.

Thought we might give it a go again? the wolfer said.

Again? she said. She laughed.

I say something funny?

She balled her fists and punched them to her hips and stood with her arms all akimbo and her face shaped into a dour expression. She finally said, Deddy was right about you.

Oh? said the wolfer. He smoked. And what was he so right about?

She seemed to study him sitting before her as if his very presence was an affront to some well-guarded sensibility. For he to utter anything at all a great violation.

Everything, she said after a very long moment. Then she said with great reluctance, Your eggs'll be up soon.

Then she turned and walked away. Both he and the boy watched her go. When she was gone, the wolfer said, Don't ever promise them a thing. That there's a hole you can't climb out of.

26

They finished breakfast and paid and headed out. In the glaring light there were three men standing next to the wolfer's truck. All of them wearing black. All in hats. Two of the men smoked. The other just stood there with his thumbs hooked in his belt. The sight of them made the wolfer stop and he held out his hand to stop the boy from going any farther. The one with his thumbs in his belt spoke up.

Hidy, Virgil, he said.

The wolfer said nothing.

Having breakfast? the man said.

He took a step forward.

Who's the kid?

Just giving him a ride, the wolfer said.

Where to?

He's trying to get to Black Elk.

Why you goin a Black Elk, kid?

Kilt did not answer.

The two a you need to learn some manners, the man said.

He sucked his teeth and then spit in the dirt.

Where's my money, Virgil?

You got your money, the wolfer said.

No, I did not.

Paid you last week.

You paid the balance but you didn't factor the interest. There's interest to these things.

You said nothing about no interest.

If you go to a bank, the man said, and they lend you money, you think they're lending that money outta the goodness of their hearts?

The man shook his head.

No sir, he said. So why would you think borrowing money from me is any different?

I paid you, the wolfer said. We had a deal and I paid you.

The man clicked his tongue.

See, he said, I just made a long trip this morning to come hear you say anything but that. So maybe you want to try it another way.

There is no other way, the wolfer said. Paid in full. We're done.

The man laughed.

Tell you what, he said. Maybe I wasn't clear enough. I'm goin a believe that you truly didn't think there was any interest involved.

The man looked west.

You're headin west?

The wolfer didn't answer.

I'll meet you in Deer Lodge in two days, the man said. I need to see the Fultons about some debts come due.

He looked in the back of the truck at the dead wolf.

You go get your bounty, that should help with your predicament.

The wolfer stood completely still. He hadn't taken his eyes from the man.

Okay, the man said. Two days.

He winked at the kid.

Drive safe, he said.

27

They drove west with the sun rising behind them. When they got to Bozeman they pulled off onto Main Street and the wolfer slowed the truck and rolled down his window and set his arm there. The road was muddy like it had rained but it had not. A streetcar ran down the middle with the electrified wires running overhead. The stores were opening for the day. Shop owners in white aprons were setting up their signs. There were butcher shops and saddleries and a blacksmith and a mortuary. There was an oriental rug shop and the proprietor was a small Chinese man with long mustaches and he was draping the ornate pieces on a kind of drying rack. There was a store for tack repair and a store that sold chocolate. On the corner there was a bank and behind that the gray granite government building. The year it had been built was chiseled into the stone.

The wolfer swung the truck off of Main Street and parked in front of the government building and jammed it into neutral and shut off the engine. He leaned and pulled a pocketbook from his hip and opened it and took out the bills therein and leafed through them and slid a dollar free and held it out to the boy.

You stay with the truck till I get back and you can keep this, he said.

Kilt only watched him.

You want to come in? the wolfer asked.

Don't matter to me.

Don't matter to me either.

The wolfer put all the money back in the pocketbook and put the pocketbook back in his hip.

Tell you what, he said. We'll split it. Two dollars for you. Two dollars for me. That seem fair enough? I spoilt your campin trip, after all.

He winked at the boy.

Come on, he said. Let's go make some money.

Together they passed through the doors of the building with the man holding the wolf pelt bundled in his arms and the boy behind him. They passed men in suits and men in shirtsleeves. Some of the men were trailed by a retinue of assistants. Some men were walking slowly and talking in low, muted voices. But none of the men nodded at the wolfer. Most of them hardly even looked up.

At the door with the words ACCOUNTS RECEIVABLE printed in gold leaf over the pebbled glass transom, the wolfer stopped and looked down at the boy and then at the doorknob and said, You mind? My hands are full.

Kilt opened the door and the two entered. Behind the long steel counter was an old man with a green transparent visor like a poker dealer might wear and he was sitting in a tall chair with a pipe hanging limp in the corner of his mouth tallying some figures in a thick leatherbound ledger. To either side of the accountant were piles of wolf pelts stacked like rugs. Behind the counter were a dozen or so gray wolves noosed around the upper jaw and hanging from the ceiling, limbs limp like their bones had been removed. Either concentrating or deaf, he did not look up when the wolfer and the boy entered. The door clapped shut and the wolfer cleared his throat but it elicited no alarm in the accountant. In fact, the old man was entirely ignorant to the man and the boy's presence, so much so that when the wolfer dropped the pelt on the steel counter beside him the old man looked first at the pelt then at the wolfer as if he'd just been dealt a great injustice.

The accountant wore thin-wired glasses with circular lenses and the glasses were propped precariously on the end of his nose. His right hand was stained with ink. He looked at the wolfer over the top rims of his glasses then he looked at the boy and then looked down at the pelt. Then he went back to his ledger.

Shot or trapped? the accountant said. His voice was flat and without expression.

What's that matter? asked the wolfer.

The accountant took the pipe from his mouth and glared up at him.

Shot or trapped? he asked again.

Shot.

Public land or private?

One pay out moren the other?

Same reimbursement. Four dollars.

Then why you askin?

I am asking because it is my job to ask. Public or private?

Public, I suppose.

You suppose?

Didn't see no one's name of it.

Are you trying to make some attempt at a joke, sir?

No.

The accountant eyed him. He took a deep breath.

Very well. Public.

He wrote it down in the ledger. Then he turned the pelt

over. He tugged at it like it was some kind of garment. He studied the head. He studied the tail.

Very well, he said again.

Then he punched something into a register and a bell within the register chimed and the money tray slid forth. The accountant removed four dollars from it and handed the money over the steel counter to the wolfer.

Good day, said the accountant, and he went back to his ledger.

They left the room and walked down the hall and stepped through the building's door out into the morning. The streets were lively and there were men riding horses with their hats low against the sun and horses pulling wagons being driven by women in plain dresses and children sitting at their side. There were Model As going up and down Main Street and the air smelled like hay and horse manure and exhaust.

The man cranked the truck and got in and handed Kilt two dollars without saying a word. Then he backed out and drove on.

28

They left town with the low eastern sun printed on the back window of the truck like a rippling coin. The wolfer's face was shadowed under his hat with the cigarette flaring occasionally at his lips and the shadow of the truck was stretched out down the road before them, dark and as long as a fallen tree. The man drove with the window down and the wind and the tires on the road were loud and because of this there seemed no reason to talk so they didn't. Kilt sat stealing a glance from time to time at the man who chewed the inside of his lip and smoked.

Finally Kilt said: Who were those men back there?

What?

The man leaned closer to hear over the noise of the wind.

Who were those men?

Hold on.

The man rolled up his window.

What now?

Kilt asked again.

Back where? the wolfer asked.

At the café. The ones who wanted your money.

Just some old friends.

They didn't seem like friends.

You don't got to worry about them.

The wolfer turned and winked at him. It was quiet again. They drove on. There were cattle in the fields. Like specks of coal in the tallow grass.

Earlier, Kilt said, when you said all that stuff about promises and holes you can't climb out of and wolfers not drawing water, you weren't just talking about trapping wolves, were you?

The man turned his face slightly. He squinted an eye at the boy.

What makes you say that?

Cause it seems like you were talking about something else.

Maybe it was just talk. Maybe that's all it was.

Was it?

You askin me if I meant it as a metaphor?

A what?

You think I was talkin about something other than what I was talkin about?

I don't know.

Well, I don't either.

You said it, though, Kilt said. Seems if you said it you must've given it some thought.

Well, the wolfer said, maybe that's all it was. Just a thought. Maybe I just said that thought out loud.

They were coming to a bridge crossing the Madison River and just before the bridge there was a turnout and the gravel road there turned down toward the river and the man pulled off and drove the truck through the stands of willow and cottonwood and stopped the truck along the shore. He turned off the engine and for a while he just sat there listening to the river. Then he passed a canteen to the boy.

Go fill this up, he said.

Kilt took the canteen and opened the door and went to the river and knelt at the bank and stove the canteen into the cold water and he watched the rippled image of it and he watched the river pass. There was wind in the higher leaves of the tall cottonwoods but nothing moved in the low willows or across the surface of the river. Later in the day the caddis and mayflies would be hatching and the trout would be splashing and leaping after them, but right now it was quiet. All seemed completely at peace.

When the canteen got heavy Kilt lifted it from the water and screwed on the cap and stood and went back to the truck. The man had his arm laid on the door and he had a cigarette balanced between his fingers. Kilt handed the man the canteen but the man waved it off.

You ain't thirsty?

Nah.

The man looked through the windshield studying the sky. A hawk dove from one of the cottonwoods with its wings folded back and at the final moment outflung its talons and both the man and the boy expected to see the bird beat skyward again with its prize seized in its feet but they never did.

You read the Bible? the man asked.

No sir.

Can you read?

Yessir.

Then why the hell you ain't read the Bible?

Never got around to it, I guess.

Well, you get around to it.

Yessir.

Anyway, he said, Matthew 5:5. It says: Blessed are the meek for they shall inherit the earth.

Yessir, I've heard of that.

You have any idea what that means?

No sir.

It means you mind your Ps and Qs and all this will be yours one day.

He raised his hand, palm up, like a curator presenting a piece on display.

The problem, he continued, is the ones who ain't so meek. They're the ones you got to be wary of. They're the ones who take take take, and once it's all gone what's left for the meek, huh? You ponder that sentiment long enough you start to wonder if it's even worth it.

He looked down at Kilt who was looking back up at him with great solemnity and then the man looked out at the sky again.

You're born into a caste, kid. Shit, we all are. And unless you get very lucky or just plain lie to yourself, you'll be indentured to some bastard born higher than you for the rest of your life. That's probably not what you want to hear, being so young and all, but there ain't no other way to tell it. People are mean and the world ain't fair. All you can do is show a little grace and take what you can get. And I mean anything. Anything laid out there, you go ahead and take it because someone else will. You'll die one day and they'll tell you you can't take it with you, but to have is a hell of a lot easier than to not. So you let the meek be meek. Don't let anyone take what's yours.

The man held out his hand.

Hand me that canteen, he said.

He took a long drink. Then he snapped his tongue.

You ever doubt that there's goodness left in this world, he said, you come back to this river and take a drink.

29

They stayed by the river all that day and camped there that night. The next morning they set off. All day the sun held its place high above the Tobacco Root Mountains. Cast about in that vast blue was a chevron of geese beating toward somewhere, but so far away they were they appeared like an etching of geese on some painter's canvas. There were a few clouds like pulled cotton moving in the wind, the world's turning.

Later the man pulled off the highway and started down a dirt road.

Where we going? Kilt asked.

Want to check on something.

What do you want to check on?

Don't worry about it.

He ground the gears and the truck lurched on. There were cows at the fence and they lifted their heads at the truck with their tails swishing and their jaws working mechanically. They passed under the shade of a giant oak tree. The clapboard house stood stark against the green grass in front of them. A big barn with the white paint beginning to curl like wilted flowers.

Who lives here? Kilt asked.

John Fulton, the wolfer said.

Who's John Fulton?

An old friend.

The man kept driving, never taking his eyes from the house.

Maybe it's nothin, he said. He spoke it in a soft voice. Barely even audible. Almost like he didn't even want to say it.

What's nothing? Kilt said.

Nothin, the man said. Nothin's nothin.

He stopped the truck in the gravel turnaround at the foot of the porch. The man leaned over the wheel and watched the house, waiting for something to move but nothing did. He retarded the throttle and the engine cut out. Then they sat there in silence with Kilt looking at the man watching the house, and the man trying to figure out what to do next.

You wait here, he finally said to the boy.

I don't want to wait here.

You scared?

No.

It's okay if you are.

Well, I'm not.

Then wait here.

I don't want to wait here.

The wolfer breathed deeply, trying his best not to lose his temper with the boy.

All right, he said. Come on. Just don't go runnin off in there.

They climbed the porch steps with the man leading and Kilt trying to see around him. The man knocked on the screen door. The door behind it was wide open. The man could see the back door was open and the wind was being sucked through the house.

The man knocked again.

Then he said: John? You home in there?

No one answered. He went around to the big picture window and cupped his hands and looked in at the living room. A coffee table had been overturned. A vase lay on the floor and its flowers were scattered over the rug. Books had been pulled from the shelves and lay folded open on their spines. The man stepped back from the window and went quickly to the screen door and pulled it open.

He closed the door behind Kilt and the wind tunneling through the house quit and everything became very still. Despite the light of the day the house was dimly lit. Every curtain save the one on the picture window was drawn. There were lines of dust hanging in the cuts of slanting light. The house smelled like someone had cooked bacon. Like stale coffee and a little bit like woodsmoke.

John, the man said. John, you home?

They went from room to room with the man leading and Kilt following close on his heels. They walked to the foot of the stairs and then he looked at the boy.

You want to stay down here, that's up to you.

Kilt shook his head.

They climbed the stairs and at the head the man stopped and he stopped the boy and held a finger to his lips.

John?

Nothing.

Let's just wait and listen for a second, he whispered.

All the doors but one were open and the light through them was printed on the hallway runner. They could hear a clock ticking somewhere. Kilt held his breath. Dust was floating aimlessly in the bands of light. Other than that nothing moved. The man cocked his head and started down the hall and the boy followed.

The man stepped slowly. At each open door he looked in and surveyed the room. All the beds were made. There seemed nothing scattered about the floors. The windows were open and the thin lace curtains lifted and collapsed in the wind. Nothing seemed out of place. They moved on and didn't stop till they reached the closed door. He stood listening, his ear angled.

After a moment he pushed in the door and the old hinges creaked. The man saw a pair of boots sticking out from behind the bed. The stiff points of them pointing toward the ceiling. He held out his hand at Kilt so as to stop him from going any farther.

Stay in the hall, he said.

But—

Stay in the hall.

The man stepped into the bedroom and saw Mrs Fulton lying on the bed with her housedress torn at the collar and her throat had been cut. There was a wide dark stain spread across the mattress and her face was hidden beneath a pillow. The wolfer was cautious as he moved across the room. Like the woman was only sleeping and he was afraid to wake her. The floorboards squeaked and he stopped as if waiting for something to move but nothing did. At the bed he lifted the corner of the pillow covering her face. Her mouth was open like she was trying to catch her breath and her dead flat eyes were staring up at him. He put the pillow back down and went around the bed to where he had seen the boots and he found John Fulton lying there in denim overalls covered in mud and chaff like he had been out working and had come inside quickly without changing out of the dirty clothes. The wolfer stepped around him and saw he'd been shot through the neck. The floor wasn't level and the man's blood had run out in a slow current under the bed frame.

The wolfer heard the footsteps of Kilt over the wood as he entered the room and Kilt said, Are they dead?

Kilt took another step.

You stay right where you are, the man said.

Kilt said, Are they dead?

Yes, he said. They're dead.

Someone killed them?

The man looked back at Kilt and squinted like the boy reflected something very bright and then looked back at the dead man lying on the floor.

The man turned and came around the bed.

We got to go, he said.

The boy didn't move. Didn't speak. Nothing.

Kid. You hear me? Got to get out of here.

The man took Kilt by the shoulders and faced him around to the door and walked him out of the room and then shut the door behind him.

30

In the long purple twilight they made camp along the river and the man got a fire going and Kilt sat with his knees against his chest and his palms extended toward the heat. The wolfer was set about gathering firewood, dragging the long brittle limbs like some hunter his kill. When he was satisfied with it he came back to the fire and squatted and warmed his hands.

He stole glances at Kilt. Watched the fire rose his face. Saw the flames lapping in the boy's black pupils like they were not eyes but distant shores that no one could get to.

The man pitched in a stick and the fire burst and the sparks hissed into the darkening air and then were gone forever. The man didn't know the best way to ask it so he just went ahead and asked.

Is that the first time you've seen one?

Seen one?

A dead body.

No.

You tellin the truth?

Yessir.

The man held his hands out to the fire. He studied the boy. Then he watched the flames dance around.

It was those men who did it, Kilt said. Wasn't it?

I don't know.

But you think it was.

Yeah, the man said. I think it was.

You think they're waiting for us in Deer Lodge? Like they said they would?

Maybe, the wolfer said. But you don't have to worry about that.

You keep saying that.

Yeah.

Is it because I don't have to or because you don't want me to?

The wolfer spit between his feet. He wiped his mouth with the back of his hand.

Both, he finally said. Then he said, You're too young to have seen that.

I'm fourteen.

Yeah. That's too young.

Kilt watched the fire.

Do you think they knew it was going to end like that?

You mean John and his wife?

Yeah.

I don't know.

You think if they did know they would've done something different?

I don't think that would've mattered.

Why not? If they weren't in that house then they wouldn't have died. Those men wouldn't have found them.

Maybe not. Maybe you just go when it's your time to go.

Because Death isn't picky. Doesn't care if you're in a house or in a field or shopping or dancing or having some fun or crying or laughing. Death doesn't care. When it's your time it's your time. Nothin you can say or do to get out of it. The only way to avoid Death is to not be born.

What if you could know?

If I could know it was my time to go? To let Death have me?

Yeah.

I wouldn't want to know that.

Why not?

Cause that ain't no way to live, kid. I got enough to look over my shoulder about as it is.

The man stood from the fire and sucked his teeth.

You got a blanket or anything? he asked. Then remembering said, Course you don't.

He went to the truck and opened the door and reached under the seat and pulled free two wool blankets and came back to the fire and handed one down to the boy.

You take the back seat, he said. You'll be able to stretch out back there.

He sat by the fire then lay down and stretched out his legs and crossed one boot over the other and spread the blanket over his legs and pulled it up to his chest and then angled his hat over his eyes. There was only the faintest paling in the west now and the first stars were coming out. It was not long before Kilt heard the man begin to snore. Kilt stood with his blanket and went to the truck and lay down in the back seat. He watched the sky darken through the window. And then soon it was all dark. And then soon he was asleep.

Kilt had a dream in which he was walking down a road in a place he had never seen. A place so foreign the dim burning colors he saw might not even have had a name. The land was flat like a vast sheet of metal and the dirt road was starlit and faded away in the distance until it could no longer be seen. To either side of him the forests had been burned and the threadbare woods were black as the sea bottom. Shored up along the ditch like tide debris were the random bones of things real or not. The sun hung low in the flat dead air, skull-colored like a ghost of the sun and it felt to the boy like night could fall at any moment. He had been walking for a long time and his legs were tired and felt heavy and every step seemed a great effort like they were sticking to something but it was only dirt that was beneath his feet. Nothing made a sound and nothing in those burned woods moved and all along the side of the road the bones were piled. He was just about to sit down and rest when the sound of birds made him squint. Not birdsong but astringent bickering like something being fought over. Down the road he saw a murder of six crows jumping and careening. Their black wings beating against each other and the birds rising into the air with their terrible heads downward and then diving with sickled beaks agape. Kilt kept walking and soon was upon it. The crows leapt away and flew and then landed and stood watching the boy. They had been picking at the remains of a headless body that had been gutted and burned. The ribs of it flayed open and stark white against the charred sinew. Its legs were gone from the knee down and the boy saw that the missing parts were stacked neatly at the roadside. The bones arranged like you'd build a fire and the skin stripped away and heaped like dirty clothes. The crows had moved off and were chattering at each other and Kilt saw another similar disfigured body down the road and another after that. And another. And another. And as Kilt looked down the road the pale sun fell and then only the faintest image of that wasteland could be seen and then it clapped out into darkness and from behind the boy heard a roar like the draft of an immense hot fire and when he turned he had only enough time to close his eyes.

31

The roar of the fire was not a fire but the man shaking Kilt awake. From dark to dark he felt the man looming over him. Kilt was about to scream when the man clapped his hand over Kilt's mouth. A harried look contorted on his face. The boy writhed in an attempt to get free but the man wouldn't let him.

Shh, the man whispered. Quit wigglin.

Kilt tried to bite his hand but he couldn't open his mouth.

Quit it, said the man.

The dark of the truck cab was perfect in its blackness. A colorless void absolute. Then the image of the man came slowly into focus and in his hand was the boy's Luger.

The man said, I'm goin a let go but don't go screaming. I ain't goin a hurt you. You just got a listen to me. Okay?

Kilt struggled a moment longer then calmed and the man said, Okay?

Kilt nodded.

Okay, the man said. I'm taking my hand away. Don't scream. He took his hand away from Kilt's mouth. Take this, he said. Take this and run.

What?

Run. Run into the brush and hide. Don't make a sound. Don't move.

What?

You ever see a baby deer hiding in the grass? You do that. You run and hide in the brush and you don't move no matter what you see or hear, okay?

Kilt didn't answer. Only stared up at him.

Okay? the man said.

Kilt nodded.

Tell me you understand.

Okay.

Tell me.

I understand.

And don't move from that spot till either you don't hear nothin or I come and find you. Okay?

Okay.

Kilt took the gun and climbed out of the truck and stood there looking at the wolfer who was looking down the road into the darkness. The fire was blazing and the light of it shadowed half of him. He turned back to the boy with a scornful look.

Go!

32

Kilt didn't stop running. The grass of the brush came to his waist. It was wet from the night dew and soaked the boy's trousers. He turned once to see the man looking into the darkness. The fire was at his back. Kilt stopped and fell to his knees and sat there panting, gazing back at the man through the grass. The man looked crazy. Like he was in some phantom standoff. Like in some spectral duel with the night itself. The fire was burning and coppering the man. The burning light ratcheting upon the man's shoulders as if he too were on fire. Then from beyond the fire came the headlamps of a car.

Kilt was about to stand and call to the man when the car pulled to a stop and out of the darkness a figure formed and then another. And then another. All three of them men. All three dressed in black. Kilt recognized them instantly. The one in the center spoke. At that distance it was diminished but the boy heard him. The man said, You were in Fulton's house today, weren't you?

You do it? the wolfer said.

Do what?

The man laughed.

You're a coward, the wolfer said. John didn't deserve that.

The man said, Maybe he did and maybe he didn't.

You're goin a hang for it.

The man lifted his right hand and held within it was a pistol. The wolfer looked at the man to the right. Then at the man to the left.

The man in the center said, Don't look at them. You look at me. They ain't got no questions for you.

The man seemed to look over the wolfer's shoulder.

Say, he said, where's that kid?

What kid?

The one traveling with you.

He run off on me when I went to get the bounty office.

Run off.

The man shook his head. He smiled.

You know what I think? he asked. I think you're a goddamn liar.

The wolfer looked at the man on the right again.

I told you not to look at them.

A little wind came up and stirred the grass and for a moment Kilt couldn't hear what they were saying. Saw the man's mouth moving, though. Then there was some kind of malevolent laughter amongst them. The wind fell and the grass calmed and it was very quiet again.

The wolfer had not moved. Had not even shifted. As if that which he awaited had yet to come. As if the three men were only in the boy's imagination. The air was totally still and there was nothing in that night to drown them out. Not a coyote's yammer, not an owl. Nothing. Then a quick flash followed immediately by a pop was witnessed and the wolfer dropped to the ground. The man stood over him and fired again. Then once more. Each shot's report fleeing into the night and dying somewhere out there.

The man holstered the pistol and took off his hat and wiped at his forehead. His face showed raggedly in the firelight. He muttered something to the other two which must have been some kind of order and the other two knelt out of view and then came up with the body in their arms and a shower of sparks raced into the air as the body was heaved onto the fire. Then without ceremony the man put on his hat and two of the men walked to the truck and the third to the car. They cranked the engines alive. Then Kilt heard the sputter of them and the gears grind and then they lurched around and drove off into the night.

33

Kilt hadn't slept a minute that night. Hadn't even closed his eyes. The morning dawned like the morning after a battle. It was gray and windless and there was woodsmoke hanging like fog. Kilt sat up and looked out over the tops of the grass. The night's fire had an anemic tendril of smoke twisting into the morning air. He heard birdsong and then as if to prove its existence the tiniest of wrens landed on one of the dusty tips of grass in front of him, and it stayed there just long enough for him to blink and then it was gone.

It started to rain and Kilt stood and made his way to what was left of the fire. The blackened corpse was smoldering amongst the burned wood. The dead face turned into the ashes. All of his hair had been burned away and the skin of his skull was stretched and tight and looked like dried leather. The rain was hissing in the dying embers and the wolfer's dead body was smoking. Kilt didn't know what else to do besides look on in silence so that's what he did. He looked for a long time. As if trying to parse out some reason for it. Trying to circumvent the absolutism of death.

The rain fell on him and the fire and the burned body and Kilt realized at some point that he was shivering but he did not know how long he had been shivering for. He wanted to do something for the man but there was nothing to be done. There are consequences in this world that have no remedy.

34

Alone again. Trotting on with little to eat. His small legs weak with exhaustion. He followed the sun as it traversed the sky, a burning compass that raced on without him.

Days of heat and wind. The smells of sage and cattle and woodsmoke carried on the air. Maybe a car or two to break up the monotony. Kilt would hide in the grass out of fear of seeing the wolfer's Ford. But none was his and none stopped. A pensive face stamped in the window. A subjection for the have and have not.

He swore he watched years pass. The sun setting like lead. And each morning the horizon rupturing like blood from cut skin.

See the boy squatting in the shade with his head downcast and labored in his arms like he was sleeping. Rocking in his languid stupor as the wind and the dust carried in the wind whirled about him. As if to hide him. As if to take him back.

The nights were long and cool. Kilt sheltered wherever he could find it. When it rained the rain was cold. Kilt made small fires with which to warm his hands. Careful to keep them small so no one would see them. He slept fitfully. Coming awake at the softest of sounds and blinking wildly into the dark searching for danger. And then he would rise and set off again.

Late one morning he came to the outskirts of a town and stopped and stood and watched it like he didn't trust it. He hadn't eaten in two days. There was a filling station and a little diner attached. Kilt could smell hamburger meat cooking.

He crossed the road and stood for a moment outside the door. He saw his reflection in the glass and almost didn't recognize himself. Face smudged in dirt and soot. His clothes looking more like rags and filthy.

A man's voice came from behind him. Said, Well, you goin in or not?

Inside he asked the woman working the register where he was.

What do you mean?

Where am I?

You don't know where you are?

No mam.

Well, where'd you come from?

Bozeman.

Last place you were in was Bozeman?

I think so.

Well, you're west of Bozeman.

Where's that?

St. Ignatius.

Where's St. Ignatius?

West of Bozeman.

The woman leaned on the counter. She said, When's the last time you ate?

Kilt shrugged.

You eat today?

He shook his head.

Come around here with me, she said.

She called some man's name and told him to bring a plate and then she led the boy to a table.

While he ate, the woman watched him. Then after a moment she said, Where's a boy like you going all by himself?

Mouth full, he said, Black Elk.

Black Elk.

Yes mam.

What's your name?

Benjamin.

Benjamin have a last name?

Benjamin Kilt.

What is Benjamin Kilt got going on in Black Elk?

I don't know. Some ranch I'm supposed to find.

What ranch?

Triple . . . Triple something.

Triple Nine?

Yeah.

Why you want to go to the Triple Nine?

You've heard of it?

Yes.

She watched him a bit longer. There was food falling from the corners of his mouth. When he drank from his cup the water spilled down his chin.

The woman said, You want another hamburger?

I don't got any money for another.

On the house.

What's that mean?

Means it's free.

Why you giving them to me for free?

Cause you look like you could use a break.

She watched him eat another hamburger.

You want a ride to Black Elk? she asked.

Are you going there too?

No.

Then why you offering me a ride?

Cause you need one.

After a long pause Kilt wiped his mouth with the back of his hand. The woman handed him a napkin.

Use a napkin, she said. So you want a ride or what?

35

He had been in Black Elk for almost two weeks. His refuge a church with a small congregation. The pastor let him sleep in one of the pews. In the evenings he would listen to the choir practicing their hymns. He read the Bible. Listened to the pastor rehearse Sunday's sermon. A future for them all predicated on the sins of man. A future given over to the will of God.

During the day the pines and the rock under the hot sun gave off a sweet smell. Every afternoon the clouds would gather and there would be a thunder and then quickly it would end and the sun would return and the ground would dry in the sun and start to smoke.

One afternoon Kilt went into a drugstore. He walked the aisles because he had nothing else to do. He still hadn't found a way to get to the Triple Nine Ranch. He was hungry. Down one aisle he saw a glass jar of jerky. He lifted the lid and pulled a piece free and was about to put the jerky in his pocket when he felt a hand come down on his shoulder. A man was standing behind him with an expression of mild amusement.

The man said, I hope you are planning on paying for that

jerky. And the boy said he was. And the man said, How it works is you take it to the counter and give the nice man there your money and then you can put it in your pocket or throw it on the ground or give it to a dog for a little treat. It's your jerky, see? Can do whatever you want with it. Just have to pay for it first.

Kilt nodded.

The man said, So let's see it.

See what?

Let's see the money you're going to use to buy that jerky.

Kilt didn't move. The man frowned. The man said, Where you from, young man?

Minnesota.

Minnesota? Heck, son, you're a long ways off. Why you pick Black Elk of all places?

Someone told me to come this way.

For what?

For answers.

Who told you to do that?

Someone back in Minnesota.

What's that person's name?

Nick Mercy.

Mm hmm, the man said.

You don't have a mother and father, do you?

Kilt didn't move.

The man said, That's why you're sleeping in the church, isn't it?

Kilt looked up with wild eyes and the man knew what that meant.

I know all about it, the man said. In fact, there isn't anything that happens in this valley I don't know about. A sweet woman drove you here, didn't she?

Kilt watched him.

Yes, the man said. Sweet woman.

The man held out his hand. He said, Hand me that jerky.

Kilt hesitated.

Go on, the man said.

Kilt pulled the jerky from his pocket and handed it to the man. The man turned it in his hand, held it against the light like a chemist.

Pretty thin piece, he said. Here. He handed the jerky back to the boy. Go on and get you another one. Get you one of them big pieces there. One of them thick ones.

Kilt finally spoke, said, You ain't going to call the sheriff on me?

Nah, the man said. He waved his hand. Just a little misunderstanding. Owner won't mind in the least.

You know the owner? Kilt asked.

Yes, I do. Very well, in fact. His name is Royal Wainwright. Sort of a big deal in these parts.

Kilt watched him. There was a smudge of something on one cheek. His little mouth moved wordlessly like he knew what he wanted to say but didn't yet know how to say it. Finally it came to him.

That's you, ain't it? Kilt said. Royal Wainwright. That's you.

The man smiled at him. He started to nod.

You are a smart young man, Mr . . .

Kilt told him his name.

The man said, That's what your mother decided to name you. Good name. You go by Ben or Benjamin?

Either one.

What do you prefer?

Don't matter. Either one.

We'll go with Benjamin, then.

Okay.

The man held out his hand for the boy to shake. He said, Royal Wainwright. But you already pieced that together.

Kilt shook his hand.

Wainwright said, I tell you what. Let's get some more of this jerky then we'll head out to the ranch. Get you some answers.

He took his pocket watch from his waistcoat and clicked it open and then clicked it shut. He said, Mrs Wainwright should be getting dinner ready here soon. You'll come out, have a bite to eat. Heck, you can eat as much as you can fit into that belly. What do you say?

Okay.

Wainwright nodded. Looked down at him. Said, What do you know about horses?

36

The Triple Nine Ranch sat on a spread just shy of twenty thousand acres. A man named Royal Wainwright was the sole proprietor, but the ranch had been Royal's father's before him and his father's father's before that. They ran cattle and raised horses. Royal's mother had been an heir to a British tea company and rode dressage and extolled the virtues of horses onto her son. The Triple Nine was widely known for its breeding and training of Arabians and Thoroughbreds. There was still plenty of cowboying being done, but the trainers outnumbered the punchers and most of the punchers spent most of their time in the mountains seeing to the cattle, coming down only to get drunk in St. Ignatius.

On the way out to his ranch Wainwright spoke without pause as if reciting a rehearsed monologue. He was profound, he was theatric. He spoke to the failures of East Coast capitalism, the people choking themselves on the dirty crowded air of its cities. And for what? he said, A dollar? Some power? No, he said, it's all greed back there. Sure, there's greed here, but at least we can see the stars.

He drove and as he drove he pointed out the names of the landscape, of birds and animals, the peaks of mountains. My father named that one, he told the boy. All of this he spoke with a low timbre, his voice booming like distant thunder. He talked about art and his love of poetry, of Baudelaire, novelists like Balzac and Melville. He spoke of the great composers.

Whose bones, he said, may lie buried beneath our feet, but their greatness, which is to say all greatness, never dies.

He talked about his admiration for Theodore Roosevelt and his detest for Woodrow Wilson. He's a bean counter and a bigot, Wainwright said, and he's going to lead us straight into war. He talked about that and more and Kilt watched him and listened without interruption, but more than anything the man talked about horses.

They turned off the road onto the gravel apron where the tall ranch gate of heavy timber spanned the drive. The words TRIPLE NINE RANCH were stamped into a metal sheet gone ocher with years, hanging in the center, with the ranch's brand, three cascading 9s, on either side.

Here we are, Wainwright said.

They drove under the entrance and Kilt looked up at it in awe like it was some grand monument. The shadow of it passed over them with the sun still high and the grass of the valley green and redolent and the mountains still holding snow on the shaded faces, and with the long gray drive cutting these green fields Kilt had the feeling he was being delivered to some holy place.

The house appeared after a long way. It was huge and magnificent. Made of old growth and granite. Kilt counted five chimneys. A covered porch wrapped the entirety of it. There was a stream off to one side. There were flowers everywhere. Hollyhocks and gladiolas and dahlias. Beyond the house was the barn and stables. There was a training corral and a fenced field where close to two dozen Arabians stood with the grass reaching their bellies and their long black tails working back and forth through the air.

Wainwright parked the car near the front, and when he did a woman came from inside, wiping her hands on her apron and then holding a hand to her eyes like a visor and squinting at the boy sitting in the car.

That's Tillie, Wainwright said. She keeps the house in order.

That's your wife?

No. Mrs Wainwright is undoubtedly preparing to make your acquaintance.

She knows I'm here?

Of course. She might be the one person in this valley who knows more about the goings-on even more than I.

That night they ate at a long mahogany table with Wainwright at one end, his wife at the other. There were candles going the length of it. A big silver platter of steaks in the center. Bowls of mashed potatoes, yams, and gravy. A plate of butter rolls. In the grand room off the dining room there was a fire going in the hearth and from time to time a woman in a plain gray dress would tend to it. Another woman would bring more wine, clear plates away. And all of it done without a sound. There were two others in attendance: a boy of about eighteen, and a girl about Kilt's age. The boy and the girl ate without a word, but the boy seemed to watch Kilt with a gauged amount of concern. Maybe even malice.

Wainwright spoke endlessly, most of the time with his mouth full, like some scorned lord. There was a glass of scotch next to his plate and the bottle was not far.

He said to his wife, You of all people should despise Wilson. His outlandish views of women's suffrage are enough to make every woman in America march over to Washington and beat his door down.

Please, no politics at the table, Mrs Wainwright said.

Well, what else is there? Wainwright said, leaning back in his chair and throwing his hands up in defeat. The union is on the brink of collapse. We'll be at war any day. Mark my words, Martha. War. All of us and everything we hold dear, all of it laid to waste. Am I wrong?

You hate tyranny, Martha said. Would going to war be a tragedy?

All war is tragedy, he said.

I don't like you talking this way in front of the children, she said.

They should hear it, Wainwright said. Especially the boys here. He pointed at them individually. The boy across the table watched Kilt begrudgingly as he cut his steak. Wainwright said, They'll be the ones sent over there. Trench warfare and mustard gas and bombs going off and God knows what else. Shooting and killing each other because some bean counter in Washington is trying to prove a point.

And what about this ranch? Martha said. She looked up at the ceiling. She looked at the walls. She tapped the table.

What about it? Wainwright said.

You think we're sitting here now because the Flatheads just gave all this land to us? One can't be selective on their opinions regarding tragedy, darling. Nor on what constitutes a war. Death is death. Only the victor gets to assign what is evil and what is not.

Wainwright threw up his hands, knowing he could not beat her on this.

Martha looked at Kilt. She said, Whatever it is he promised you, it's not too late to run for the hills.

Kilt's mouth was full and he covered his mouth with his hand and chewed and when he was done chewing, he said, Didn't promise me anything, mam.

What did he tell you, then?

Yeah, said the boy across the table. What'd he tell you?

Don't interrupt, Sidney, Wainwright said. We've spoken about this.

The boy cut into his steak again. Kilt watched him then looked at Mrs Wainwright.

Invited me for supper is all, Kilt said.

He offer you a place to stay? Martha asked. He offer you work?

No mam, Kilt said. Just the supper.

Supper, she said. She sat back in her chair. Lifted her wineglass from the table. Took a sip off it and never once let her eyes fall from the boy. You're the boy from Minnesota. The one sleeping in the church.

Yes mam.

Pastor there says you like to read.

Yes mam.

Well. No place for a boy to be sleeping. You sure Mr Wainwright didn't offer you anything else?

No mam.

Well, she said, he should have. Mr Wainwright seems to be losing his manners like he's losing his hair.

She sipped her wine and then set the glass down on the table and took the napkin from her lap and dabbed the corner of her mouth and then placed the napkin back in her lap and looked at the boy and said, There's a room in the bunkhouse. Been empty for a while now. It's yours if you want it. Be nice to have some extra help around here. You like horses?

I don't know one way or the other, mam, Kilt said. Never been around them much.

Seems an odd place to turn up, then, don't it? Sid said.

The girl sitting next to Sid giggled into her plate. Mrs Wainwright gave her a look.

That's enough, you two, she said. Then she said, looking back at Kilt, You'll get used to them. The horses, that is. You might even come to love them.

37

Kilt made his arrangements in the bunkhouse. It was a nice room, which he had all to himself. A nice bed. The linens were clean and soft. He was told breakfast was served at five thirty each morning and that if anyone wanted to eat they should not be late. When he first arrived to the room that night he found a stack of books on his bed with a note from Mrs Wainwright that read: *This is a well with no bottom. Drink up.*

The next morning a man named Lou set him up with a pitchfork and showed him how to muck stalls and pitch hay into each stable. Then he nodded at the boy and went away.

Kilt was forking up hay out beyond the barn when the shadow of a horse and then the shadow of a rider sitting the horse darkened the ground before him. When Kilt turned to look the sun was directly behind the rider, nimbusing him in white light, and Kilt had to squint against it. He stuck the tines into the earth and fashioned his hand into a visor to shield the sun from his eyes. The rider had a rifle laid across his lap and when he spoke he spoke like he was delivering some kind of eulogy. He said, So they tell me you're supposed to be my brother.

Who said that?

Wainwright. That's the reason you're here, ain't it?

I don't know, Kilt said.

What do you mean you don't know?

Means I don't know. I've never seen you before a day in my life.

Well, you either is or you ain't.

Okay.

So which is it?

No one told me either way, Kilt said. How would I know?

You follow me out here?

I don't even know who you are.

Why you in Montana?

Because I am.

That's not a good reason.

Only reason I got.

I'm from Minnesota, Sid said.

So am I.

I know you are, Sid said. Mr Wainwright told me so much. I think he sent for you. Just like he sent for me.

A guy named Nick Mercy told me to come here.

Nick Mercy. Mr Wainwright. Same thing.

Why would Mr Wainwright do that?

Guess he must have had a thing for our mother. Made trips back to Minneapolis in the summer, checking in on his beef supply out there. Said he met her at some kind a hotel. Said she had two of us. One—he pointed at himself—she didn't know where it was. The other, she said—he pointed down at Kilt—was up in Duluth. You believe that?

Not really.

You ever remember her leaving for a week or two? Making some excuse to take off?

Kilt didn't move. Didn't answer.

The boy said, That means you do. Well, that's where she went. Down to Minneapolis to meet up with Mr Wainwright. He really cared for her, you know. Took real good care of her.

The boy leaned in the saddle and spit. He looked off toward the Missions then he looked up the valley and then looked down at Kilt. Then he said, So I'm gonna ask it again. Why you here?

I don't know, Kilt said.

To the north there were dark clouds and the wind was such that it had the feeling of rain. The tall cottonwoods near the river were luminous against the darkening sky and their leaves rippled with the first winds coming down the valley.

So how'd Mercy do it?

Do what?

Get you to rob a bank for him.

How do you know Mercy?

That wasn't my question.

Didn't rob a bank for him, Kilt said.

But you were there. So what'd you do? Run a distraction? Steal some lady's purse in the teller line, run out a there, make the guard chase you?

How do you know who Mercy is?

Why do you think it is that I'm out here?

I have no idea why you're out here.

Because I robbed a bank with him, Sid said. Just like you.

I didn't rob a bank.

You did something. What was it?

Bosco squinted at him. Then he closed one eye. Then he leaned in the saddle and spit again. Then he clucked his tongue.

You were the getaway driver, weren't you?

Kilt shifted on his feet.

Yep, Bosco said. That's exactly what you did.

That what you did?

I wish.

The horse bent to eat and Bosco let it, easing on the mecate. The horse started moving toward Kilt, eating the hay at Kilt's feet. The horse's mouth was inches from his toes.

Best watch your feet, Bosco said. Nibble them toes right off.

Kilt stepped aside.

Bosco stood the rifle with the butt on his thigh. He had his hand on the stock and his finger hooked through the guard.

What do you know about horses?

Nothing.

You know what that is around that colt's nose?

Kilt shook his head.

That's a bosal, Bosco said.

Bosal, Kilt said.

No, Bosco said. Bosal. Like bow. Bosal. This rope here's a mecate. And that leather strap around its ears is the hanger. Altogether it makes up a hackamore. And a hackamore is a bridle without a bit. You know what a bit is?

No.

You'll learn, Bosco said. He leaned and spit. You wanna see a fun party trick? Bosco handed down the rifle and then let go of the mecate and covered his eyes with his hands. He made the horse back up. Made the horse turn in circles one way. Then made it turn in circles the other. He got the horse going at such a pace that the dirt rose up and the dust clouded its hooves. Then all at once he stopped it, said: Take a bow, horse. And the horse knelt a little and lowered its head.

That's a good trick, Kilt said.

Sure, Bosco said. He snapped his fingers at Kilt for the rifle and Kilt handed it up. Bosco laid it across his lap again and sat the horse.

So what's he doing back there? Bosco said.

Who?

Mercy.

Ain't doing nothing.

Has to be doing something.

Not if he's dead, he don't.

He's dead?

Kilt just squinted up at him.

You the one who did it? Bosco said. You and that German peashooter you carry around. He gave that to you, didn't he? He sucked his teeth then he laughed through his nose and said, Nah. You didn't do it. You ain't got the salt for that.

No, Kilt finally said. Wasn't me who did it.

You seen him dead?

Yes. The four policemen standing around were the ones to do it.

Four of em?

Yeah.

How many bullets they get him with?

A lot of bullets.

Fuckin law, Bosco said. He spit a thick gout onto the ground. Mr Wainwright'd whip me if he heard me say that. He's got some kind of hard-on for the law. Sense of right and wrong and all that bullshit. You ask me, the law's just as bad as the bad guys. What do you think?

Never thought about it.

Well, you should. Should be thinking about it all the time. You're a bank robber now.

No, I ain't.

You robbed one, didn't you?

I just drove the car.

That's the same thing.

No, it ain't.

You fuck a sheep, what's that make you?

I don't know.

Makes you a sheep fucker, Bosco said. You robbed a bank and now you're a bank robber. And you better get wise to the law and you better get that way pretty damn quick because the law don't like bank robbers like us and they're going to be on your ass till the day you die.

Bosco hooked his finger into his lip and snapped away the wad of tobacco. Then he turned in the saddle and pulled something free. Then he leaned in the saddle and handed Kilt his Luger.

Don't leave your gun unattended, Bosco said. Can't trust anyone these days.

Then he nodded at Kilt.

Got to get you a hat, he said. Then he turned the horse and rode off up the valley with the sky darkening and the wind coming on.

38

That evening before Tillie called him in for his supper he stood at the window and looked out on the landscape, at the pasture and the horses in the pasture. The hushed dusk settled in through the valley, spilling its rose light so brightly that the horses' backs nearly reflected the sky.

A little later the moon finally rose over the opaque ridgeline of the Missions all white and swollen like it was infected. The hard blue light throwing shadows stark as blood.

That blue light came through the windows of the dining room where they all sat at the long table saying little to one another with the only sound being their cutlery on china, the measured footsteps of Tillie coming and going from the kitchen. The girl was sitting beside Bosco as she had the night before. She would steal glances at Kilt between bites. There was a glint to her eyes that wasn't flirtation but something akin to it. The intrusive stare of a child. One of curiosity, one that sought possession. Kilt felt it sear into him but refused to acknowledge her attention. It was Mrs Wainwright who finally spoke without looking up, saying, Carlee, you're staring.

The girl, however, showed no embarrassment. She only smiled down at her plate. She seemed to relish being caught.

The woman spoke again. This time to Kilt. She said, I understand you found an empty bed in the bunkhouse?

Yes mam.

Is it satisfactory?

Yes mam.

No damn church pew, is it? Wainwright said.

You won't talk that way at the table, Mrs Wainwright said.

Mr Wainwright's lips went tight in a hidden smile. He looked at Kilt and winked.

Sidney tells me you're rather handy with the pitchfork, Wainwright said.

Sir?

You're a hard worker, he said.

If you got a job, Kilt said. He forked up some potatoes, ate them, swallowed. You better do it, he continued.

You better do it, Wainwright echoed. That's good. I like that. You got a job, do it good.

Do it well, Martha said.

Yes, Wainwright said. Forgive me. Grammar and all that. I'd a feeling I'd like you.

Sir? Kilt asked.

Nothing, Wainwright said. For another time.

Mrs Wainwright set her eyes on Kilt just as she must have on Bosco and Carlee in the days or months or years before and pursed her lips and dabbed the corners of her mouth with the linen napkin and then lay the napkin on her lap as she prepared to speak and finally said, The world is full of very stupid people, and if you are to be a part of this ranch certain, oh—she flung a hand oddly as though at odds with herself—traditions.

Rules with respect to a more refined time must be observed. It is not *ain't*, for example. It is not. *Ain't* is not a word.

Yes mam, Kilt said.

Have you attended school in the past?

Yes mam. I went through the second grade.

Have you read any of the books I left for you?

Yes mam, Kilt said.

All of them?

No mam. But I like them. Thank you.

There is much to learn, Mrs Wainwright said. In addition to your work on the ranch, you'll be expected to attend lessons provided by me and Mrs Foster.

Who is Mrs Foster?

She is a woman in Black Elk. Well established in the subjects of mathematics and science. Do you know anything about mathematics and science?

You mean like counting, mam?

Don't say like. Just say, you mean counting.

Yes mam.

But yes. Counting and problem-solving and physics.

Don't know nothing about physics, mam.

Language, too, she said.

Language?

Linguistics. Grammar. No double negatives.

Yes mam.

She smiled at him. She said, There's a whole world left to be learned.

I'll try my best, Kilt said.

And I'll have some more wine, Wainwright said. He shouted, Miss Tillie!

She appeared in the doorway, the shadows from the lamplight hiding most of her and the line of shadow rising up the front of her dress like a theater scrim as she entered the room.

Yes, Mr Wainwright, she said.
We got any more of that wine?
Of course, Mr Wainwright.
Keep it coming till I tell you otherwise.
He raised his glass to his wife. He said, To Benjamin's future.

39

Kilt lay in bed that night with the moonlight printed as a crystalline strip across the floor. He thought about the ranch and he thought about the Wainwrights, thought about Sidney Bosco and he wondered if what the boy told him about their mother was true or false. When he closed his eyes Kilt could still see her in that small room in that cold town in Minnesota with her pale shoulders all full of bruises, and he could hear the words she would always speak when she believed her son was asleep. Words that almost took the place of promises. An encapsulation of her love and regret and hope and fear entire. You were wrong, he wanted to say. No one is fully their own.

Kilt thought about this and more, most of which had no answer or no answer he was capable of understanding and not long to follow he felt the soft pull of sleep. Then a sound no louder than a pencil hitting the floor stirred him and he turned away from the wall and faced the door and saw the outline of the girl's back as she closed the door behind her. She turned to him and he watched her as if he had forgotten her name. She crossed the room without a word. Her feet were bare and she was wearing a white cotton dress that seemed to move of its own volition. Floating in absence of a body. It looked like a white sail ghosting across a dark sea. She passed through the bar of moonlight and he saw that her eyes were mascaraed and that her hair had been plaited in French braids. At his bed she stood. She said, Are you awake?

Yeah.

Get dressed.

Why?

Just get dressed. I want to show you something.

What do you want to show me?

I want to show you where the ghosts live.

Ghosts?

Just get dressed.

She turned around so he could dress but she didn't stay turned and peeked once or twice. When Kilt was dressed she said, Come on.

They left the bunkhouse and crossed the yard and set out into the night. Carlee was leading him. She was running through the grass and the grass was wet with dew and her cotton nightdress clung to her skin.

Where you taking me? Kilt asked.

She turned with her face smiling and her teeth glowing in the dark. She held a finger to her lips.

Shh, she said.

The cemetery lay blue under the moon and the headstones cast long shadows. She led him to a hill that overlooked the grounds. She was practically skipping over the grass. When they got there she sat down and tucked her knees to her chest and wrapped her arms around her knees.

What are we doing here? Kilt asked.

She held her finger to her lips again.

Shh, Carlee said. You don't want them to hear us, do you?

Who?

They were whispering now.

The ghosts, Carlee said.

They sat in silence for a long moment. Kilt never taking her eyes from Carlee. The wind was moving very slowly in the trees and the shadows of the leaves trembled over the blue grass. Finally Carlee's look changed and she turned to Kilt.

I come here listening for bells, she said.

Bells?

My mother had a bell here. But they took it down. I come to listen to see if I can hear anyone under there.

Your mother? Kilt asked.

When they bury someone they always put a string into the ground, tied around a finger. Then the string goes to a bell on a stand above.

Why would they do that?

In case they're alive, of course.

Are they ever alive?

Sometimes.

They can't tell if someone is dead?

I heard Mrs Wainwright talking about it. Something about the water. People drink bad water and it puts them into some kind of sleep. Makes it seem like they're dead. I don't know. But they get buried without being dead. And if they wake up they can ring that bell.

Who's going to hear?

There's always someone working at night. That's their job. To listen for the bells ringing. The graveyard shift. That's why we have to be quiet. So no one hears us.

Your mother had a bell?

They all do. At first.

She turned and regarded him intensely, squinting like someone with bad vision. Finally she said, Mrs Wainwright isn't my mother, you know.

Okay.

She adopted me.

Okay.

So are you going to stay?

Stay where?

Here.

You mean at the cemetery?

You know what I mean.

No, I don't.

I mean at the Triple Nine.

I don't know, Kilt said.

You don't know.

Her face tightened. She took a deep breath. Then she let it out. The smoke tumbled from her lips.

You don't want me to stay, do you?

No, Carlee said.

Why not? Kilt asked.

Because I don't want you to hurt him.

Hurt who?

The girl only stared at him. Her eyes like dark globes. The mascara fencing in a deep malice, perhaps. Like a well with no bottom.

He knew you were here in the valley, she said.

Who did?

Told me he was going to kill you if he ever saw you.

Who wanted to kill me?

I told him you were here. That you were just hanging around. I told him you were practically asking to be killed.

I don't know what you're talking about.

I thought he was going to do it that day he rode up on you. Had that rifle laid across his lap. Thought he was going to shoot you dead right where you were standing.

You were watching us?

No, she said. Just you.

Why were you watching me?

She shrugged.

I've never seen anyone shot before, she said.

Where were you? Kilt asked. When you were watching me.

Near the stables, she said. You know he's a little sweet on me. Told me he's going to marry me one day.

Okay.

Don't you want to know what we were doing in the stables?

No.

We were kissing.

Kilt didn't answer. He only sat there and looked at her.

She slid toward him over the grass on the hill.

You ever been with a girl? she asked.

He did not answer.

You ever kissed one?

No, he said.

You want to?

Do I want to kiss a girl?

Why do you keep repeating my questions back to me?

I'm nervous, I guess.

I make you nervous?

Yes mam.

You don't have to call me mam. Not much older than you.

Then she leaned across and kissed him. She parted her lips and then she pulled away. Then she stood from the grass. The cotton dress was wet and stuck to her skin and Kilt could see a lot of her under the fabric.

You might want to think about leaving, she said. Sid gets jealous.

Then she started down the hill back in the direction of the ranch. Kilt didn't know if he was supposed to follow her or not. So he didn't. He just sat there in the quiet night, looking out at all the still headstones under the moonlight. The black mountains beyond.

40

It went on like that for nearly a month. Kilt working the stalls. Dinner every night with Mr and Mrs Wainwright. With Bosco and Carlee. And never did he get comfortable with it all. Carlee always wearing that same coquettish look, Kilt never knowing if Bosco knew what had gone on between them. Never knowing if what she had said was even true.

Till one day, not even dawn, when Bosco kicked the leg of the bed awakening Kilt like a pail of water had been thrown on him. He lay there blinking wildly trying to bring it all into focus. Could've been the middle of the night for all Kilt knew. Coming into focus was the shape of the young man and soon thereafter Kilt could see it was Bosco.

He was standing there with an extra hat in one hand and a biscuit wrapped in a cloth napkin in the other.

You been layin there for almost five hours, he said. You can sleep when you're dead.

Feel like I'm dead, Kilt said.

Well, you ain't. Not yet, anyway. You been out with Carlee in the cemetery again?

No.

Mm hmm.

Then he nodded and tossed the hat on the bed beside Kilt and set the biscuit next to the hat.

The hat, Bosco said, is from Mr Wainwright. Thought you'd stuck around long enough to warrant a hat. And Miss Tillie told me to bring you the biscuit. Don't want you thinking I'm getting soft on you. Doing you any favors and all.

Bosco kicked the bed frame again.

It's almost light out, he said. Git up.

The sun was still well below the ridgeline of the Missions but a blood-colored light was leaking up behind it and in the valley to the west there hung a thin fog left over from the cold night.

In the barn Bosco handed Kilt a pair of hay hooks and told him to buck each bale into the bed of the Ford. The steel was cold in Kilt's hands and he held them awkwardly.

You ever used them before?

Kilt shook his head.

Put that T between your middle and ring finger. Then chuck the hook into the hay.

Kilt did as he was told.

Now lob it up here.

Kilt tried to swing the bale off the stack and up to the bed but it was heavy and the weight threw him and he landed on the ground with the hooks still lodged in the bale. Bosco just stood there grinning. Then he leaned and spat.

Mm hmm, he said.

Bosco jumped down and held out his hand to Kilt and Kilt took it and stood and wiped the chaff from his trousers.

Got to use your leg, Bosco said. Get some leverage on it. Here.

Bosco took hold of the hooks and deadlifted the bale then

drove his knee into it and in a single deft motion twisted and bucked the bale onto the truck.

There, Bosco said. Do it like that.

Bosco jumped back up and dragged the bale to the front of the bed and turned it athwart then took out the hooks and looked down at Kilt.

Come on, sweetheart, he said. Truck ain't goin a load itself.

41

The bells of the Black Elk courthouse were tolling noon as they drove into town with the truck loaded down. Bosco asked Kilt if he was hungry and Kilt said he could eat and Bosco found a diner and parked the truck in front of the storefront window.

They walked into the diner and took a booth along the wall. Opposite the wall was a long lunch counter and every stool was taken. The place was loud. There were men drinking coffee and men smoking. A few women sat fanning themselves with paper menus. Kilt and Bosco sat and Bosco leaned back sideways in the booth with his boot kicked up on the bench. He looked around like he was bored.

What do you think of it so far?

Think of what? Kilt said.

This.

The diner?

The diner. The town. Townsfolk. This life. Bosco swiped his hand around. All of it.

It's fine.

Bosco's face pinched up. Then he shook his head.

Can't stand it, he said. People couped up like this. Spendin their money they worked hard over. Just so they can go back to work to spend it all again. I work hard at the ranch. Work hard for Wainwright. And I'm happy to. I'm indebted. But at some point there's got to be more. You don't get nothing of your own by workin for someone else. Sometimes you just have to go take it.

What are you talking about?

Bosco looked around the diner and then waved a hand. Said, My point is that people are suckers. People are scared.

What are they scared of?

Shit, Bosco said. They're scared of everything. People like them are afraid of it all. Afraid that whatever they got is going to disappear. Poof. Gone. Left with nothing. So what do they do? They work to make money to buy things to surround themselves with. He tapped his temple. And those things, they think, are some kind of wall that protects them from all the bad things we do to each other. But their things are just things and things are just things. And a man with all the things in the world will bleed out like everyone else. And where's that leave you?

Bosco could tell Kilt was wondering what he was talking about. So he said, Leaves you dead, Benny. That's where it leaves you.

The waitress came over and asked them what they'd like and Bosco ordered a steak and fingerling potatoes and then said, Why don't you bring a couple a them orders. He'll have the same. Bring some coffee too.

A little look of suspicion on her face.

You boys drink coffee?

Yes mam. Since I was a baby. Bosco smiled and pulled his papers and tobacco from his shirt pocket and rolled a cigarette. He lit it and leaned back and blew away the smoke.

She went away and came back with the coffee and told them their steaks would be along promptly. Bosco sat sidelong in the booth and smoked and when he spoke it was like he was speaking to someone in another table.

You ever been drunk?

Drunk?

No.

Then we're gettin drunk tonight.

Okay.

We'll swipe some from the old man's collection.

He won't mind?

Shit yes, he'll mind. We just won't tell him.

Bosco smoked then held out the cigarette to Kilt.

Go on, Bosco said. Git you some.

Kilt took the cigarette between his fingers and brought it to his lips and soon fell to coughing. Bosco laughed and took the cigarette back.

You'll get the hang of it, he said.

When Kilt had finished coughing Bosco said, You think it's strange we ain't never met till now?

I don't know, Kilt said. Never thought about it.

Then think about it.

I guess it's stranger we had to meet out here.

You mean all the things that had to come together to get us in the same place?

Yeah.

You think it's strange we don't have the same last name?

No, Kilt said. Different daddies.

You think your daddy's name was Kilt?

Probably. Why not?

Maybe she just made up names for us.

You think Mama would do that?

Shit, Bosco said. Left me on some doorstep. I think she'd do just about anything.

Don't talk about her like that.

I'll talk about her any damn way I want.

Still your mama, Kilt said.

Not anymore, she ain't.

The waitress came and set the platters of steaks and potatoes before each of them and refilled their coffee. Bosco stubbed out his cigarette and then thanked the woman.

Thought about changin my name, Bosco said.

Why?

What the hell kind a name is Bosco?

Kilt was about to ask what he would change his name to when the bell over the door rang, stopping him from continuing on, and outside parked in the sunlight was the dead wolfer's truck and the three men he had seen that night entered and Kilt just watched them and didn't know what to say at all.

42

The men moved slowly through the diner, staggered in a line one before the other. They all wore pistols and black Stetsons with the crowns belled out. Kilt couldn't take his eyes from them. Bosco had been eating and looking down at the platter and not looking at Kilt but when he did he could see that Kilt was scared. Bosco spoke with a full mouth. He said, What's wrong with you?

After a second Bosco asked it again. Then he turned in his seat and leaned out of the booth to see what the hell Kilt was staring at. The place was full and to Bosco Kilt could have been looking at anything. But the three men were different and when Bosco looked he knew they were the ones scaring Kilt.

You know em? Bosco said.

Kilt didn't speak.

Benny?

Kilt finally looked at Bosco.

You know them men?

Kilt nodded.

How you know em?

Kilt told Bosco about the night Virgil was murdered. About how they had shot him dead and burned his body without remorse. How he was still smoldering in the gray morning.

Them men did that?

Yeah.

How'd they know him, this Virgil guy?

I don't know. He owed them money, they said.

Bosco watched the men. Their backs were turned. They were still wearing their hats. Bosco squinted. Picked at something in his teeth with his tongue. He seemed to be squaring some kind of rationale in his head. Righting a possible wrong. Then as if settling on it he nodded his head. Said, Mm hmm. Then he went back to his food, cutting into his steak. Taking a small bite and eating it like an aristocrat.

The men were lined up at the counter, shoulder to shoulder. They did not speak. In the backbar mirror Kilt could see their faces were hidden under the brims of their hats. He only saw the slow working of their jaws as they chewed.

They hadn't been seated more than twenty minutes before one of them merely raised a finger from the counter to signal the bill. The waitress came with the slip and laid it down and one of them set a dollar and several coins on top of it and in unison the three stood and made their way to the door with the little silver bell chiming as they stepped outside.

When they were gone Bosco laid down some money for the food and some for the tip and tapped the table and looked at Kilt and said, Let's go.

Bosco drove at a distance behind the dead wolfer's truck, following the men to a filling station. They pulled to a pump and an attendant came from inside and came around and leaned his palms against the door and must've asked them how much. Then he turned to the pump and took the handle and flipped the pump lever and turned back to the truck and unscrewed the fill cap and inserted the nozzle.

Bosco had parked the hay truck at the far end of the station and sat there smoking and watching the men. He didn't say anything for a very long time. When he finally did he said, You sure those the guys?

Yeah.

Awfully dark at night. Could've been anyone.

It was them, Kilt said. That's his truck. And that one sitting at the passenger door is the one who shot him.

Why they here?

I don't know.

They seen you, yeah? Knew where you was headed?

Yeah.

Bosco leaned and spat out the window.

I got a feeling they're lookin for you, he said.

Me? Why they looking for me?

Cause you were with him. And maybe they think you saw them do it.

Bosco reached behind to the shotgun in the gun rack and wheeled it around skillfully and broke it to make sure it was loaded and then he closed it again and opened the truck door and stepped out. He flicked his cigarette to the ground and stamped it out in the dirt.

Where you going? Kilt said.

You just stay here.

Then he closed the door behind him and reached around into the truck bed and took up one of the hay hooks and stuffed the handle into his belt with the parabola curved away at the small of his back. He leaned into the open window.

Don't move, he said.

Kilt watched him cross the lot to the pump. The attendant was busy washing the truck's windows. Kilt could see the men's heads silhouetted in the glass. It was only a little after noon and Bosco cast no shadow. It was as if the sun passed right through him. As if irrefutable laws did not pertain. As if he were not a young man but the mirage of a young man whose sole purpose was to deliver retribution in its most unwavering form. The hay hook caught the light and the steel winked in the sun. Bosco sauntered with the shotgun resting on a shoulder, his hand on the barrel, without hurry as though returning from a prizeless hunt.

At the rear of the truck the attendant took notice of him and called out. His voice muted to Kilt sitting in the cab. Kilt slid over the seat so he was behind the wheel and he leaned his head out the window so to better hear. He heard Bosco say something to the attendant but it was too far and it only came across as a mutter. The attendant showed slight alarm as Bosco approached the driver's door with the shotgun, and the attendant started to come around the back of the truck in protest but quickly cowered and dove to the dirt as Bosco wordlessly opened the door and spun the shotgun from his shoulder and fired twice into the cab. Each head bursting and painting the back window with blood.

The passenger door flung open and the man spilled from it to crabwalk on his hands and knees. Bosco went around the front of the truck and broke the gun and the smoking shells ejected in a silent arc and he thumbed in two more. The man was scrambling over the ground with the dust rising and his bootheels slipping. Bosco's hat was low and his face was daubed in shadow. Unhurried as he was, he appeared the manifestation of some dubious executioner. A shape of death in disguise. A reckoning one could not conceive and therefore all the more sinister in its possibility.

The man said something to Bosco, pleading for fortune, and he held up his hand to attenuate any malice but Bosco fired with the shotgun at his hip and blew away the penitent hand. The man collapsed and began to scream. He clutched his wrist, looking on in disbelief at the shards of bone, at the blood cascading down his arm. Bosco came around and took the hay hook from his belt and swung the point down into the man's collarbone and began to drag him toward the garage of the station like a bale of hay. The man grabbed the hook with his good hand while the stub of the missing flailed about like torn fabric. The man kicked as if trying to run. Or like slipping on ice.

Kilt watched it all with a kind of detached horror. Then suddenly the attendant got his wits and stood from behind the truck and crouch-ran to his own car parked at the edge of the station lot and found a pistol and started back in that same awkward run as if he were trying to hide behind something. He knelt at the wheel well in an attempt to stay out of view. He opened the cylinder and checked it and then closed it again. He stood from behind the truck and aimed the pistol at Bosco. Bosco looked up and saw the drawn gun. He wrinkled his face knowing what was about to come. And the attendant was about to shoot when the bullet from Kilt's gun punched a hole just above his temple and a gout of blood burst from the other side and the attendant fell into the dirt.

Bosco opened his eyes and saw the attendant lying motionless on the ground. A strange hush fell around them. The white sun was glaring down. The dying report of the Luger was the only thing that seemed to make a sound. Even the hooked man had quieted. Bosco turned his attention to Kilt. The Luger in the boy's hand was trembling. The gun in his small hand looked huge. Then his arm fell slack and Kilt just stood there.

Benny, Bosco said. Benny!

Kilt looked like he had been sedated.

Brother! Bosco said. Give me a hand here.

43

The man writhed on the floor in the dark garage. Bosco was just sitting in a metal chair with the shotgun stood on its butt watching the man when Kilt came through the door with the Luger still in his hand. Slats of light cut the dark and the hard mud floor was checkered with it. The place smelled like grease and gasoline. A little bit of mildew. Across the squares of light printed on the packed mud was a track of blood glistening red from black to black. There was nothing for the man to reach or grab so Bosco just let him be. Kilt was stock-still in the doorway and Bosco looked up. The gun heavy in his limp arm. Bosco nodded and then said: What do you want to do with him?

Then he said: Do you want to kill him?

Said: Do you want to kill him?

Finally said: Okay. I'll kill him.

Bosco stood from the chair and knelt to the man and asked something of him. Under the hat, God knows what expression. The man shied like Bosco was holding a venomous snake.

I'll ask again, Bosco said. Have you put forth enough in this life to meet God and let your soul be set free?

The man's lips moved but he did not speak. Bosco leaned closer.

Say that one more time, Bosco said.

The man's dry lips broke and his tongue murmured something Kilt couldn't hear.

Bosco leaned away. Put his hands on his knees and balanced there on the toes of his boots and clicked his tongue. Then he stood, rising up like some terrible judge with his eyes hidden, and said, That ain't good enough.

He crossed the garage passing through bricks of light. His face always shadowed, his shoulders illuminated momentarily before going dark again.

Where you going? Kilt said.

Find some rope.

Rope?

Can't haul him up without rope.

At the workbench Bosco set about rummaging through the old wares. Knocking cans of hardware to the floor. Split clutches. Carburetors chewed with rust. A clamor of disarray tossed and thrown.

Kilt stepped into the garage, light to dark, and walked to the man. The man was holding the hook with his good hand. His face all puckered up, his eyes all but narrow slits, trying in vain to bring about any amount of peace. But there was no peace to be had and there would be none to come and the man must have known he was going to die because he began to plead and call out to God. Glops of foam and spittle were hurling from his mouth in this futile attempt at salvation.

The brick of sunlight spilling into the dark garage held the man in an alabaster spotlight. The blood from the hook and the blood from the missing hand was running all over the place. It was pooling beneath him and he was just sitting in it.

Bosco was throwing cans around and the abrasive aroma of motor oil and gasoline filled the garage.

The man opened his eyes.

You don't have to do this, he said.

Kilt couldn't speak.

The man said again, You don't have to do this.

Kilt watched the man. Then he looked at Bosco. Then he looked back at the man.

You did it to us, Kilt finally said.

Did what? I don't even know you.

You know me.

You don't have to do this.

I should set you on fire.

Fire?

Like you did to him.

Did to who?

You burned him.

Didn't burn nobody.

If we let you go you'd do the same to us.

Who the hell are you? I don't even know you.

Stop saying that, Kilt said. You shot him that night. You shot him over a little bit of money. Then you burned the body. I was there. I saw it all.

The man blinked in a strange moment of clarity. But it did not last and soon his eyes pinched shut in pain.

I won't, the man said. I'll disappear. You'll never see me again.

You think I'm stupid because I'm young.

No, I don't.

Yes, you do. And if I let you go, first thing you're going to do is shoot us dead.

I won't. I promise. I'll be gone. You'll never—

But he didn't finish because Kilt shot him through the chest. And then shot him again. And he kept shooting till the magazine was empty and only the hollow click of the action falling against an empty magazine was heard. The garage was suddenly very still and nothing made a sound. Bosco turned and saw his brother still pointing that gun down at the man. And he didn't say a word because there was nothing to be said.

44

That night both boys were quiet at dinner. They sat side by side with Bosco huddled over his plate and Kilt sitting with his back against the chair and a fork in his hand and the tines of the fork poking at the potatoes. The girl Carlee watched them from across the table, her eyes darting back and forth between the boys like cats. All of it did not go unnoticed to Mrs Wainwright.

You are in quite the contemplative mood this evening, boys, she said.

Bosco lifted his face and spoke for the both of them.

Big day is all, mam.

Then why are you not all eating? Carlee said. Think you'd work up an appetite.

I am eatin, Bosco said.

He isn't, Carlee said.

Truckload a hay ain't nothing, Bosco said. Tired's all. Ain't that right?

He elbowed Kilt who didn't seem to be paying attention.

Hmm? Kilt said.

Ain't that right? Bosco said.

About what?

Bein tired.

Yeah, Kilt said. Tired.

Well, Wainwright said, if it's too much a job we can find work elsewhere on the ranch. No shortage of work here.

No sir, Kilt said. Work suits me fine.

How did the drop-off go? Wainwright asked.

Fine, sir, Bosco said.

They credit you or Tomlin just give you the money?

Credit, sir.

Wainwright nodded.

Very good.

Bosco looked up at Carlee sitting across the table and seeing through it all she squinted at him. Then she looked at Kilt who was still looking down at his plate. Then she said: Tomlin didn't credit you.

Yes mam, he did.

No, he didn't.

Bosco sat back in his chair and tongued at something between his teeth and crossed his arms and said: Yes, he did.

I know he didn't, she said.

And why's that?

Cause Tomlin wasn't in town today.

You keepin tabs on him?

Don't need to keep nothing cause he was out here at the ranch. Isn't that right, Mr Wainwright?

Yes, Carlee, Wainwright said. Here most of the day. He's got a mare he's looking to sire.

Well, Bosco said, still looking at Carlee, never taking his eyes from her, maybe it wasn't Tomlin who credited me.

Who credited you, then?

New guy, Bosco said. You don't know him.

Someone new in Black Elk?

Yeah.

Who?

You don't know him.

What's his name, then?

Bosco threw the napkin from his lap onto his plate and slid out with his chair tipping over and crossed to the window and tapped his knuckle on the glass at the truck parked in front of the barn.

You see any hay on that truck? he asked.

I'm sitting at the table, Carlee said. I can't see anything out the window.

Then stand up.

Children, Mrs Wainwright said. Her voice calm and judicial.

You think I'd load a truck full of hay, Bosco said, just to dump it somewhere?

Maybe you would if you were trying to hide something?

Hide something? Pssh. Girl, you're dumber than you look.

That's enough, Mrs Wainwright said. Sidney, I think some fresh air is needed. Take Benjamin with you.

Carlee was trying to hide a smile.

Mrs Wainwright chided her and said, And don't you provoke them.

Bosco came back to the table and stood his chair and slid it in and took up the napkin and wiped his mouth and then tapped Kilt on the shoulder.

Come on, partner. Let's go check on the horses.

45

Later that night there was lightning to the north where it flashed like great burning sutures deep within the blackness. Hanging in the sky for several seconds. And so bright and clear and precise they were they seemed to be cracking the very firmament to reveal something never before seen beyond.

Bosco came out onto the porch with a bottle and two coffee mugs. He sat down on the porch steps next to Kilt and set down the mugs and uncorked the bottle and poured two measures and then handed one mug to Kilt. It was late enough that everyone else was asleep in the house. No one said anything for a long while. They just watched the lightning and waited for the rolling shutter of thunder but no thunder ever came. Out in the pasture the black horses were standing not like animals coveted or revered but like the statues of horses with their manes and tails slack in the cool windless air and the only thing giving them away was their hot breath smoking in the moonlight.

The lightning was far to the north but over the pasture and

the ranch the sky was clear. The stars were shining like alabaster, burning out there in places that had no names and never would. Places free of anything anyone could imagine, far from God or even God's comprehension.

When someone did finally speak it was Bosco and Bosco said: That girl can be a real bitch sometimes.

Who?

Carlee. She knew what she was doing. Fixing to rat us out.

Maybe.

No maybe about it. She's too smart for her own good.

Thought you said she was dumber than she looks.

You know what I mean.

You don't like her?

Like got nothin to do with it.

You think she'll tell Mr Wainwright?

Tell him what?

That we killed them men.

Them men were already dead. Dead men walking.

You think she'll do it?

She ain't got no proof.

You just said she was fixing to rat us out.

You know what I—

He didn't finish what he was saying and instead finished by shooting Kilt a look.

What if they track us back to it?

Who?

Anyone.

Ain't no one goin a do that. Hell, this is Black Elk, Montana. And unless you're stealing from the damn governor hisself, ain't no one goin a take a second look.

What about that gas attendant?

Shit, Bosco said, that was self-defense. He was aiming to open me up. And if you hadn't stopped him he would've too.

They stared out at the darkness and at the lightning where

some erupted within the thick columns of cloud and illuminated them like mythic pantheons.

Then as if picking up in the middle of the conversation, Bosco said: That attendant had it coming. Everyone with a gun thinks they're a goddamn cowboy. You draw that piece, you better know what's coming your way. Taught him a good lesson.

He's dead, Kilt said. Can't learn no lessons when you're dead.

Well, Bosco said, at least he ain't goin a make the same mistake twice.

They were quiet again and Bosco leaned and looked into Kilt's cup and then reached for the bottle and bit the cork and poured some whiskey into the mug and then stoppered the bottle and set it back on the porch step.

This working on you yet? Bosco said.

My toes are tingling a little.

That's good.

I'm worried.

Bosco took a thoughtful sip and winced a little at the bite of it and said: Goin a finish the whiskey then tomorrow we're goin a take the truck into Ronan and go make some real money.

How we going to do that?

We're goin a rob a bank.

Kilt squinted at him.

You crazy?

I told you I was goin a do it.

I thought that was just talk.

Ain't talk, baby brother.

Maybe this ain't the right time.

Perfect time.

There will be people looking into the gas station.

Then they'll be there instead where we're goin.

Bosco sipped the whiskey.

Ain't like you've never done it before, he said. You know how it goes down.

I just sat in the car, Kilt said.

Then you follow me in. Let your big brother handle it.

There was lightning again and this time the ripple of thunder came. It suddenly felt like everything beyond the ring of porchlight was untouchable. Like some deep chasm one cannot return from.

You just follow me, baby brother, Bosco said. Nothin to worry about. Easy peasy.

46

In the morning Kilt got his breakfast in the kitchen while Tillie moved about in the early gray light. His head hurt from the night before and he half wondered if what Bosco had said was only a dream. Some fabrication of the sottish mind. Though he knew it wasn't a dream when Tillie said: Late night?

What? Kilt asked.

She was tending to a tray of biscuits with her back turned. It was as if she were speaking to someone else but it was only him in the room.

What were you boys going on about?

She set the tray on a wood cutting block and turned, wiping her hands on her apron and then crossing her arms and resting back into the counter.

Nothing, Kilt said.

Saw the porch light on, she said. Her eyes narrowed. She frowned. You want to stay up and do whatever it is boys do, you do it without the lights. Keeping me up.

Yes mam.

Come get you a couple biscuits while they're still warm. Go on.

Kilt ate at the kitchen table and when he was finished he brought his plate to the sink and washed it before Tillie could take it away from him and then he thanked her and went out.

The air was cool and he turned up the collar of his coat and started out for the barn. He thought maybe Bosco or even Wainwright might already be out there because the man door on the side had been left open but he saw no one. There was a pond beyond the pasture and there were ducks in the pond and geese and there were cattails rimming the shore and redwing blackbirds balanced on the bursting tips. The wind of the day had not yet come up so the surface of the water was like a plate of glass and printed upon it was the pale image of the Missions, gray and austere because the sun had yet to touch them. The little mountain creek that fed the pond was making sounds that reminded him of the sounds a baby makes and he could hear the horses in the pasture and they blew and nickered and watched him from the grass that came to their bellies so they looked half-sunk, and save for the horses and the creek and the birdsong of the redwings nothing made a sound out there.

He was about to start for the barn when he heard a gun fire and then the report of the shot dying out over the valley. He heard another shot and then he heard his name called. From behind the barn he saw Bosco emerge, Kilt's Luger dangling from his hand. Then he waggled it in the air and what frail light there was caught in the dull metal and almost cast a reflection.

Didn't I tell you not to leave this thing unattended? Bosco said. He waggled it some more. Works pretty good.

I know it does. What are you doing with it?

Just trying it out, Bosco said. You got something you need in the barn?

Was going to muck the stalls.

Did that already.
You did my job? Why you doing my jobs?
Come on, Bosco said.
Where we going?
I already told you.

47

Bosco parked the truck on the corner of the intersection across from the Ronan Bank and Trust building and killed the engine and the two of them just sat there watching the building without saying anything. It was still early and the bank wouldn't be open for another two hours and that is exactly what Bosco wanted.

If it ain't open, Kilt said, how we going to get in?

We'll get in.

But if it ain't open.

Not to customers, it ain't. But we ain't customers, are we?

Bosco set out explaining the plan. About the money delivery every Thursday morning, two hours before the bank opened. About the two delivery guards, the one bank teller, the manager, the secretary. About how they always go in through the back and leave the door wide open.

They're practically beggin for it.

What about guns?

We got guns.

So will they.

Damn right, they will.

You're fixing to get us in a shoot-out.

Naw, Bosco said. No shoot-outs for this outlaw.

He explained how he'd been coming here every Thursday morning for the last eight months and not once had he seen them bring their guns with them. Always leave them in the truck, he said. He said, Always the same two guys too. Said: A robbery's the last thing them guards are expecting in Ronan. We'll go in there, guns ablazing. Nothin to it. Easy peasy.

What if you're wrong?

I ain't, Bosco said. You just walk in there and shove that thumb buster in someone's face and they'll have no choice but to oblige you.

What if they don't?

Bosco was watching the front of the bank. How the early light had coppered the granite. He was biting his thumbnail in excitement. When Kilt repeated his question Bosco paused and turned and said: Then you'll pull the trigger.

Bosco reached behind his seat and lifted up two silk bandanas. He tossed one to Kilt. Kilt looked down at it like some feral cat had just jumped onto his lap.

What do you want me to do with this?

I want you to wipe your ass with it. Bosco shook his head. You're goin a wrap that around your face, he said. You don't want anyone recognizing that pretty smile of yours, do you?

Kilt lifted it. Stretched it taut. Stared into the fabric like the black silk held some kind of answer.

Black? he asked.

We're bank robbers, baby brother. True blue.

48

They watched for ten minutes. Twenty. At 7:05 a.m. a truck came around toward the back of the bank. The faces of the men flashing behind the glass momentarily in a brilliant wash of gold, both men squinting at the low sun, before their faces went dark again.

That them? Kilt asked.

That's them.

They don't look like guards.

What did you expect them to look like?

I don't know. Different. Meaner maybe.

Shit, Bosco said. You get between them and that money, you'll see all the mean you can handle.

Bosco got the shotgun down from the window rack and laid it in his lap and broke it and removed the bird shot then took two shells of buckshot from his shirt pocket, thumbing them in, and then stuffed a handful of shells from a paper box into his pocket. Then he closed the gun and set it on his lap and just watched the doors of the bank for a while.

There's a little over fifteen hundred dollars being delivered through those doors at this very minute, he finally said. All of it packed neatly into two canvas bags. One for each of us. All we got to do is carry it out.

He squinted his eyes like he was looking into the sun but there was no sun in his eyes.

Behind those doors is our future, baby brother, Bosco said. Behind those doors is our freedom.

A man walking a dog passed the doors of the bank but he did not stop. Bosco followed him with his eyes till the man rounded the corner and was gone. Then he tied the silk bandana around his face.

You ready?

Kilt nodded.

Then Bosco opened the door and stepped out of the truck and the early light caped his shoulders and his shadow stretched long before him.

The two boys walked one in front of the other toward the bank and around the corner to where the door was still open just as the guards had left it, and within minutes of entering, if anyone was close enough, they would have heard the flat claps of a shotgun, one chamber expiring then the other, and then a pause as Bosco reloaded and then two more in quick succession, and one might have thought it was all over till a fifth shot buckled the silence, a sound not of a shotgun but a pistol and then it did fall silent. Five shots in all. One for each delivery guard, one for the teller, one for the manager and the final bullet for the secretary. And from the outside anyone would think it was any normal morning, but no one was out so no one saw or heard a thing.

The boys came around the corner holding a bag each and the silk bandanas stowed away in their hip pockets with the morning light slipping down the front of the bank like a theater curtain and the songbirds in the trees.

PART 3

It should hardly need to be said but the world is not only unfair but cruel to women. The decisions provided to us are only a masquerade. Our memories are based upon the actions of another that have since come to fruition, and our future has but one path that already lies cemented in the past. This all sounds very cynical and I don't mean it to be but it is a truth, like stating the weather or summer turning to fall, and like the changing of that season it is something we must get through, only to be exactly where we were when it started.

Until I was stolen, I lived with my mother and father in Alberta. I close my eyes and I am back there. Though I don't see every detail, I see the face of my mother, the face of my father. The faces I see still hold joy. I never saw them again and I can only guess that joy faded, is perhaps even gone altogether.

The school I was forced into was dismal and I won't go into the details here. But I mention it because it was my first notion that free will does not exist for people like me. The decisions I make now were formed long ago, and the outcomes of these decisions were engineered to benefit a select few.

I'm telling you all of this because my memories are haunted. I don't know if anyone is truly alone in the memories they hold, but I know I am not. There is always someone there. Not all of them are dead but all of them are ghosts. All the vague faces that occupy the shadowed corners waiting for me to close my eyes. I suppose this is not unique to me. We are all fated for the same. All of us are haunted by memories.

49

(1935)

They drove for miles and miles through the night. The headlights of the Coupe struggling against the dark. No stars to be seen and the only color in the sky were the electric lights of Missoula paling the clouds behind them.

Bonnie in the passenger seat looking out the window, saying nothing for the better part of an hour till she finally did, saying, Are you mad?

No, Kilt said.

Yes, you are.

No, I'm not mad.

Then why ain't you talking?

Cause I don't feel like talking at the moment.

Cause you're mad.

Cause there's nothing to say.

There's everything in the world to say.

Like what? Kilt asked.

Like there are three more dead back there. Three more dead because of me.

They ain't dead because of you.

If it wasn't for me they would still be alive.

Maybe at this very second they might be. But tomorrow, the next day, the day after that? Kilt shrugged. Dying's all the same, kiddo. There's no beating that.

I've been called that before, you know. What those men said. Won't be the last either.

Will be if I have any say in it.

Just because you're saying it don't mean it's going to stop it all. They'll be saying it till that word doesn't exist. And that's never going to happen. That'll last forever.

Then I'll just keep shooting, Kilt said.

You'll run out of bullets.

This is America, kiddo. Bullets might as well grow on trees.

Down the road they caught deer in the headlights and in the headlights they were colorless save for their blazing eyes burning red back at them. Kilt did not slow the Coupe and the deer stood completely still till the last moment when their ears switched and their heads turned and in twos and threes leapt the ditch and then the fence, fleeing the light into the safety of darkness. Kilt could tell Bonnie was looking at him. Even in all that dark he knew she was faced straight at him and on that face there was nothing but skepticism and more than a little dread, and he turned to look at her because he knew she wouldn't stop until he did.

That's not the person I am, he finally said. The one you saw back there.

Sure seems it to me, Bonnie said.

You know, in all the years doing what I do, all the banks I've held over, if I told you I've only fired my gun once would you believe me?

No.

It's the truth, he said. And I've regretted it ever since.

Well, you seem good at it.

Good at what?

Killing people.

Gun does most of the work.

This ain't funny.

I know it ain't. It ain't funny and it ain't fun. It's as serious as it gets. This—he made a sweeping gesture with his good hand—all this is in support of an end.

And what end is that? You dead? Me along with you?

Like I said, there's no beating it.

So you just going to die on me?

Yes mam. Someday. Like those men back there. Like my mama. Like Nick Mercy. I'm going out the same way. Eyes open, maybe, see it all coming at me at once, but I'm going.

What about me?

You?

Yeah.

Nah. You ain't going out like that. You're the only thing I've ever seen that ain't.

Why?

Cause you're innocent in all this. Pure. And purity doesn't die. That's why God invented diamonds.

Bonnie was quiet for a long moment. She rested her forehead against the glass window and looked up at the sky. The constellations burning in the darkness. The stars shimmering like gold. Finally she said, God had nothing to do with it.

Then she turned back to Kilt and said, So where you taking me now?

Kilt squinted out at the road. The brown grass on the roadside was captured for only a moment in the headlights before being drawn back into the darkness.

I said where you taking me?

Just a little place down the road.

A little place?

Horse place.

Place wouldn't have anything to do with those three dead men back there, would it?

No mam, Kilt said. Just the one. And he ain't dead. Not yet.

50

They drove into the town of Black Elk a little after ten. All the storefronts dark with the streetlamps catching the metal of the Coupe and slipping over the surface like illuminated water. The image of the Coupe rippling in the warped glass of the stores as it passed. Only the saloon open at that hour. Men in hats, both of town and country, lingering just without, all of them smoking and all of them watching the Coupe as it paraded by.

You think they can see in? Bonnie asked.

See in where?

The car.

Just ignore them.

Bonnie stared out the window and as they passed the group, one of the men made an obscene gesture with his tongue between his fingers, and he, along with the rest of them, fell to laughing.

Outside of town the moon was stamped above the mountains. It was ringed in a silver halo and so bright it was it threw shadows like it was not the moon but some kind of cold sun.

Almost eleven o'clock by the time they reached the Triple Nine. The entrance to the ranch had a gothic look to it and Kilt did not remember this quality the last time he left. Black iron oil lamps hung at each corner and a larger lamp with a wickerwork pattern like some metal spider's web was stationed in the center and backlit the Triple Nine's brand, which was a series of cascading *9*s so that the shadow printed upon the ground below the burning light was three upended *9*s. The *6*s flayed out with the fire behind the tempered glass gave the shadowed edges a trembling look as if the very earth was quaking. As if a deep shudder were occurring somewhere underfoot.

Kilt stopped the Coupe and leaned forward over the wheel and peered through the glass up at the blacksmithed image of a stallion in full gallop below the Triple Nine brand. The fire from the oil sawed behind it and did so with the illusion that the stallion's mane and tail were on fire, some horse sired by fire. Its punched-out eyes aflame and burning and its mouth agape and consumed with heat, and the horse poised there to race over the dark plain, to thunder silently through the night for eternity.

Bonnie leaned forward in the same manner and Kilt turned and saw the flames from the lamps dancing in the girl's dark eyes. The stars were fanned out across the sky and slipping in a slow arc and perhaps those stars were somewhere within the girl's eyes too but Kilt saw only the burning horse, and so omnipotent the sight was that he had to shy and turn away and look ahead to where the road leading to the ranch faded away.

Bonnie looked over at Kilt and said, This is where you grew up?

Kilt put the Coupe into gear and let out the clutch and said, Not here.

They drove under the plangent gate with the blazing lamps high above, burning for guests welcome or not, and the thick shadow bar of the horizontal timber dimming the cab of the

Coupe like a cloud passing under the sun. But unlike a passing cloud there was no light to return, only the headlamps cutting the dark in a narrow band, and as all that came to pass, Kilt said again, Not here.

Bonnie turned in her seat and watched the flames in the lanterns till the road bent around a low headland and each oil lamp popped out one at a time and then there was no light.

They drove for a mile or more. The black outline of the mountains against the black sky. The only color other than black was the brown gravel road and the lighter brown of the tall roadside grass that was powdered with dust and almost white. The air was still and so the grass did not move and as pale and unmoving as it was there seemed a strange plague-like sight to it. As if the earth had wilted. As if anything still alive would not be for long.

When the house finally came into view every window was lit and the house gleamed like a ship at sea. There was the barn and bunkhouse and the bay doors to the barn were thrown open and electric light spilled over the ground. They could see shadows moving within that light, coming and going like dark fish in limpid water. From the darkness they saw a man leading a black Arabian through the bay doors. Its coat rippling with light like it was coated with oil.

Kilt parked the Coupe in the gravel turnaround and killed the engine and just sat there a moment. He had a look like he was trying to resolve something. Bonnie watched the house. Despite all the lights on it looked empty. She turned to Kilt. She said, What do you want to do?

I want to sit here a minute, he said.

So they did. One minute. Then two. Not long after, however, the porch door opened and a woman in a nice dress and her hair in a long blond bob stepped out and walked to the edge of the porch. She looked like she was dressed for dinner. She crossed her arms and leaned against the post. She didn't know the car but perhaps she was used to visitors at odd hours because she showed no concern or impatience. Kilt sat back in the seat. He shook his head.

I haven't seen you in years, he said quietly. Almost to himself.

What? Bonnie said. Who you talking to?

Ain't talking to no one.

He opened the car door and stepped out and leaned his good arm over the open door.

The woman straightened and Kilt could see her squint into the darkness then relax her posture. Maybe in relief or maybe not.

The prodigal son, she called out.

He stepped from around the door and closed it and crossed the turnaround and stopped at the bottom step of the porch and took off his hat and passed it to his slinged hand and smoothed his hair with his good hand.

Hello, Carlee, he said.

She led Kilt and Bonnie through a large anteroom where riding boots were stood under a long bench and various tack and riding crops hung from the walls of some type of dark hardwood. It was a room Kilt had passed through many times before but like the ranch gate, like the house, he recognized none of it. The décor had changed. The mood. He didn't remember the wood so dark. Even after all the years Carlee said nothing as she led them into the main room. Didn't even turn to look over her shoulder.

In the grand room Carlee held out a hand to a maroon damask sofa and Kilt and Bonnie sat. Carlee sat at the edge of a tall armchair and crossed her feet at her ankles and laced her fingers on her lap.

The floor was of milled old growth and a large area rug

lay under the sofas and chairs. The ceilings were vaulted and the timbers were joined in black iron fittings and an enormous baroque chandelier was suspended from a giant beam. There were hunting trophies and elk antlers and antlers of antelope and deer and the heads of bison and a towering grizzly bear rearing on its hind legs with its claws outflung and its fangs snarling. Several red-tailed hawks, a coyote with a lank mink captured in its jaws. A gray wolf with its head raked to an unseen moon howling. Throughout there were oil paintings of horses and hunting dogs and men on horses and there was a portrait of Royal Wainwright and there was one of Carlee in a black evening dress. Another with only her and Wainwright, him seated and she with a hand on his shoulder. Kilt lingered on that one longer than the others and then looked at Carlee and then looked back at the painting. When he looked again at Carlee she was smiling thinly with her lips together.

How long has it been, Benji?

A few years.

Seeing you here now makes me wonder about something.

And what's that?

After Sid left, she said, I always wanted to know what kept you here.

Nothing, Kilt said. Nothing kept me here.

It did for a couple years.

So what?

So what kept you here all those years ago? It wasn't the education. It wasn't the work. Seems to leave only me. Doesn't it seem like that?

What're you doing here, Carlee?

I live here, she said. This is where I live.

Where's he at?

Where is who *at*?

You know who.

No, I am asking in confirmation of that question. The

question in which you just posed. The way you asked it. Have you forgotten how to speak?

I really don't want to play this game right now.

Don't you want to ask me how I have been?

Kilt sat back in the sofa and crossed his legs and examined the palm of his slinged hand halfheartedly and traced the lines therein with his middle finger. Then he looked up at her. Sighed.

How you been, Carlee?

Oh, she said. You know.

She raised a hand like such a thing couldn't be measured.

Kilt looked at the far wall then he looked up at the ceiling. Then he looked back at Carlee. Carlee shifted her eyes to Bonnie.

And who is this? Carlee asked.

This is Bonnie.

Looking at Bonnie, Carlee said to Kilt, You always have liked pretty girls.

Ain't like that, Kilt said.

No?

No.

You once thought I was pretty, she said. Do you remember that? Do you remember when you thought I was pretty?

Kilt only stared at her. Her shoulders were bare and the dim light from the chandelier made her skin look like it was painted gold. Then she shrugged.

What happened to your shoulder, Benji?

Cougar bit me.

She made her hands into claws and bared her teeth and made a little growling sound. Then she nodded at his missing finger.

And your finger? Cougar get that too?

That's what I'm trying to figure out.

You had your finger one day then the next you didn't. What's there to figure out?

You going to tell me where he is or not?

How could I tell you where anyone is if I don't know of whom you speak?

Since when you start talking like this?

Talking like what?

Like you give a damn.

She smiled that same thin smile. Then she said, There are only two people I suspect you care enough about to return after all these years, at this hour, to ask me about.

And they would be?

She smiled again. She leaned forward and her dress fell away and if he wanted to look he would have seen her breasts but he didn't look. He didn't even shift his eyes.

One of them, she said, is here in the house. And the other was.

But isn't now.

She sat back in the chair and crossed her legs. The slit of her dress went high on her leg and the skin of her thigh was smooth and pale and at that he did look.

Why you wearing that dress? he asked.

What dress?

The one you got on. You look like you're trying to impress someone.

Am I impressing you?

No.

She turned to Bonnie.

Do you like this dress?

I don't know, the girl said.

It's a very easy question.

I guess it's nice.

You guess.

It's a very nice dress, Bonnie said.

Have you seen many nice dresses?

I've seen a few.

And how many were very nice dresses?

Carlee, cut the shit.

I'm only asking to gauge her reaction.

You done asked, Kilt said. Now close your mouth.

You've never asked me to close my mouth, Carlee said. If I remember correctly you always liked me with my mouth open.

Kilt pulled the Luger from the small of his back and laid it on his lap and looked down at it like it was something to be revered. Cherished, even.

And as though it were some strong tonic, Carlee reeled back in joy and began clapping her hands excitedly and stood from the chair.

You still have it, she said.

She stepped closer to him. She positioned herself so that she was straddling one of his knees. One leg hidden behind the dress. The other free from the slit and gleaming like polished stone.

May I? she said.

She bent at the waist and lifted the pistol from his lap. She rose up and turned it in her hand, examining it. She held the barrel to her nose. She leveled her eyes at Kilt.

This gun has been fired recently, she said.

Kilt did not respond. She gripped the pistol by the handle and then pointed the barrel at Kilt. A strange smile bloomed on Carlee's face.

Bang, she said.

Then she let the gun fall to her side and hang there limply from her hand. Then she turned it and offered it back to him by the barrel.

I'll let Tillie know we have company.

Tillie's still here?

Of course.

Why you got a let her know?

So she can make up a bed. You are staying here, are you not?

Wasn't planning on it.

You have to plan for *something*, Benji.

After a long moment he conceded.

Of course, she said. One bed, then?

Her eyes slipped to Bonnie.

It's not like that, Bonnie said.

Well, I am happy to hear that, Carlee said. A heart can only break so many times.

She winked at Kilt.

Kilt was about to stand from the sofa when a familiar voice stopped him. It clapped against his ears like some wave that had been a long time running in open water to finally expire as it burst upon a breakwater. He looked across the room to an open doorway and through it came a crippled man being pushed by Tillie. Wainwright was in some kind of high-backed wheelchair. There was a woolen blanket laid atop his legs. Even through the blanket Kilt could see they were like the legs of a crane, thin and gaunt and the bulb of the knees looked like some kind of strange root. His hair was mostly gone, a few long white strands hanging to his collar. His cheeks and his eye sockets were sunk and within those dark pits his eyes flared and winked like sapphires unearthed from coal. Kilt stood.

Mr Wainwright, he said.

Benjamin.

The voice was brittle and aged. He sounded like he needed to cough but he never did. His hands were brittle too and long and on the skin were blotches the color of prunes. Kilt crossed the floor to him and held out his hand and Wainwright took it in one and laid his other over Kilt's. Then he patted it paternally then made a gesture for Kilt to sit. He twisted in the chair to Tillie. Said, Thank you, dear. And then Tillie went away. Wainwright turned back to Kilt and just watched him for a long moment.

It's nice to see you, sir, Kilt said.

Wainwright shrugged dismissively.

I am sorry that you have to see me in this state. When you left I was not so old. Now.

He made another gesture with his hands.

A man does not think he will age. Mortality is understood but it is always for someone else. Death is never in anyone's plans.

Well, it's nice to see you.

I've thought about this day for a long time.

Yessir.

The day you left I knew you would return but I did not know when that day would be. The years passed and I heard nothing. One starts to dwell on things, you know. One thing age has delivered is a strong sense of morbidity. My inclination toward meliorism has faded. When you get old like me you realize how fickle the ideals of a young man can be.

Kilt looked around the room. He looked at Carlee. He looked at Bonnie. He realized it was only the four of them in the room.

Who are you looking for? Wainwright asked.

Where's Mrs Wainwright?

Wainwright smiled. He patted the arm of his wheelchair.

Do you pray, Benjamin?

Do I pray?

Yes.

What do you mean by that, sir?

I mean, do you pray? Do you submit yourself to something more than you? Do you seek reflection and forgiveness?

I'm not sure I've got much to reflect on or be forgiven for, sir.

Nonsense, Wainwright said. Everyone has the opportunity

to be forgiven. Forgiveness is what sets us apart from the beast, after all. Empathy, Benjamin. Reason. Order. Three things free of any statute of limitations.

Why you telling me this?

Because I think there needs to be more forgiveness in your life.

I thought your meliorism had faded, Kilt said.

You misunderstand me, Benjamin. Do not confuse my enlightenment for some kind of altruistic tendency. Who's to say enlightenment is exclusive to good fortune? I have found answers to questions and a lot of those answers are not happy ones. True, I do not believe the world can get better. Nor do I believe that humans can aid in its betterment. I do believe, however, that prayer and supplication to something beyond this world is our only salvation.

Kilt looked around the room again.

That why you kicked Sid out all those years ago?

Wainwright gave Kilt a thin smile.

I gave Sidney a choice to admit that he stole from me and repent, he said. Or leave.

He was just a boy, sir.

All the more reason to admit wrongdoing.

Kilt looked around the room again.

Where's Mrs Wainwright?

Wainwright smiled. Carlee came around from behind the chair.

Isn't that obvious, Benjamin? he said.

Sir?

She's right here, he said. She's standing right in front of you.

Carlee placed her hand on Wainwright's shoulder and Wainwright placed his on hers.

I want you to sleep well tonight, Benjamin, Wainwright said. You're home now.

He reached out and touched Kilt's slinged hand. Looked pensively at his wounded shoulder, his missing finger. Then looked Kilt hard in the eyes.

Nothing can hurt you anymore, he said.

Wainwright turned his head and kissed Carlee's fingertips.

I will say good night to you now, Wainwright said. In the morning we will find the answers to all of your questions.

He turned in his chair and called for Tillie. She appeared promptly and came into the room and took her place behind Wainwright.

You'll find all the arrangements satisfactory for you and your friend.

Wainwright nodded in a suggestive way.

Ain't like that, Kilt said.

Wainwright shrugged.

It's not my place to judge, he said. Then to Carlee he said, Please don't be late to bed, my darling. The bed is so terribly cold without you.

Then he motioned subtly with his hand and Tillie pushed him out of the room. Carlee sat back in the chair and crossed her legs and laced her fingers over her lap.

Such a sweet man, she said.

They all sat in silence in the great room with the oil lamps burning and the shadows of the lamps dancing on the walls. And no one said a word till Carlee finally said, He really does just hate a cold bed. And then she stood.

Sleep tight, Benji. Don't let the bedbugs bite.

And then she left the room.

51

It was quiet in the bunkhouse as Kilt made his way down the dark hall from the bathroom to his room. Behind the closed walnut doors some of the men were snoring. The bunkhouse smelled of hay and tobacco smoke and sometimes of horses. Stood outside each door were the hands' boots, squared off as if in phantom attention. Passing Bonnie's door he noticed it slightly open. He fingered the handle and tried to pull it closed without the hinges moaning in their gudgeons but they did. Bonnie sat up and said, How long you wanting to stay here?

You need to keep this door closed, he said. You need to lock it.

How long you wanting to stay here?

I want to stay here till he comes back.

What if that doesn't happen?

He'll turn up.

How do you know that?

Cause he's looking for me as much as I'm looking for him.

How do you know that?

Cause Carlee done said so much.

No, she didn't.

Might as well have.

I got a bad feeling.

It's only feeling. It ain't real.

What if it is real?

Then I'll be wrong.

But you can't be wrong.

Then I won't be. Now go to sleep.

He was closing the door when she said, Ben?

What?

Will you stay in here with me? Just a little longer. I got a bad feeling.

Kilt looked at her lying in the bed. Her hair pinned up. Her skin pale. The square of moonlight laid out over the sheets.

No, he said.

Then he closed the door.

Kilt lay in bed and watched the far wall where the window print of moonlight hung like a framed blank canvas. He had the window open and the air coming into the room was cool and spilled over the sill like water. The air was sweet-smelling and dewy and he could hear animals out in the darkness and he could hear crickets and things that sounded like cicadas but he knew there were no cicadas here. He lay with his hands laced behind his head. He'd no idea what time it was only that it was late and he marked the advancing hours by the moonlight slipping on the wall.

He must've closed his eyes at some point and fallen asleep because when he opened them again the moonlight was stamped on the door and when he heard the sound of the doorknob turning and the door swinging on its hinges he sat up and reached for the Luger on the nightstand. He pointed it at the door and he was about to call a warning when she stepped through the door.

You going to shoot me? she said.

Carlee came in and closed the door behind her and stood there for him to look at.

You look lost, Mrs Wainwright, Kilt said.

She was standing before him in a thin cotton dress the color of milk. She pulled the straps from her shoulders and the dress fell to the floor and she stood there naked with her alabaster skin burning in the darkness. She stepped from the pooled fabric and crossed the room to slip between the sheets smoldering against him. Her legs fell around his lap and she looked down at his face in the blue half dark and without a word she tried to kiss him. He turned his head but she held his chin and forced him and her lips pressed to his and then parted. She moved one of his hands to her breast but his hand recoiled like her skin was too hot to touch. Like it was not skin but fire. She sat up, looking down at him.

What are you doing here? Kilt asked.

Isn't that obvious.

Don't you remember you're Mrs Wainwright now?

Mr Wainwright and I have an agreement.

An agreement.

I care for him and in turn he gives me certain liberties.

Like sneaking into other people's bedrooms in the middle of the night?

I can leave if you don't want to.

I don't want to.

Of course you do.

She sat back. The moonlight and the shadows the moonlight propagated draped her naked skin like a piece of torn lace.

Just look at me for a while, then, she said. Pretend it's Lindsay Marie. Tonight let's pretend I'm your sweet Lindsay Marie.

When she said that he swung her off and he swung his legs off the bed and stood and went to where she had undressed and lifted the cotton dress and turned and flung it back at her.

What do you want me to do with this? she said.

Want's got nothing to do with it, Kilt said. What you're going to do is put that back on, get the hell out of my bed, and run back to that big house of yours. Back to your husband.

It's just a little fun, she said. Like when we were kids.

We ain't kids, he said. We ain't been kids for a very long time.

I'm sorry for the way I acted tonight. I wasn't being very nice.

You've never been nice.

Civil, then.

You never been civil.

Give me a little credit.

Credit for what?

For coming out here tonight. For looking after myself for a change.

You know how crazy you sound right now?

I'm not an old woman, she said.

No one said you were.

This place out here is lonely.

Then leave it. Go somewhere else.

You know I can't do that.

Sure you can. You get up and put some shoes on and walk away.

A woman with choices, then, she said. Is that your argument?

No argument, he said. Just the way it is.

Do you really think that's true?

Yes mam.

What if I asked that girl of yours? Carlee said.

I already told you, Kilt said. She ain't my girl.

Okay, Carlee said. *That* girl, then. What if I asked her?

Asked her what?

If she was free.

You already know the answer to that.

But she is a woman, is she not?

It's not the same and you know it.

That's easy for you to say. You are a man. Any opposition and you just chop it down. Those who make the rules can do what they like. You see, any protest I make is eventually met with frustration. And a man's frustration is often resolved with violence. No, there is no freedom for me. The cages I'm confined to may not have bars but they restrict me just the same.

Just put your dress back on, Kilt said. I ain't come back to have some existential chat about your feelings.

She sat on the bed with her legs folded beneath her, clutching the dress in her lap, naked from the waist up. She shook her head.

All you men are the same.

No, we ain't.

Yes. It is either life or it is death. There is nothing in the middle.

There're some things that don't have a middle. Some things either are or are not.

Then you are a fool, she said.

I ain't telling you nothing you don't already know but I know you've seen him. And when you see him again you tell him he ain't going to like what I got planned.

Perhaps it is each other you deserve. To go out together bloody, shot full of holes.

If that's what fate has in store.

Please.

She gestured with her hands. She dismissed the whole conceit. She stood from the bed and bent and stepped through the dress and pulled it up and slipped each arm through its strap.

Fate, she said. To be so arrested in your choices as to throw up your hands and bend to some oblique whim.

Fate, she said again, shaking her head. I never expected such indifference from you, Benji.

No mam, not indifference. Indifference wouldn't have brought me back here. I know damn well why I'm here. I know exactly what's coming down that pike.

Carlee looked down and then smoothed the front of her skirt and then looked up at him with tears in her eyes. She crossed the room, passing through the bar of moonlight not like a young woman but the ghost of a young woman and she stopped before Kilt and took his face in her hands and kissed him and once more called him a fool. Then she left the room, closing the door behind her. Then he heard her beyond the bunkhouse walls, heard her crying through the open window. He watched her walk back to the main house and then climb the steps and then she was gone and the only thing out there that night seemed to be the moonlight on the grass.

52

He awoke the next morning and the light through the window was gray and the room was cool. The air passing through the window had the smell of rain but it had not rained and when Kilt rose and peered through the warped pane of glass he saw the ground was dry and that a dry dust was being risen by a horse being worked in the center of the corral.

He pulled his pants and shirt from the chair and dressed in the brittle light. He went to the window and leaned on the sill and watched the man in the ring with the horse and the horse was rearing and kicking and tossing its head and the man at the end of the long rope seemed to have no control of the animal whatsoever. More than once Kilt watched the man be lurched on the rope and brought to his knees only to rise again humiliated and cursing the horse.

At the corral's fence line he saw Bonnie standing in a long skirt and boots and an oversized ducking jacket. She had her elbows resting on the top board and her chin was resting in her hands. Even from behind, not seeing her face, she had the look of someone not casually observing. Kilt finished dressing and pulled on his boots and left the bunkhouse and stepped into the cool gray morning. There were songbirds calling and a couple of border collies went trotting over the gravel near the stables and when they saw Kilt one of them barked but neither altered its pace and soon they were gone.

Bonnie had not moved nor did she when Kilt came up beside her. Not even her eyes shifting. As if Kilt weren't even there.

You like horses? Kilt asked.

Everyone likes horses.

No. Not everyone.

She turned her head.

You don't like horses?

Not particularly.

What do you mean you don't like horses?

I didn't say that. Just said I don't really care for them.

So this whole cowboy look is all for show?

She nodded down at Kilt's boots. Kilt lifted each boot in turn and shrugged.

Don't have to be a cowboy to wear boots.

How did you grow up in a place like this and not ride horses?

Never said I didn't ride.

So the boots are just to make you look taller, is that it?

Kilt stepped back from the corral with both hands laid atop the top board and looked down at the dirt and spit through his teeth then looked up at the colt trotting in circles with its eyes wild and rolling and its coal-black mane lifting and falling with each step.

I heard you talking to someone last night, Bonnie said.

Not me.

Was it that Carlee woman?

It might have been.

What did she have to say?

Nothing important.

She came to your room for something.

Kilt frowned at the girl. He said, Girl your age shouldn't be talking like that.

Bonnie turned back to the corral and watched the colt with her chin in her hands. The trainer in the center of the corral was turning with the colt keeping both hands on the rope like the horse was going to burst into a gallop at any moment. From time to time the colt would squat and buck sidelong, sliding the trainer on his bootheels over the dirt. Then it would jerk its head and set once again into a trot, letting the trainer think he was in control.

What's that trainer's name? Bonnie asked.

I do not know.

Well, he ain't doing it right.

She lifted her chin from her balled fist and pointed out at the horse.

That horse's bar is sore.

What makes you think its bar is sore?

Doesn't matter what I think. It is what it is, and that colt's bar is sore.

How do you know that?

The skin there's all puffy.

Kilt squinted to better see.

He's using a snaffle bit, Bonnie said, and it's hurting the horse's mouth. That's why it's bucking the way it is.

You can see all that from back here?

Can't you?

Kilt squinted again.

Well, now that you said it I can.

Bonnie set her fist on the top board and set her chin back on her fist.

You know what to do, don't you? Kilt said.

What do you mean?

If the bit is hurting the horse. What would you do?

Probably the same thing you'd do.

Maybe a mullen bit. Or get that bit out of there altogether.

I'd use a hackamore, Bonnie said.

So would I.

Kilt spit between his teeth again and then nodded at the trainer.

Why doesn't he know that? he said.

Bonnie shrugged.

But pulling on that rope, Bonnie said, like he's doing isn't helping anything. You can like a horse all you want but if it doesn't like you it never will.

Kilt turned and watched the girl.

You got a plan hatching, don't you?

No, she said. No plan.

You're a bad liar, he said. Anyone ever tell you that?

People tell me all sorts of things all the time. Especially men like you.

Men like me.

Yeah.

She hadn't taken her eyes from the horse.

You and Carlee must be talking behind my back.

There was a commotion in the corral and the horse reared and jabbed its forefoot at the air then turned and punched a rear hoof at the trainer. The trainer fell backward into the dirt and scuttled blindly with his hat fallen over his eyes till he hit the corral boards. The colt pounded off seesawing wildly with smoke pouring from its nostrils and thin ropes of spit swinging from its lips. The trainer rose up and took off his hat and knocked the dust from it against his leg and swept back his hair and then squared his hat.

You better go on and show that cowboy how it's done before he gets himself killed.

And before Bonnie could protest Kilt whistled at the trainer and the trainer turned as he was reaching down for his rope.

Girl says you're doing it wrong, Kilt said.

Like he hadn't heard him correctly, the trainer straightened up and tilted his head and narrowed his eyes. Then he faced around and laid his hands on his hips and looked down at the dirt and spit in the dust and looked up again at Kilt.

The hell ye say?

Said you're doing it wrong, Kilt said. According to her.

Kilt cocked his thumb at Bonnie.

The trainer took a step forward.

Doin what wrong?

Whatever the hell that is you're doing with that poor colt.

Breakin it, the trainer said. They call it breakin.

Seems like you're aiming to kill it.

The trainer leaned his head like there was someone standing beside him and shook it. And then he looked back at Kilt and spit.

Ye got a problem with the way I work?

No sir.

And how the hell would ye know what kind a job I'm doin?

Not me, Kilt said.

Then why the hell ye talkin?

I'm a talker, I guess. Just like to talk.

The trainer pointed at the big house.

Well, ye can go over there and talk, he said. I'm sure one a them women folk inside's just dyin for a little gossip.

Kilt looked at Bonnie then stepped back from the corral and spit between his boots.

You know the difference between a snaffle bit and a—

He looked at Bonnie.

What'd you call it?

Hackamore.

Hackamore, Kilt said. Yeah. Then to the trainer he said, The difference between a snaffle bit and a hackamore?

The trainer spit a molasses-colored gout through his teeth

then looked over his shoulder at the horse like a trick was being played on him.

Ye got some brass, the trainer said. You know that?

Shoot, Mister, Kilt said, don't mean nothing by it. And I ain't trying to start nothing either. Just an observation is all.

Ye want to come out here and giver er a go?

No, Kilt said. No, I do not. Anyway, I'm not the horse whisperer. She is.

Bonnie shot Kilt a look. The trainer laughed.

Ye think I'm just goin a give this horse over to a Indian girl?

I don't think you have any choice in it, Kilt said.

The trainer laughed again and went to the far side of the corral with his spurs ringing in the cool morning air and took a coiled rope down from a peg and walked back to the center of the corral and held out the rope for the girl. Bonnie didn't move.

Ye want me to bring it to ye, I will.

When Bonnie still didn't move the trainer looked down and shook his head. They heard him laugh again. Then he called out.

Ain't got all day, sweetheart. Ye goin a come show this cowboy how it's done or ye just goin a stand there and pout?

I'll go talk to him, Kilt said.

And he was taking his boot from the bottom board when Bonnie stopped him, saying, No.

She climbed the boards of the corral and swung one leg at a time over the top board taking care not to snag the hem of her dress as she did and then she climbed down and wiped her hands on her skirt to flatten it and walked out toward the trainer who was still holding out the rope.

Bonnie reached for the coiled rope and Kilt heard the trainer say, Go on and get ye some buckaroo.

The trainer patted her on the head as he passed and walked over to Kilt who had a boot jacked up on one of the boards and his arms slung over the top board. The trainer leaned back against the wood and took his papers from his shirt pocket and rolled a cigarette and handed it to Kilt and then rolled one for himself. He popped a match and lit Kilt's then his own then he waved out the flame and tossed the spent match to the dirt and then crossed his arms and stood there smoking.

Ye done sent that little squaw to a early grave, he said.

They watched her stand there in the middle of the corral. The coil of rope in her small hand. The colt seemed to know why the girl was standing there like she was because it nickered and stamped its feet and punched out a hoof and tossed its head like it was trying to shake a cloud of flies.

But the girl didn't move. Not an inch. Kilt could only assume she was waiting it out like a child in a tantrum. Then all at once she stepped forward. The colt stopped moving and stood there watching the girl with its eyes walled and half-crazed. The girl didn't stop till she was about ten feet away. There she knelt and took up the rope lying in the dirt like a dead snake. The colt was suspicious. It started tossing its head, slowly at first. The girl stepped closer. The colt looked at her like she was a lioness, and as it was already uneasy, Bonnie stepped on a small pebble that popped under her shoe like a gunshot and the colt lurched into the air, taking up the rope, and vaulted at the girl with its teeth chattering. Not more than a second and those teeth came down upon her forehead lighting up her brow in an eruption of blood. The colt was scared and reared again thinking the girl might rise from the dust. The colt brayed. The colt jeered and cried out and finally kicked once at the board and then took off like some equine dervish.

The girl stood and gathered herself with the blood running into her eyes. Her hair wet and matted she looked some nightmarish incantation. She raised a hand to her brow and touched the gash and looked at her fingers glistening and red but showed no sign of horror or alarm. And then as if to prove it were real she brought her fingers to her mouth to taste the blood.

She bent and took a handful of the hem of her dress and tore two strips away and wrapped one strip around her head. Then she went to the corral's edge and pulled in a long stick and tied the second strip to its end. Then she turned back to the colt and walked toward it and knelt for the rope and gave it a sharp tug like there was a dog on the other end. The horse tried to jerk its head but the girl popped the rope again. She started circling the horse with the horse mirroring her movements, and the whole time she did this she was waving the stick with the strip of dress tied to it. Every time the horse did something she didn't like she'd tug on that rope and wave the stick. Horse and girl patterning each other in some choreographed dance.

She worked the horse that way for around fifteen minutes, never taking pressure off the rope and never taking her eyes from the colt.

She ain't goin a quit that horse, the trainer said, is she?

Your guess's as good as mine, Kilt said.

Bonnie tugged again and all at once the colt softened and stood there with its eyes blinking and its ears switching. Bonnie stood stock-still. She spoke to it. Some ancient homily perhaps known only to drovers and gauchos and mystics. Then she took the stick and slapped it against the colt's feet with the colt not bucking but simply stepping away. The girl did it again and again the colt stepped away.

Bonnie dropped the rope and didn't make a move. She stood there looking almost impatient. She leaned her weight to one foot and put her hand on her hip. Occasionally she'd swipe the stick up and down with the piece of dress chucking against the wind but the colt never moved. It hardly even blinked. Then the girl walked calmly to the colt and put out her hand and touched its nose and ran her hand up between the eyes and the colt blinked and tossed its head in a sort of playful way and then Bonnie undid the straps of the halter and slid it down the colt's face and took the snaffle from its mouth and examined the swollen lip and spoke to it again. She dropped the halter and bit to the dirt. She stepped away and turned to the men.

You got a hackamore around here? she asked.

The trainer pointed to the far side of the corral.

A moment later the trainer said, I'll be goddamned, as the colt began to follow Bonnie across the grounds like a pup.

At the edge of the corral Bonnie took down the hackamore from its nail and turned to the colt behind her and slid on the bridle. Then she led the horse by the mecate to the middle of the ring.

She rubbed the horse all over from poll to croup. Then she brought the mecate around and leaned her body against the colt's flank, lightly at first to see what it might do and then with all her weight. She reached over its withers and swung a leg over its back. The horse stepped from side to side with the girl saying something and correcting it when it went somewhere she didn't like. Then the horse fell still and she sat it for a moment. She leaned and rubbed the colt's shoulder. Then she set it into a trot and she rode past Kilt and the trainer. She circled the corral once, twice, with her black hair trailing and lifting and falling with the horse's gait and when she came upon the trainer she halted the colt and looked down from the animal and said, Open the gate.

The trainer agreed without a word and swung the latch and pushed open the gate and Bonnie rode the colt out of the corral and over the gravel drive toward the barn. At the barn she stopped and dismounted and laid the mecate over the colt's neck and opened the bay door and then led the horse into the barn.

I'll be goddamned, the trainer said again.

Not today, Kilt said. I think that girl just done saved your soul.

53

When he found her that afternoon she was brushing down the colt. She was talking to it but Kilt couldn't hear what she was saying. He leaned against one of the stalls and crossed one boot over the other and stood there watching her. She looked at him for a moment then went back to brushing the horse.

You have a way with them, Kilt said. They trust you.

I've never met a horse I didn't trust, she said. I don't think that horse exists.

I'm sure there's one out there. One that'd give you willies.

No, she said. Horses don't have that in them.

So when you leaving? he asked.

Leaving?

Yeah.

I never said I was leaving.

But you are, aren't you?

You could come with me.

No, I can't. You know I can't.

You staying here for good now?

He's coming. I don't know when. But he'll turn up and I want to be here when he does.

You're stubborn.

Okay.

She looked up at him. She said, I can see why she ran off with your brother.

She didn't look away when she said that. Just stared him in the eyes. Tried to get something out of him that she hadn't seen before. But there was nothing. He didn't show her a thing.

Figured I'd take the car, she said.

Kilt shrugged.

It's your car.

A horse blew down the bay and they both looked at the same time and they saw the heads of the horses black and gleaming and their eyes were shining and their ears were turned like they were listening.

So when you leaving? Kilt asked. So I can say goodbye.

Morning, I suppose.

You all packed up?

Got nothing to pack.

Kilt nodded like he knew that answer already.

If you stay here, Bonnie said, something bad's going to happen.

You think so?

Yes.

Like me dying?

Yes.

You want to come in and get something to eat?

No, she said.

Kilt nodded.

Don't run off without saying goodbye, he said. Okay?

Then he turned and walked out of the barn. The air was cooling in the late afternoon and the sky to the west was pink and the west faces of the Missions were pink and the shadowed valley to the north was a pale lavender and the air was still and there were songbirds calling and there were horses in the pasture looking west toward the fled sun and their faces were rosed in the light. Kilt turned once and looked back into the barn and saw Bonnie talking to the colt and rubbing its nose and its neck, speaking to it in a language Kilt did not know nor ever would. And seeing her like that he felt nothing but contempt for the world and all the men in it. How the evils of a few negate all else till it is all corrupted. He wanted to tell her this and other things like if how the world was left to people like her things would be different and there would be no violence and perhaps even suffering wiped away. But the world would not change because nothing ultimately changes and in the end some kind of darkness lingers, waiting for us all.

54

He was in the bathroom of the bunkhouse washing his face in the porcelain water basin when he heard the motor of the Coupe crank up. He took the hand towel from the hook near the mirror and wiped the water from his skin and he went to the window as he dried his hands.

She was small behind the wheel. Her hands were on the top of the wheel and she was looking over the tops of her hands. She looked around at the seat beside her like she had forgotten something. Kilt pushed open the window and he heard her grind the gears and then the car bucked and stalled. She started the engine again. The tailpipe coughing out little puffs of blue smoke.

Kilt turned from the window and left the room and went down the hall and pushed open the door to the bunkhouse and in the ashen twilight he watched Bonnie drive off, the trail of exhaust swirling like some dry wake, and he watched her go till the drive bent at the headland and the car disappeared. Only the faint rattle of the engine fading. Only the lingering exhaust to prove she was even there.

He was about to turn back into the bunkhouse when he

saw Carlee standing on the porch. She was in evening attire and she was watching Kilt. After a moment she said, Come in for a cocktail.

They sat in the great room with their drinks. A fire was going. Carlee was having champagne and she held the flute delicately between her finger and her thumb. It was just the two of them. They said little to one another but Carlee had not taken her eyes from him. Finally she said, Do you mind if I come and sit next to you?

Free country, Kilt said.

She stood and crossed the room. She wore a dress with a plunging neckline and when she sat beside him she leaned with intention but Kilt kept his eyes up and it did not go unnoticed to Carlee and she smiled from the sport of it all. She arranged the skirt of her dress, running a hand down her thigh.

Last night was a mistake, she said.

There are no mistakes.

I don't want you to think less of me for it.

I don't.

Well, that makes me happy to hear.

She sipped the champagne.

Are you sad to see her go? Carlee asked.

No mam.

Not even the smallest thread?

No.

Aren't you worried for her?

I suppose.

And that doesn't make you sad?

Sadness and worry ain't the same thing.

No, she said, but they are certainly related, are they not?

If you say so.

She reached out and touched his leg.

How is your whiskey, Benji?

Fine.

I want to ask you a question. In fact, I have been wanting to ask it since I saw you.

Okay.

Do you believe we can change?

We?

Us. Anyone. Do you think people are capable of change?

That's the burning question you've been wanting to ask?

Yes.

No, he said. I don't think people are capable of change.

Why not?

We are who we are, Kilt said. People are lazy. Takes a lot to do something different.

Don't you think there is at least one person out there capable of this?

It's action against thought, ain't it? Person might want to quit the whiskey, for example, so he does. But that ain't going stop him from being a drinker. Ain't going stop him from thinking about it. He may not drink, but that don't mean he ain't a drinker.

Are you saying there is some sort of purity in thought?

I'm saying you are who you are. Up here. Kilt tapped his temple. You don't change up here.

She sat back in the sofa. She crossed her legs and the length of her thigh appeared like blood suddenly spilling from a gash.

It must be wonderful to live your life so simply, she said. To see things as one or the other.

No, Kilt said. Things either are or aren't. True or false. There ain't no variation.

So what does that make me? Sitting here in this dress. Drinking champagne. Talking to you as a married woman. That make me some kind of whore?

You ain't done nothing.

She sipped the champagne.

Yes, she said. But I thought it. I even tried. So what does that make me?

Her eyes reddened and began to well but before Kilt had a chance to answer he heard Wainwright bid them a good evening. Kilt turned and saw Wainwright in his high-backed wheelchair with Tillie behind him.

My dear, Wainwright said, you did not tell me you and Benjamin had started cocktails.

Carlee breathed in and dabbed a finger under each eye and then put on a smile and turned on the sofa.

My darling, she said. I was just about to send for you. Benji here has absolutely captivated me in his conversation.

Perhaps before he extinguishes all of his interest, Wainwright said, we be seated for dinner.

Of course, darling.

And Benjamin, Wainwright said, you left this hanging on the wall near the door.

He held out Kilt's Luger in its holster. Kilt crossed the room and took it up.

Thank you, sir.

They were seated at the long walnut table with numerous candles burning the length of it. It was all but dark save for the light of the candles and the glassware sparkled from the light of them and the windows of the dining room too. The varnished wood shined like a mirror. Or like another kind of sky with the specks of flames awash in some foreign celestial formation.

Wainwright sat at one end of the table and Kilt the other. Carlee sat adjacent to Wainwright like a decoration. Laid out on the table were platters of steak and fillets of trout. There were wedges of tomatoes and pyramids of corn. Potatoes and bowls of salad and bottles of wine and for the epergne there was a gilded candelabra and the guttered candles spilled their wax like things seen in caves.

Carlee ate primly with one hand placed in her lap. The bites of food she took could hardly be called bites. Like she was merely bringing an empty fork to her mouth. Like she was some stage actor in the middle of a scene. She snuck furtive glances at Kilt who looked as if he was indentured to his place at the table.

Wainwright spoke without pause. He spoke of horses and bloodlines, and he spoke of the ranch in its current iteration and he spoke of his plans for it in the future. He spoke of politics and how the country was changing and he spoke of the arts and how it seemed they were paramount to this change and that it was this balance that was lacking. He said that to restore civility one had to figure in religion. He said the only prosecution for one's God is another's God and that there is no reconciliation beyond that. He said the only cure for such blasphemy is surrender, unequivocal and complete, and that to believe otherwise is a damnation of the soul.

Wainwright drank his wine and his food went untouched. He continued on.

There are few constants in this world, he said, greed and war among them, which are the same thing. The same desire. And that every generation has known this and every one to come. And that the foolishness, however, is that even though this is understood, detailed in our history, we commit the same acts, the same mistakes, so that our failures are reborn again and again and again.

Then he paused as if for effect and then leaned back in the wheelchair and angled his head at Kilt.

You must know, Benjamin, he said. That I loved your mother very much.

My mother?

Yes. I told her that I would care for the two of you like you were my own. That I would always care for you no matter what. I even asked her to come out here and live with us just before she died. Martha, of course, would never have it.

Wainwright shrugged.

Why are you telling me this now?

Because it is something I wished I would've told you years ago. From the beginning.

Why didn't you?

Fear, I suppose. I don't know. I feared if you and Sidney knew the truth you would leave.

What about Nick Mercy?

Martha's son. She loved him dearly.

Why did he leave, then?

Some boys, like Nicholas, like Sidney, cannot get out of their own way.

So you send them away?

No one can be sent away when they are already gone.

Wainwright sighed deeply.

I know why you are here, Benjamin, he said. And I must warn you, there is no good in it. These oaths that are paid for in blood can never bring closure.

At this Wainwright lifted a brittle finger and tapped his temple.

These things, he said, which are paid for in blood and blood only will never die, will never end. They will always live on. And one day, perhaps in years to come, perhaps longer, they will return to you. And of course you will not be the same man and perhaps that man will have had other experiences and this will lead that man to a different perspective. A perspective of grace maybe. Of humility. Perhaps even one of forgiveness.

He shook his head.

This bloodlust for your brother has consequences none of us can comprehend. To commit such an act will only lead to torment and you will dwell there for eternity.

Wainwright paused. Kilt pursed his lips and tapped a finger atop the table.

I've already heard this story, sir, Kilt said. One brother

killing the other. But what if one brother is already dead in the mind of the other? And that brother slew at the hands of him. What then?

Wainwright shrugged like such a question had no answer.

If that is true, Wainwright said, then that brother shall have a mark on him. That brother shall be a fugitive and wander the earth accompanied only by guilt. He shall know only suffering and anguish for his actions.

A fugitive, you say?

Yes.

Like a bank robber.

No, Wainwright said.

Where is he? Kilt said. You tell me where and I'll go. I'll leave this place and you won't have to worry about it anymore.

This desire, Wainwright said, is lurking at your door. You are filled with anger and contempt. But you must master it. You must overcome—

Wainwright had only just uttered that final vowel when the bullet entered just forward of his ear and punched a hole out the other side. Carlee was spackled with the blood and when she looked down at herself she screamed.

Wainwright's head slumped forward and hung there limply with the blood runneling out of the ragged opening. Kilt had leapt up with the chair tipping over behind him and he had the Luger drawn. The room was quiet. So silent it was only the grandfather clock in the great room could be heard ticking. Then from some other room came the unmistakable sound Kilt had only previously heard in a dream. A sound that seemed to usher in some depthless dark. A sound Kilt knew only as death. From the other room came the gentle ringing of a bell.

Then he stepped into the dining room, smiling.

Hello, baby brother, he said.

55

Lives are parsed into the then and that to come. There is no present. The faulty predilections that we can escape suffering doom us. That to live purely in the light will be our undoing.

The lamplight peeled down his face and his eyes were shadowed under his hat. He was dressed in black with a black hat and a black shirt and black boots. The jacket he wore was long like an undertaker's. His teeth seemed to be glowing amongst the black beard. He had a silver bolo tie at his neck that flashed in the light. He crossed the room to the dining table and pulled out a chair and sat and then removed his hat and set it on the table and smoothed his hair down. He rested the butt of the pistol on the table beside his hat and with his other hand he rubbed his face like he was tired or had just come in from the sun. But there was no sun and he was not tired and he let out a deep sigh and then laid the pistol on its side. Bits of Wainwright's skull were littered over the table and Bosco swept them away with his hand like they were crumbs. Then he laced his fingers together over his stomach and sat back in his chair.

Why don't you put that thumb buster away, Bosco said. Never liked chatting with a gun jammed in my face.

Kilt didn't move. Carlee sat there breathing like her lungs didn't work. Bosco leaned a little in his chair to better see Kilt. Then he nodded his appraisal.

You've looked better, baby brother, he said. What happened to your arm?

Still Kilt didn't move.

Look, Bosco said, if it's the old man you're upset about, it wasn't up to me. He was about to say something I didn't want to hear.

When no one said anything Bosco threw up his hands.

All right, he said, let's hear it. What's got you all clammed up?

Then he looked across the table at Carlee and he looked at her like he hadn't noticed her before.

Ah, shoot, honey, he said. I'm sorry. I got your dress all dirty.

He went to stand but when he did Kilt stepped closer. Bosco held up his hands.

Just goin a help the lady over there, he said. No need in anyone getting shot over this.

He didn't take his eyes off Kilt.

I'm goin a stand now, okay? And when I do you ain't goin a shoot me, all right?

Kilt didn't move.

Standing now, Bosco said.

He stood slowly and pushed the chair out with the back of his legs. With one hand still aloft he took up a linen napkin and held it out for Kilt to see as if to prove he had nothing to hide.

Goin a walk round the table now, he said.

He made his way around the table. He passed Wainwright slumped and dripping in his chair. He pulled out a chair beside Carlee and started to dab the napkin at the blood on her face.

Old man got you all messy, Bosco said.

She tried to pull away but Bosco grabbed her face and held it in place. He dabbed the napkin at her neck. He dipped the napkin into Carlee's champagne flute and ran the napkin over her skin, down her chest. She was trembling. The blood loosened up and funneled between her breasts.

Sorry to ruin your dress, honey, he said.

Then he wiped the hair at her forehead, the hair at her temples. She had her eyes squeezed tight.

We'll go into town tomorrow, he said to her, get you a new one. Pick you out any one you like. My treat.

Then he stood and leaned and kissed the top of her head and went back around the table and he patted Wainwright on the back and then he sat down and took a deep breath.

You can take that gun off me now, Bosco said. And would you sit down, goddamnit. You're clutterin up the room.

After a long moment Kilt moved forward and took up his chair that had fallen over and stood it up and sat down and laid the butt of the Luger on the table.

You ain't goin a put that away, are you?

Bosco threw up his hands. Fine, he said, have it your way.

Bosco took his hands from the table and tried to move them to his lap but Kilt stopped him.

You move them hands another inch, Kilt said, and I'll put a hole right between your eyes.

So it does speak, Bosco said. He laid his palms on the table before him. I thought all that dirt had done something to your voice box.

Voice box is just fine, Kilt said.

Bosco looked over at Carlee.

So what've you and Benji been talkin about? He been flirting with you?

Carlee just sat there all bloodstained and silent. Then Bosco looked at Kilt.

You can if you want, he said. Flirt with her, I mean. Can do more than flirt for all I care. Hell, maybe you already have.

He directed his attention to Carlee again.

How about it, honey? You let him have a poke? I bet a man back from the grave would appreciate a little warmth like that.

When no one answered, Bosco said, Hell, what's everyone so upset about? If I knew no one wanted to catch up I'd have stayed home.

Then Bosco snapped his fingers and pointed at Kilt.

Just dawned on me, he said. You're mad at me. Aren't you?

Bosco shrugged.

Shit, he said, guess I'd be a little mad at me too. Suppose it wasn't very nice to leave you like that. But it wasn't like I left you with nothing.

That's exactly what you left me with, Kilt said.

You talkin the bank box with those flyers in it?

Bosco snorted a laugh.

Yes, he said, that was cruel. But you have to understand, baby brother, you dealt me the same hand.

You buried me alive, Kilt said. I would not consider that the same hand.

Oh, but it is. You needed some kind of abandonment in your life.

That's all I ever had, Kilt said. And you know it.

Bosco laughed in disgust.

Think back, baby brother. Can you picture Mama's face? Go on. Close your eyes. Picture it. Cause I can't. I never even seen her face.

This conversation again, Kilt said. Save it for someone else. Save it for God for all I care.

Don't be so dramatic, Bosco said. This should be a happy night. Us reuniting. I'm willing to put it behind us. Start clean. Bygones be bygones.

He clucked his tongue.

So how'd you find me anyway? Lonny have anything to do with it?

Kilt only stared back.

It was Lonny, Bosco said, wasn't it? That Jew bastard. Have to go have me a talk with him when I'm done here.

Where's Lindsay Marie? Kilt asked.

You're just diving right in, Bosco said.

Then he leaned back in his chair. He smiled. He reached for his hat and upended it and took a folded piece of parchment paper from the greasy hat band then turned his hat back over and waggled the paper in the air and then laid it on the table and slid it to Kilt. Kilt palmed it.

Go on, Bosco said. Give it a read.

He unfolded the paper cautiously, one corner at a time as if within contained some incomprehensible evil. As if contained therein were the answers dooming not just him but all he knew. The scrolling words were penned in black ink and his eyes dashed across the lines because he knew what they were leading to. He knew it was she who had written them but this was not her, this could not be her.

Don't start crying on me, baby brother.

Bosco sucked his teeth and grabbed Wainwright's glass and finished the rest of the dead man's wine. He reached for the bottle and poured another glass.

You ain't goin a sull up on me, are you?

He sipped the wine.

These things, he said, these things, they happen. People change their minds all the time. Falling in and out of love. That's just life. What you got a do, baby brother, is move on. Find someone new. Like Carlee here. Fine woman right here in this room.

Bosco leaned in his chair.

Look at them legs, he said. Long enough to wrap around you twice.

He sipped the wine again.

She can do these things with her tongue, Bosco said. I ever tell you about that? Shit that'll make your head spin.

One more thing out of your mouth, Kilt said, and it'll be the last.

How about her mouth?

She ain't mine to tell what to do.

Okay.

Then in one deft motion like a magician's sleight of hand the flash of a pistol appeared from beneath Bosco's jacket and winked in the candlelight and he pulled the trigger and he shot Carlee twice in the chest in rapid fire. The force of the shot knocked her over in the chair like a tin cutout in some carnival arcade. Kilt reared up and swung the Luger at Bosco and he pulled the trigger only to hear an empty click. Kilt turned the gun in his hand and then trained it back at Bosco and again pulled the trigger. Bosco just sat there shaking his head.

Never leave your gun unattended, baby brother. How many times I got a tell you that?

He put the little pistol back in his jacket and sat forward and took up the wineglass and drank. Then he set it back on the table and sat back in the chair.

Now, Bosco said, it's just me and you. The way it ought to be.

You're a dead man, Kilt said. You don't know it yet but you're already dead.

So much killing, he said. Let's just call it what it is.

And what would that be?

Bad luck. Wrong place, wrong time.

You're describing fate.

Well. Bosco shrugged. If not that then what?

Fate didn't put me in the ground. Left to die. You did that.

I came back, Bosco said. Maybe a moment of clarity. Maybe I just changed my mind. Like right now, for example.

Right now what?

You're alive. Could've been like those two in a blink of an eye.

Bosco snapped his fingers as if to prove it can all happen that quickly.

Then why didn't you? Kilt asked.

I wanted to give you a chance to be the hero.

The hero?

Save the girl.

Kilt pointed at Carlee on the floor.

She's already dead.

Bosco let out a strange small laugh and shook his head.

Not her, he said. That soulmate a yours. The one and only. Apple of your eye.

Kilt straightened in his chair.

Save her from what? he said.

Bosco pointed. Kilt stood and by the time he got to the window the barn was already on fire.

56

He ran from the dining room, down the hall toward the front door. Tillie lay on the floor in a pool of blood with her throat cut. One hand was laid out the front door like she was trying to crawl away.

He leapt over her body and bound down the porch steps and ran over the gravel toward the barn. The smoke tumbled and eddied like it was caught in a tide. The burning barn looked like the pillar of fire rendered in Exodus and the flames leapt wildly into the dark night and the sight of it arrested him there in the dirt.

In the enormous oak tree near the stables the trainer was hanging dead from a long rope and his body twirled gently. At the end of the rope the colt Bonnie broke stood stock-still with the rope dallied around the saddle horn. Kilt ran toward the hanged man and took a knife from his pocket and snapped it open to cut the man down but in the fire the doors to each stall must have given way because a flood of burning horses raced from the barn wheeling and kicking and screaming horribly with their manes and tails trailing like comets, and Kilt watched as the herd afire pounded into the dark leaving nothing in their wake but the afterimage of torment and finally dropping in the distance one by one to collapse in a mound of orange and yellow and red, colorful flames to sear the hot flesh until the final heart's beat. Colorful flames to keep the blood from cooling until the last flame died. The dark plain then became silent and the final voice of a horse receded, consumed by the darkness. The last horse to be heard. The last horse of the world.

Kilt turned away and was about to cut the man down when through the open bay door he saw Lindsay Marie tied to a chair. Her hands were bound behind her back and her ankles were tied to the chair. She was in the dress he last saw her in. Her head was bowed and he called her name and through the snarls and booms of fire she must have heard him because she looked up. His feet were cemented to the ground. He couldn't move. Her eyes were full of water and caught within the gloss the flames danced as though in some strange celebration. Eyes that appeared destined for this moment. To hold his eyes in some profound revelation, to prophesize that the end was a certainty and that to continue on was not possible. That to continue in any sense is ultimately corrupted with time.

He stepped forward. He called her name again. And in that very moment the beams gave and the roof caved in and the barn collapsed around her. A shower of sparks burst forth and he howled in anguish. How he howled. How he howled.

He ran toward the burning heap as if to pursue some futile attempt of salvation and in his fervor he didn't hear the gunshot and his leg gave out and he fell to the dirt. He tried to kneel but another shot came from the pitch dark and hit him just above the kidney. He lay in the dirt, holding himself, his face pressed into the dirt. The ground smelled of iron and he didn't know if it was the iron of the dirt or the iron of his blood. The bullet had traveled all the way through his abdomen and come out the other side and when he pulled his hand away it came away slick and warm.

He rolled over onto his back and saw Bosco come slowly from the shadows to stand over him, now bathed in the rippling light of the fire. His eyes were nearly hidden under his hat but what of them Kilt could see appeared like hollow caverns. Like wells one peers into where depth is lost and only the cold breath of the earth is felt. Yet within those voids a tiny speck of light burned and more ominous for it because within that lightless place there lived a soul stricken by darkness and it cried out with an eerie clamor. And looking up at him Kilt did not see his brother, but death.

Pity, Bosco said. I didn't think the barn would fall that fast.

Bosco kicked Kilt's hand away from his stomach and pressed his boot into the wound. Kilt cried out. Bosco pulled his boot away and cocked it to the light and the gleam of blood sparkled on the leather.

You're bleedin, baby brother, he said.

He wiped his boot against Kilt's trouser leg.

Well, he said, I bet you want a explanation. Figure I owe you that.

I don't want nothing from you.

You ain't curious as to why you found yourself in that hole?

Kilt spit at him. The gout of spittle was red, full of blood. Bosco looked down at it on his trousers and swiped it away with the barrel of his pistol.

You ain't wanting to know why that little girlfriend of yours is lying under that burning barn? Why everyone on this ranch is now dead? Ain't you wanting to know that?

You're just going to tell anyway, Kilt said. So just get it over with.

You got a ask me.

I ain't got to do shit.

Come on, baby brother, play along a little. Don't have to be like this. Just ask me before you bleed out and leave me a only child.

Why?

You mean why did I kill all them people and set the barn on fire and tie sweet Miss Lindsay Marie to that chair and bury you alive? Why did I do all that?

Sure.

Bosco knelt beside him and leaned to his ear. He spoke in a quiet voice.

Because I'm the devil, he said. That's why.

He stood from his crouch. He patted his leg with the barrel of his gun.

My leg feels better, he said. Remember that? I was all shot up around the campfire that night? Had ourselves a bit of a snafu on that last job, didn't we?

Why'd you wait so long?

Why'd I wait so long for what?

To kill me. Why didn't you just do it sooner? Had all the chances to.

Figured it would be better to let it marinade. I knew I was going to do it, just didn't know when. But the longer I waited the better it got. I figured when it finally happened there'd be some kind of release. That sound crazy?

Yes.

I wanted to strip the happiness away all at once.

What happiness?

When I saw you lookin at Lindsay Marie that day. The way you looked at her and the way she looked at you. There was a lot of happiness there. That's the straw that broke the donkey's back. Everyone I've ever known has only done me wrong. Those kinds of people aren't good people. And if good people aren't good then that makes them bad. That makes them bad people. And we don't need bad people in the world. There's enough badness as there is.

You know how stupid that sounds?

Maybe.

Bosco stood there with the pistol at his side, looking down at his bleeding brother. Then the pistol rose and fired and he shot Kilt through the kneecap. Kilt cried out.

You see what happens when you say mean things to me?

Bosco squatted and pushed his hat back with the barrel of the pistol then he scratched his chin with it then he lay both elbows on his knees and let the gun dangle there between his legs. Then he sighed like someone running out of patience.

It's not my fault I'm like this, baby brother. You might think it is but it ain't. Shit. You think I wanted all of this to happen? All of it to turn out this way? This is because of them. This is their fault. After the old man kicked me out I tried to make it right again. Did he ever tell you that? Did he ever tell you how I wrote to him, asking for forgiveness? I bet he didn't. The old man just wrote me off.

He gave you a chance, Kilt said.

Pssh. I heard what he said tonight. All that blood oath shit. How I'm goin a dwell in torment for eternity and whatnot. How I'm marked as a fugitive and cursed to wander the earth alone and blah blah blah. The old man evangelized things he was capable of himself. The old man was full of shit.

Well, if that's true, Kilt said, if you already got the mark, then you best get on with it. You're wasting my time.

You're just like him. Turned your back on me just like he did.

The hell I did.

You ran out of that bank. You're the one that got me shot up. Hung me out to dry, just like the old man.

You're a liar.

Bosco smiled. He cocked his hat forward and stood from his squat. He looked down at Kilt.

We had a good run, baby brother. But nothin good ever lasts, does it. Eventually it all comes to an end. Some ends just come sooner than others.

Bosco raised his pistol.

There anything you want to say? Bosco asked. Never gave you that opportunity before. Wasn't right of me. So, if there's something you're wantin a say, now's the time.

Kilt lay in the dirt holding his stomach. All the life was draining from his face and his skin was going pale. The fire was flashing in his dimming eyes.

I don't believe you, Kilt said.

You don't believe me what, baby brother?

That you're all bad. You ain't all bad.

Hate to spoil your rosy image, but I am. I'm as bad as they come.

No, you're not. You're my brother and there's good in there. I know there is.

Sorry, baby brother. I really am.

You ain't making it out of here, Kilt said. Sure as I'm going out, you're going out with me. You can count on that.

Bosco shook his head. He clicked his tongue.

You say hi to that whore mother of ours, Bosco said.

He thumbed back the hammer of the pistol and trained the gun on Kilt's heart.

See you in Hell, baby brother.

The shot rang out and Bosco faltered. He looked down at his chest where his shirt was suddenly going wet. He rose his hand to it and his hand came away slick with blood. He turned dumbfounded to where the shot had been authored and Bonnie was standing with a rifle leveled at Bosco. She fired again and then again, striking Bosco in the heart and he fell to his knees as if in repent. He swung the pistol around and fired recklessly into the darkness about her but none of the bullets found their mark and then he fell forward and died there in the dirt.

Bonnie ran to Kilt. She knelt at his side and cupped his head in her arms. She took his hand from his stomach and the blood shimmered in the firelight and she put his hand back again.

Thought you ran out on me, Kilt said.

I came back.

I think I'm dying.

You're not dying.

I feel cold.

Can you stand?

I can stand.

By the time she got him to the Coupe he hardly knew where he was. He was slumped in the front seat watching the blurred fire.

Don't close them eyes, Bonnie said. You got to stay awake.

She turned the Coupe around in the gravel roundabout and sped off. There were horses smoldering on the roadside.

Are those horses? he asked.

Shh, Bonnie said. Don't talk. And don't close them eyes. Going to get you some help.

You got any water? he asked. I'm thirsty.

You just stay still. Going to find you some help.

They passed under the ranch gate but when Bonnie tried to turn toward Black Elk Kilt labored and reached and took hold of the wheel.

Don't, he said.

Let go, she said. Got to get you some help.

No, he said. He tilted his head. Go that way.

There's only mountains that way.

Just go.

Ben, she said, we got to—

Just go that way.

He coughed and he could taste the blood in his mouth.

Please, he said. I don't want to ask it again. Just get me up there.

She sat there unmoving behind the wheel. Just watching him. Just staring.

Go!

She turned the Coupe reluctantly toward the dark hills and the darker mountains beyond and they drove till they couldn't drive anymore and when they got there he asked her to help him out and she did and then he asked her to sit with him and talk to him so he could listen to her voice.

He lay on the ground with his palms upon the dirt and his heart skyward facing whatever heaven might be up there, and he felt the moonlight cool on his face and he closed his eyes to it and listened to the wind in the trees and to her voice, and he sensed it all passing before him, slowing for nothing or no one, favoring neither the young nor the old, not the fortunate nor the stricken, not the evil nor the good, nor lightness nor dark, and with his eyes closed and his palms outflung he tried to coax the world to move slower or to at least not abandon him but he knew that was not possible, not for him nor any living thing.

He opened his eyes and saw Bonnie sitting beside him and she took his hand and she spoke to him for a long time about goodness and hope and redemption and love until her voice became the wind and the stars and the world's turning, and in hearing her voice he was no longer scared of dying which meant he was scared of nothing and when her voice finally drifted away it was like nothing at all and that's all there ever would be.

EPILOGUE

In the dream I often have he is walking through a field of wheat. The sun is setting and the first dew beginning to wet the grass and the air is heavy and sweet. The dying light in the west bleeds through the sky to pink the clouds like blood in water. And amongst it all there is a woman standing in the grass. I do not know her but she has been waiting. And I do know that when she sees him she does not need to wait anymore.

I am visited by that dream with such regularity that I wonder if it is not my imagination but rather Benjamin Kilt attempting to reassure me that even in the end there is promise. I did not have this dream when I was young; it is a dream that has only recently found me. I am too old now to doubt the existence of souls nor argue against the possibilities of God, so I cannot excuse the thought that Benjamin's spirit is trying to extend some kind of courtesy. On the other hand I cannot refute the tangibility of solipsism and that all of this matters little and that to believe otherwise is foolish. The benefit of age is that it doesn't really matter one way or another. The only thing that matters, that holds any kind of relevance, is that the good outweighs the bad. That in the end we tried our best to live in the light, to attenuate darkness whenever we could. And it is this that I take from the dream: that Benjamin Kilt chose the light.

ACKNOWLEDGMENTS

To begin to thank everyone involved in the making of a book is daunting. It is also impossible. But Harry Kirchner has been with me since the beginning, before there even was a beginning, even before the possibility of a beginning. They tell you repetition makes things easier, perhaps even perfect. This does not apply to writing. Writing is still as hard as it was that very first day all those years ago and it will never be perfect and I assume will only get harder. Yet Harry is the type of editor who makes it all feel possible. He works on a manuscript as if it's his blood being spilled. Most of the superlatives in this world would be a paltry summation of his kindness and generosity. So, once again, my friend, thanks for believing in me and trusting me and calming me down time and time again. Thanks for all the hours at Rory's talking writing and books and publishing and baseball. All my love.

Thanks to Dan Smetanka for his excitement around this novel. To be in a tier of writers who can garner your time and attention is still a little wild to me. Thanks to you, each one gets better. I got one coming down the pike that I think will knock your socks off.

Halloween of 2024 was the day I got a call from Julia Kenney. We talked for an hour, and I don't know if you could tell, Julia, but I was trying my best not to sound like a total nitwit. When we hung up I just walked around for the rest of the day, wondering if I'd just dreamed it. Since freshman year in college, you're the kind of agent I'd always hoped to get. I adore you. So thanks for the call that day. Here's to the years ahead. And thanks to everyone at Dunow, Carlson & Lerner. I still have to pinch myself.

Thank you, Mom and Dad, for everything you do. I'm certain the world would stop if the two of you were not in it. I want to thank Jenny Schumacher for all the years of encouragement, for reading everything I have written, for her unequivocal friendship. I need to thank Glen Chamberlain, dearest of dear friends—I love the hell out of you. Thanks to Megan Clemmer and Nate Wiss, two people I couldn't do without. Thanks to Molli O'Neill for all the years of friendship and for an early read—what will we call ourselves one day, parents-in-law? Thank you to DB and Little Red for putting up with me all these years (also, five easter eggs, I think). Thanks to Danny Halliday for never letting me be reverent and for reading fiction, and an even bigger thanks to his wife, Robin, for putting up with him (and me)—I lucked out in meeting you. I must thank this dude named Ryan Sallis-Mitchell. This guy first told me about the whole concept behind the dead ringer thing, and I told him, I'm going to write a novel about that. So here it is, Ryan, thanks for teaching me something new. Thanks to Lindsay Duckworth, my lifelong friend, my evil twin—let's go climb some buildings and throw snowballs at yuppies next time I see you. Thanks to Andrew Hedrick and Rialin Flores and little Izzy, I couldn't do it without you. Thank you to everyone who picked up this book, and for continuing to read fiction. And of course, I must thank the Cabin Tavern. Greg and Christian and Kay. Hearing the audiobook for *The Houseboat* played in the bathroom is a small miracle to me!

Okay, one day I'm sitting at this coffee place, editing *TDR*, and two of the coolest gals in Bellingham come and sit across from me. We had all met at this wild wedding and they asked if they could be in the book. Carlee said, Can you make a scene where me and Bonnie are riding a horse barebacked together? I said, No, but I will name two of the main characters after you. So, thank you Bonnie Burke and Carlee Bock, unrivaled and peerless. The two of you are rascals and I love it.

I want to thank everyone at Counterpoint. To: Laura Berry, Victoria Maxfield, Wah-Ming Chang, Andrea Córdova, Rachel Fershleiser, Megan Fishmann, Ashley Kiedrowski, Lily Philpott, and Yukiko Tominaga. You make cherished things in a world that often cherishes little. I'm in your debt for that.

Thanks to Callan Wink, Eli Cranor, David Joy, and Willy Vlautin, four writers I greatly admire. I'm honored that you offered a place at the table.

This novel is dedicated to my sons, Tøren and Anders. Did you know I wake up most nights and immediately think of you two? I am filled with an existential dread that the two of you are getting bigger and will never be babies again and that mommy and I, no matter what we do, have to say goodbye to those days. But then, as it happens every morning at six, you two gallop into our room, crawl under the covers, and for the briefest of moments are still and quiet and we can breathe in your hair and feel your tiny lungs going in and out and then the dread subsides. I never used to be afraid of anything but now I'm afraid of everything and I couldn't imagine it any other way.

And once again, all of this and everything in it is for Madeline. Always for you, baby. I swear the tides rise and fall to the rhythm of your breath . . .

© Kelly Bahr

DANE BAHR was born in Minnesota. He is the author of *The Houseboat* and *Stag*. He lives in Washington state with his wife and sons.